brae

TRUE NOBILITY
Copyright 2018 © by Lori Bates Wright
www.loribateswright.com

ISBN 978-1-7326738-0-9 (print)
ISBN 978-1-7326738-1-6 (ebook)
Print Edition

D1232431

Cover design by Roseanna White Designs

Author is represented by The Steve Laube Agency

SierraVista Books
104 Ovilla Rd.
Red Oak, TX 75154

SierraVista
BOOKS

To my husband, Daryl.
For your unwavering support,
constant encouragement,
and bold faith.
Your love is a gift.

TRUE NOBILITY

LORI BATES WRIGHT

Prologue

England, Midnight, 2 February, 1860

Moonlight fell through an open casement as a rising shadow crept closer to the bed. Stillness clung to the damp night air. In the distance, a night owl's warning went unheeded as the silver glint of a blade sparked a terrifying illumination before plunging deep into the satin quilt.

Across the room, a door flung open where a night-capped silhouette wavered. The shadow of a pistol, held between shaking hands, centered unsteadily at the black-cloaked assassin.

Victory, however, proved short-lived.

An empty chamber pot hurled across the dim room knocking the weapon to the floor. With a daring leap, the murderer made an escape through the open window, instantly swallowed up by darkness.

In burgundy robe and slippers, an elderly gentleman shuffled further into the room. With anxious fingers, he struck a matchstick to light the lamp on the night table.

For a brief moment, his shaking hands lingered over the smooth coverlet before pulling it back. The down-filled bolster he'd carefully arranged there earlier now sported an eight-inch knife jutting from its middle.

Pulling a monogrammed handkerchief from the pocket of his robe, he dropped to sit on the bed, then dabbed at the sheen on his brow. Unfolding a note, he reread the message he'd received not three days past.

Take every precaution!
Your daughter, Victoria,
is to be killed before
her twentieth birthday.

Cold dread pounded through his veins as he stared blankly into the flickering flame fighting for life against his heavy breath.

It was then Edward Haverwood, third Earl of Wrenbrooke, resolved to do everything within his power to save his beloved daughter from the clutches of a maniacal killer.

"Will you walk into my parlour,"
said the spider to the fly.
"'Tis the prettiest little parlour
that ever you did spy."
~ Mary Howitt

One

England, 16 May, 1860

Squinting against the morning sun, Nicholas Saberton looked out over the lush green countryside of England's Lake District as it passed along the way. Unable to enjoy the view, his thoughts were distracted by Haverwood's urgent summons.

The letter insisted Nicholas personally make the trip from his home in Georgia to escort the earl and his daughter to America without delay. A tidy sum of money had accompanied the odd request for good measure.

Ordinarily, he would disregard a haughty demand such as this, sending one of his best men to escort them instead. But having recently acquired the majority holdings of Haverwood Shipping and Trade, Nicholas wasn't keen on upsetting the English Haverwoods.

Percy Haverwood had been a good friend over the years and he'd trusted Nicholas without reserve. The least he could do was play escort to Percy's brother and niece.

Truth be told, it had been invigorating to be aboard *The Tempest* again. With his younger brother Zachery at the helm, Nicholas had enjoyed a much-needed respite from the hectic pace he'd set for himself this past year.

Wrenbrooke Hall was in full view twenty minutes before the passenger wagon rumbled to a halt in front of the stately manor. Nicholas took in the elaborate entrance, looking up at the clinging rose vines covering the trellises on either side of the portal. Swinging down from the wagon ledge, he threw his cape casually over one shoulder. Ignoring the weighty brass knocker, he rapped steadily upon the grand wooden door.

Slowly the door opened and a somber man in butler's uniform appeared.

"Nicholas Saberton, to see the earl."

The servant stepped aside to reveal a long narrow hall. "His Lordship will see you in the library."

Nicholas entered, handing off his cape into the outstretched hand.

"Saberton! Don't dawdle, man. We've much to attend to." Lord Haverwood leaned on his cane in a doorway to the right before disappearing inside.

As he followed the earl, Nicholas noted the similar design to his own library back home in Georgia. His father had built the Saberton house and had incorporated many of the same baroque elements. Nicholas was barely through the door, however, when the earl impatiently waved him in.

"Rather a large fellow, aren't you." It was a statement rather than a question. Lord Haverwood looked him over from head to foot before crossing in front to get a better look. "Passable as far as looks go, I suppose. How are your teeth?"

Teeth? Nicholas met the earl's question with a steady stare.

"Not much for conversation, eh?" The earl motioned for Nicholas to take a seat. "Well, no matter. I trust everything has been prepared for our departure?"

"The ship is ready to sail as soon as we arrive back at port," Nicholas leaned forward in his chair to rest an arm over his knee. "We can catch the morning tide, if you can be ready to leave this afternoon."

"Splendid! The sooner, the better. Tea?"

The butler lifted a china pot and poured two teacups a quarter of the way full.

Nicholas held up a hand. "None for me, thank you."

"What's this? No tea? Not given to stronger drink, I hope."

"No. I prefer coffee, myself."

"Hmmph." The earl's mustache gave a quick twitch. "Of course. You revolutionary devils forget your origins."

With a direct look, Nicholas took the affront. It was time to get to the bottom of this summons. "What exactly can I do for you, Lord Haverwood?"

"I believe my correspondence was rather straightforward. I've need of your services to see my daughter and me safely out of the country."

"Yes, that I understand." Nicholas declined the butler's offer of an assortment of sweets. "My question is, why the hurry? And why me specifically?"

"I rather expect that you are the precise man for the task. Besides my late brother's glowing opinion of you, I also knew your father's uncle quite well, you see." Lord Haverwood paused and Nicholas kept his expression closed.

"Lord Thomas Saberton was a fine gentleman. Duke of Brechenridge. We were seated together at Lords for a number of years until his unfortunate ailment took its toll."

All his life he'd heard of his father's uncle Thomas. Nicholas relaxed back into his seat and lifted his foot to rest upon his knee. "I'm sorry I never had the chance to meet him."

"Saberton's brother, your grandfather as it were, caused quite the scandal running off to the colonies as he did. Severed all ties with family and country when he chose to defend the treasonous rebels against us,"

Again, Nicholas met the earl's regard with a wary glance.

"There are no British heirs to the Saberton domain, you see. Everything has reverted to the Crown. Unless, of course ..." He lifted his cup and took a sip. "... a rightful heir was to step forward to reclaim it."

Nicholas was unimpressed. His grandfather had lost his life fighting for the liberation of their adopted country, a cause the American Sabertons had since embraced with fervor. Titles and English lands held no appeal to him whatsoever.

"Tell me, Saberton, you are a God-fearing sort, are you not? You haven't converted to some savage belief over there, have you?"

Why the senseless questions? None of this was anything Nicholas cared to discuss. Thankfully, he was rescued by the sound of a female voice drifting down the hall.

Lord Haverwood looked up. Taking his cane, he made his way over to wait by the door, ending the odd conversation.

When she entered the room, Nicholas was struck by her elegance. The stately way she moved gave her the presence of a princess. Coming to his feet, he noted she had delicate features and a magnificent mane of auburn curls. Long dark lashes framed brilliant blue eyes radiating an innocence that made him smile.

"Good morning, Father."

"I'm pleased you chose the lilac gown, my dear. Most flattering." The earl took her arm and led her over to where Nicholas stood. "Captain Saberton, I present my daughter, Lady Victoria Haverwood."

Her first thought was that the man standing before her was huge—thickly muscled and a good head taller than average. His glossy black hair fell well over his collar although he was dressed in an impeccable taupe overcoat with matching trousers and vest.

"Nicholas Saberton." He reached out and respectfully took her hand. "A pleasure to make your acquaintance."

At second glance, she decided he was a most handsome man as well. Admittedly, more masculine than the cadets from Sandhurst who visited once a year during the social season.

Lord Haverwood stepped between the two. "The good captain and I were finalizing our arrangements, my dear. All is in order for our voyage."

Reluctantly, she turned her attention back to her father, who led her to a chair opposite the one Captain Saberton stood ready to reclaim. "I'd hoped we could continue our conversation about that in private, Father."

"Nothing to discuss, Victoria. I've told you we shall travel to the colonies and that's the last of it." Her father, the illustrious Earl of Wrenbrooke, was fast becoming red in the face. "Captain Saberton is a formidable American officer and has agreed to see to our safe passage. I'll not have you offending him with your needless questions."

"I'm not offended at all." The captain repositioned himself to rest a foot atop his knee. "If you have concerns, by all means speak freely."

His candor took her by surprise. As a woman of quality, she'd never openly contradict her father's opinions.

Which was exasperating considering she had an opinion on almost everything. However, because of her strict upbringing, she had to find more subtle ways of expressing herself.

"Victoria?" She didn't miss the warning in her father's tone.

"Tori," she corrected under her breath.

Pointless, really. He would never take to her more fashionable nickname. He was stubborn and old-fashioned to a fault.

"Whatever it is you call yourself. Answer the man."

Nothing at all wrong with his hearing.

Tori glanced at the captain who didn't bother to hide a smile.

Over the years she'd found better ways of getting around her father's petulance. "I certainly won't argue with you, Father. If you say we must travel, then I'm sure you have your reasons." Accepting a cup of tea from Higgins, she added two lumps of sugar with two deliberate plops.

Her father gave her a ferocious scowl. "I'm in no mood for your antics this morning, Victoria."

Lately, he'd been in no mood for anything other than pestering her to come home early from school. Three months early to be exact. Something was definitely amiss. Her father, the only parent she'd ever known, had aged considerably since her last visit to Wrenbrooke. His usually vivid blue eyes were listless and tired. Deep lines framed the corners of his mouth. Most telling, however, was the way his bushy gray mustache twitched ever so often. Always a sure sign he was agitated.

Now he was insisting they take a spontaneous trip across the ocean to visit relatives he hadn't seen in twenty-five years. If truth be told, he didn't care much for Aunt Charlotte and never minded saying so.

So why this sudden need to travel to Savannah?

As usual, she must take care not to ruffle his aristocratic feathers.

"The captain assures me everything is ready for an early morning departure. So we shall have the carriages loaded and be on our way to the ship by this afternoon."

"Tomorrow morning? So soon?" Tori again looked over at the captain across from her. He said nothing but studied her with his eyes. Gentle eyes, deep brown, almost black. For a mere instant she had an unsettling feeling she could see her own reflection in their depths.

Scolding herself, she realized she was behaving like an untutored ninny.

"I say, Victoria. You're not listening to a word I've said."

"Forgive me, Father. Please go on."

Her father pressed an intolerant frown upon her. "As I was saying, I should like to be on our way by one o'clock. Is that suitable to the both of you?"

"Fine by me. Does that give you enough time?" Captain Saberton asked in an unfamiliar drawl.

"I'll have to send a note to Miss Mair as soon as possible. They'll have to find a replacement for me for the rest of the school term."

"Well, now there's something." Her father waved Higgins off when the man tried to refill his cup. "When I allowed you to stay on at that simpering creature's school, it most certainly was not to see you educated as a common clerk. All this training in writing and calculating numbers has you forgetting you are merely a *female* after all."

How utterly archaic. Tori made a face just outside her father's line of view.

This put her in a terrible predicament. Miss Mair would not be happy about her leaving them in such a bind.

"You are not an ignoble school mistress, Victoria." The earl picked up his spoon and rattled it against his cup. My own fault, I suppose. I should have insisted you return home the minute you made sixteen. Should have secured you in a suitable marriage years ago."

The captain discretely coughed into his hand but the grin on his face said he found her father's careless comment amusing.

Her father was anything but tactful, and when he was on a tangent there was no telling what he might say.

"Surely I don't have to remind you that your mother was married and expecting you any day by the time she was nineteen." With a shake of his gray head he gave her a disapproving mumble.

Love for him washed over her. Despite his gruff mood, she knew he adored her and she'd missed him terribly.

She'd even missed these prickly lectures he was so fond of.

"You were a headstrong little whelp even then." He turned toward the Captain. "She insisted on being born feet first, you know. Not in the least cooperative. "'Tis a blessed miracle Dr. Fitzpatrick was able to save her at all."

Tori refused to look at the man seated across from her. Her father's lack of discretion only confirmed her suspicion that something was not right.

"Unfortunately, of course, he was not adept enough to save her mother." Her father took a long sip from his cup, gazing at the opulent pattern running through the rug laid out in front of his desk.

Tori was stunned.

He rarely spoke of her mother. As much as she hoped he'd say more, airing the details of such a personal loss, especially in the company of a stranger, was not like him at all.

"My condolences, sir." The captain's consideration for her father sounded genuine. This time Tori did look over at him.

When his attention turned to her, she had to remind herself not to look away. She wasn't easily intimidated, but he had an imposing way about him and was far too free with his assessment of her. A blush warmed her cheeks, betraying her brave front.

"Now, as I said, I should like to have the baggage loaded and on our way to port by one." Her father stood and checked his timepiece. "Just after ten o'clock now.

Are we clear, Victoria?"

The maids had already packed her trunks for the most part. "I'll be ready." Searching her mind for any available reason to delay, she was running out of excuses. "But it hardly seems fair to set you off to sea again so soon, Captain. Shouldn't we wait a few days, Father?"

"No need for worry on our account." The ship's captain had a disarming smile. "We've taken on fresh supplies and our men live by the sea. They don't do well with too much free time."

"Excellent. One it is." Her father dismissed them by taking up his cane and calling for Higgins. "Captain, have you had your breakfast? Cook has set pastries out on the buffet should you care for a bite while our baggage is assembled onto the wagon. Higgins, here, will show you to the dining area."

Captain Saberton stood and prepared to take his leave.

Lord Haverwood's voice stopped him. "Oh, and one more thing I'd like you to do this afternoon before we put to sea."

"Certainly, sir." Nicholas remained where he stood, but raised a quizzical brow.

"Marry my daughter."

When thou passest through the waters,
I will be with thee.
~ Isaiah 43:2

Two

After a futile attempt to discuss her father's bizarre outburst, Tori found herself packed and on their way to meet the ship in just short of three hours. Falling back into the tufted leather cushions of her family's polished brougham, she grasped the silver filigree cross that hung from a chain at her neck.

"Merciful heavens," she whispered to no one in particular. "My beloved father has gone completely daft." Sympathy overwhelmed her as she stared blankly at the poor dear man sitting on the seat across from her.

Tori was stunned by his absurd request but had badgered him only as far as she dared.

From what she gathered, Captain Saberton was heir to the dukedom of a longtime friend. Yet the man gave no inclination that he would be at all interested in claiming his right. Even if he did, she had done her best to evade every marriage of convenience her father had suggested over the past two years. She had no interest in tying herself to a man who'd neither love nor care for her beyond the benefits of her title. When she married, she'd like to think it would be because her heart was bound by love alone.

Therefore, the only reasonable conclusion, was that her father's ridiculous proposition was proof he was on the brink of senility.

Once she pushed him, however, he insisted that he was "in full control of his faculties" and advised, in no uncertain terms, that Tori "keep her mind on their departure and quit playing nursemaid."

Her only consolation was that, for now, his delusional episode was behind them.

This chance to travel might prove to be just the thing he needed. It would give him some time away to relax and, more importantly, it would give her a chance to keep a better eye on him. He should not have been left alone for so long. With a shake of her head, Tori made a mental note to send for the ship's doctor as soon as they were underway. It was evident he needed special care. Perhaps some sort of medication might help.

She patted at a wayward strand of hair and tucked it under the neat chignon at the base of her nape. In their haste to leave she had donned a ginger-colored traveling gown with wide black satin trim bordering each of the three tiers of her skirt. The sleeves of the jacket were close fitting, as was the narrow waist and she soon regretted the decision. A silk bonnet, in the same ginger hue, lay on the seat next to her.

Absently, she stroked the small black feathers tacked to the side of the hat, watching her father on the seat opposite her. He was feigning sleep to avoid any more conversation. She watched him spy her through slitted eyes and manage an exaggerated snort.

Tori stifled a smile behind her black-gloved hand. The earl was eccentric—always had been—and she normally loved him for it. Today, however, he'd completely outdone himself.

The carriage felt warm. Shifting irritably, she whisked imaginary wrinkles from her gown. She wasn't looking forward to seeing the captain again.

Regardless of what he'd thought of her father's unusual proposition, she had not missed the stinging, egotistical smirk Captain Saberton sent her way before making his exit. Clearly, the vile man was of the opinion that her father had set a well-laid trap in order to snare him into marrying his spinster daughter.

Nineteen and unmarried was hardly considered a spinster in this day and age. Beatrice Harrington was nearly twenty-seven before she left Miss Mair's to marry the old viscount from Stratham.

Tori raised her eyes heavenward in silent prayer, rubbing her temples in an effort to erase the unpleasant memory. Glancing over at her father, she wished he'd pretend to wake up now. She had so many questions about this trip to America. He'd spent a good bit of time there before she was born.

Tori reached into a black satin reticule that dangled from her wrist and drew out a shiny silver coin. She'd met her Uncle Percy only once, when she was small, but she remembered him as a kind and generous man. He had given her the coin when she was five and to him it represented a country that he had grown to love.

Turning the piece over, she studied the lady in flowing gown, surrounded by a half-circle of stars. America seemed inconceivably far away. This venture across the sea promised a most welcome change of pace. Meeting her cousin Aurora was going to be wonderful after so many years of corresponding.

Were the people in that savage land as crass as she'd been told? Did they truly ignore social order and run amock in the streets? That would certainly explain the captain's crude behavior.

His estimation of her circumstances didn't matter a fig. Once they were settled in Savannah, it was unlikely she'd ever see him again.

The carriage jolted to a stop and Tori returned the coin to her bag. Casting an apprehensive glance out of the small square window, she set her feathered bonnet at an angle to shade her eyes.

"Harrumph. What's this? Ah, the harbor." Lord Haverwood came fully awake. "A rather pleasant drive, wouldn't you say, my dear?" He didn't wait for an answer as he climbed down from the vehicle's ledge.

Stepping lightly from the carriage step, Tori took her father's arm and covered her nose at the rancid stench of the waterfront.

A tangible breeze blew in from the brine, causing heavy ropes to flap against the towering masts. Waves washed into foam as they lapped at the huge wooden vessels. Herring fishermen lined the bay as far as the eye could see and rotting fish heads littered its banks. Gulls circled noisily overhead, and the coarse shouts of seamen reverberated through the dense fog.

"You must be Lord Haverwood." A smiling young man, by appearances not much older than Tori, bounded down the extended ramp to meet them.

"And who might you be?" Her father questioned stiffly.

"I beg your pardon, sir. Captain Saberton at your service." With that he made a formal bow and gave Tori an appreciative glance.

Narrowing her eyes, Tori gave the man a stern appraisal. She was certain they'd never met, yet his bold manner was somehow familiar.

Taking her hand, he spoke to them both. "Welcome aboard *The Tempest*."

Tori snatched her hand from his grasp and gave him a hard look for his brashness.

"Now see here, my good fellow. I don't know what your game is, but you most assuredly are not Captain Saberton." Waving his cane, he continued, "I must insist you go fetch him at once."

"That would be me, Zach." The sound of Nicholas's voice startled Tori as he came up behind them. "I see you've met my brother, Captain Zachery Saberton," Nicholas appeared unaffected by the earl's scowl.

"What's this? I specifically—"

"You specifically asked that I come and personally see to your safe transport, and that's the only reason I'm here," Nicholas interrupted. "Zach, however, is captain on this voyage and we are guests on his ship."

Tori peered at him from beneath her wide-brimmed bonnet until she noticed his bored gaze centered on her. Lifting her chin, she matched his glare with one of her own before turning away.

"Well, it won't be his first go, I trust. I should rather like to get there in one piece, if you don't mind." His mustache twitched, looking over the younger of the two men with obvious skepticism.

Zach grinned with an easy charm. "I assure you, sir, I've made this voyage several times." He directed his smile at Tori. "And with such precious cargo aboard, I promise to be especially attentive."

Tori realized now why she'd recognized that suave manner and odd dialect. Heaven help them if there wasn't two of these ill-bred Sabertons.

Summing them up one at a time with a critical eye, she noticed that Zachery had a youthful way about him and wasn't quite as tall as Nicholas. His hazel-colored eyes held a friendly sparkle, and he was quick to smile whereas his brother seemed far too serious.

Leading the way up the ramp, Nicholas permitted the younger captain to escort Tori.

"Allow me to show you to your cabins. I'll have my men unload your baggage." Zachery offered her his arm and steered her around the admiring leers of his crew.

One seasoned sailor released a loud appreciative whistle. But when he caught the dark scowl of the elder Saberton, he nearly swallowed his fingers. With a nervous jab of his elbow, he got the attention of the man next to him. Tori watched as word spread and the censured crew returned to readying the vessel for the command to sail.

"Zach, I saw McGinnis on my way up. He needs to see you about the new deckhands you hired on today." Nicholas took her hand from Zachery's arm. "I'll see the earl and Miss Victoria are properly settled."

"*Lady* Victoria," Tori corrected, bristling at his snide reference to her unwed state, obviously in retaliation to her father's earlier offer. "My father can see me to my quarters, thank you. If you'll be so kind as to point us in the direction."

She tried to snatch her hand from the muscled bend of his arm, but he tightened his hold.

Leaning close, he spoke so she alone could hear. "Where I come from, Miss Haverwood, Lady is a title one must earn." Nicholas returned her wide-eyed expression with a half smile. Surely the man wasn't serious. Tori glanced at the others to see if they had witnessed the exchange.

Amusement danced in Zach's eyes as he watched Tori

fume at the impudence of his brother. "My apologies for leaving you so soon. Please be my guests for dinner this evening."

"Yes, yes, so kind of you to offer. We shall await your summons." The earl dismissed Zach with a wave as he turned back to the elder Saberton. To Tori's dismay, he was completely oblivious to the man's rude behavior. "I say, Captain, I should like a word with you in private. To continue our previous conversation, if you've a moment."

Her father was obviously on the verge of another episode. Once again, she tried in vain to withdraw her hand from Nicholas's hold. He absolutely unnerved her.

"Follow me, I'll show you to your cabins. We can talk there. But, I will tell you this ..." The corners of Nicholas's eyes crinkled. "Though the offer is appealing, I'm not in the market for marriage."

"What an utterly absurd thing to say!" Tori couldn't help herself. "As I see it, Mr. Saberton, no one is the least bit interested in what you are, or are not, in the market for. Truthfully, you could fall off the nearest pier and I doubt even the scavenger fish would take notice." She finally succeeded in freeing her hand. "Now, sir, if you don't mind, I would appreciate it if you would *quietly* show us to our chambers."

"G-Good gracious, Victoria!" The earl blustered.

For the first time since he'd met her, Nicholas threw back his head and laughed in full, vibrant timbre.

Nicholas straightened in his ladderback chair, rubbing stiffness from the nape of his neck after pouring over the captain's log for the better part of an hour. Laying aside his pen and capping the inkwell, he closed the leather-bound volume.

Zach's calculations on the trip over had been right on track. Having noted the subtle changes in the south wind, they would make excellent time if they pulled away by dawn. Barring unexpected weather, the crisp spring breeze would provide a consistent speed that should have them stateside within three weeks.

Nicholas glanced up to find Zach standing over the carved oak desk with two steaming mugs in his hand. "Just came from the bow. We've got red skies as far as the eye can see." Zach set the cups down on the desk and straddled a chair that he pulled over from the corner.

"Your records look good. You've done an excellent job of plotting the course. We should be home in time for the Dogwood Festival." Tension eased from Nicholas's shoulders with the first sip of hot coffee.

Zach rubbed his hands together, smiling from ear to ear. "Mmm. I can almost smell that hog sizzling over a fire."

"Well, we're not there yet." Nicholas grinned. "How's the girl?"

"Lovely beyond compare." Zach smiled before taking a sip from his own mug. "But I'm not telling you anything you don't already know."

"Can't say I've noticed." Nicholas leaned back and

hooked an arm over the back of his chair. That was not the honest truth. He had noticed. But, arming his brother with that kind of knowledge was asking for teasing he didn't need. "I will say this …" Nicholas placed the log book into the desk drawer and replaced the blotter to the center of the desk. "She's a bothersome little package."

"I found her thoughtful and considerate." Zach held his mug between both hands and stared down into his coffee. "And her eyes. Did you notice? She has remarkable eyes."

Nicholas dismissed his brother's obvious admiration for his charge. "Ask me about her self-righteous airs or that quick little temper. I'd be more than happy to enlighten you about that."

Zach rubbed his jaw and weighed his next question carefully. "One of us should pay her a call once we reach Savannah."

Nicholas knew Zach was carefully testing his reaction. "Go ahead. If you've a notion to court Miss High and Mighty, have at it."

"Unless … you know … you were thinking of courting her yourself."

Nicholas threw his younger brother an incredulous look.

Zach rushed on to defer the gathering storm. "I saw the way you looked at her on deck this afternoon. She intrigues you. Don't deny it."

Nicholas gave in to the urge to laugh. "You're wrong, little brother. And you may as well save your time. Her type won't give either of us a second thought." Nicholas plunked the mug onto the table. "You're forgetting the British upper crust see themselves as superior to us lowbrow colonials. Heaven forbid she should meet one she'd actually like to get to know better."

"I thought Lord Haverwood asked you to marry her."

"That's when he thought he could get his hands on Uncle Thomas's holdings. Once he figured out I have no desire to be a duke, or to move to England, he wasn't as interested."

"I hadn't thought about it that way." Zach sounded dejected. "So are they only allowed to socialize with royalty? What happens if they meet a commoner they find interesting?"

"I'm not quite sure." Nicholas narrowed his eyes and tried to appear serious. "But I think Princess Victoria would be stripped of her tiara and flogged with the royal scepter."

"Well, I'd like her to at least consider me a friend." He leveled a frown at his eldest brother. "And a friend will look out for her. Once we get back home, she won't want for male attention. I can at least steer her away from those with less honorable intentions."

Nicholas shrugged and shook his head. Given different circumstances, he might have taken an interest in the blue-eyed beauty. As it was, he was devoted only to building up his shipping company. Commerce was an investment he could trust. "She's a bundle of trouble, Zach. See her to Savannah and bid her farewell."

"She's not that bad." Zach persisted despite Nicholas's glower. "She's nothing like Celine."

At the mention of his former fiancé, a dark shadow gripped his soul. Pushing away from the desk, he ended the conversation. "It's time we dress for dinner." With that, he left his brother staring down at his empty mug.

One often meets his destiny
on the road he takes to avoid it.
~ Elizabeth Barret Browning

Three

Tori sat miserably in the rebuke of silence.

During the awkward moments following her scandalous outburst, her father had stared at her in shocked disapproval while the captain continued laughing. The only thing she remembered about walking to her cabin was her cheeks burning along the way.

Her telltale reaction to him this morning when they'd met had been scandalous enough. Then this afternoon, the man again compelled her to forget her gentle-bred manners and make an absolute fool of herself.

Dare she try to top the performance this evening at dinner? Tori berated herself while visions of Miss Mair in a dead faint fluttered across her mind.

With a heavy sigh, she looked around the small cabin.

Stuffy, but clean, and neatly arranged. A small bunk

projected from the whitewashed wall, covered with crisp, sun-bleached sheets and a patchwork quilt. On the other side, a compact mahogany desk was stocked with paper, inkwell and pen. Behind a cream-colored screen, hooks hung from the wall for clothing and towels. Tucked over in the corner was a wash stand and basin with a simple unframed mirror hung above.

A loud, insistent knock caused her to jump. Surely it wasn't the dinner hour already. She'd hoped for more time to gather herself.

"Yes?" she asked into the closed door. "Who is it?"

"Your trunks, ma'am." The reply was muffled.

With relief, she turned the latch and swung the door wide to allow sufficient space to move about. Two shabbily dressed men entered, one at each end of her large trunk. Their caps were pulled down over their ears and the collars of their ragged overcoats were turned up high. Under different circumstances, Tori would have easily mistaken the scruffy two for common delinquents.

They flung her baggage into the cabin, scraping it loudly against the doorway as they lumbered through.

With a gasp, Tori hurried over to inspect the damage marring her fine Moroccan leather. From the corner of her eye she spotted the short, round ruffian edge over to shut the door, while the thin one inched his way behind her.

They were obviously up to no good.

Hoping to buy herself some time to get back to the door, she tried to engage in trivial conversation. "You

must be more careful. I shall have to speak to Captain—"
The man at her back shoved her hard to the floor.

A wicked-looking dagger was aimed at her chest. Tori let loose a bloodcurdling scream and rolled from under the fiend.

The knife descended striking a plank in the floor.

Too afraid to consider the consequences, she lunged for the door but was caught from behind.

The man dragged her back with both arms, keeping her in front of him so that she couldn't see his face. "Bar the door," he yelled, grabbing for the knife.

With a glimmer of defiance, Tori aimed her elbow hard into his ribs. As her arm met with his slight, boney frame, she realized he couldn't be much older than fifteen.

He caught her with a rough shake. Cold steel nicked her chin.

"You've a might feisty one there." From her awkward position, Tori could see the round villain across the room where he licked his lips nervously. His bulging eyes darted uncertainly from his partner to the door. The man resembled a greasy gargoyle, like the one looming above the entrance of St. Mary's Church in Adderbury.

Emboldened by the fact that the one holding her was merely a boy, she issued a deliberate shove, pushing hard to gain her release and earning a solid slap across her face.

A loud crack splintered the doorjamb, squashing the stubby man behind the heavy door.

Tori pulled away from her attacker, scrambling up

onto the far side of the bunk.

Nicholas was across the room in an instant. With a swift hand, he sent the knife clattering against the wall. The intruder froze before an ear-piercing shot rang through the cabin. A look of pain flickered across Nicholas's profile as he grabbed his shoulder.

Covering her mouth, Tori dared not scream again. She needed to keep her wits. Grabbing a cotton sheet from the bunk, she made her way to where Nicholas stood between the assailants.

The squatty one turned the point of the small derringer toward her. A thin tendril of smoke curled from the barrel. "I got one shot left, so you best stay put, little lassie. I'll not be wantin' to lay a hole in your bonny little noggin." His tongue slathered freakishly over his thick lips and he appeared muddled.

"Victoria, stay back." Nicholas's eyes narrowed as he watched the anxious gunman.

Tori was frantic. Nicholas had been shot. Still, he all but dared this villain to try it again. Briefly closing her eyes, she bid herself to calm down. She could scarcely take in a breath against the fear gripping her throat.

"Get yourself over by the lass, Cap'n." The thug motioned with the gun to where Tori knelt.

Nicholas didn't move. Had he not been wounded, he could easily overpower the man. Injured or not, it appeared he considered doing it anyway.

"Now, don't you be doin' anything stupid. I'll send her lov'liness to kingdom come. Don't think I won't."

The gargoyle man cocked his gun and aimed it directly at Tori. She smothered a gasp and held tightly to her cross.

To ensure Victoria's safety, Nicholas gritted his teeth and grudgingly complied, moving to shield her with his body. "What is it you want here?"

"I'll just be collectin' my friend here, and we'll be on our way." The short man inched over to where the other attacker crouched on the floor.

His mistake was in turning his back to her.

With a surge of strength she didn't know she possessed, Tori clobbered him with a well-worn pillow, sending a flurry of small white feathers raining down upon them.

Without pause, Nicholas took one step forward and twisted the gun from the ugly man's grasp. "The only place you'll be going is straight to the brig unless I get some answers."

The man's bulging eyes grew even wider.

"Zach!" Nicholas stepped to the splintered doorway and bellowed above deck. "Get down here and send for the dockmaster."

"I don't know nothin', I tell ya. Just an easy sixpence. It don't do well askin' too many questions, ya know." The short man stumbled over his own feet trying to get to the door.

Two brawny sailors appeared, and Nicholas motioned for them to take the invaders topside.

When the taller one paused to glare at Tori, she moved further behind the broad shoulders of Nicholas to block any possibility of him getting to her. The kid's collar was still raised to cover his face as he was prodded out the door.

"Amos, see that they get to the dockmaster." Nicholas started to follow but stopped when he noticed Tori.

"Princess?" His voice softened. "Are you hurt?"

His offhanded endearment gained her attention. Shaking her head, she still said nothing.

"Victoria, look at me." He clasped her hand and gave it a pat.

The enormity of what had almost happened rendered her motionless. Never in her life had she experienced anything so brutal and she needed a moment to regain her voice—and nerve.

Nicholas smoothed away the wayward curls over her brow to inspect her face. "You *are* hurt."

Touching the forgotten spot on her chin, she felt the sting of a fresh cut.

"It's merely a scratch. But your shoulder needs attention." Tori carefully laid a hand on his arm, searching his dark eyes for permission to have a closer look at his wound.

Permission was neither granted nor denied.

Since he wasn't inclined to move away, she took the opportunity to try and staunch the blood flow staining his shirt. "You were very brave." She spoke soothingly, to divert his attention from her touch, like she did when tending to one of the younger students at school.

Nicholas watched her with an unreadable expression.

Taking up the sheet, she dabbed at the wound until she could see that there was no bullet lodged inside.

Apprehension began a slow crawl up her spine as she realized how close the bullet had come to finding his heart. Her hand suddenly stilled. "Captain, you could have been murdered."

"My murder wasn't in their plan." Nicholas frowned as he looked over at the shattered door frame. "Odd that your traveling bag was left untouched. I'm guessing robbery wasn't their intent. And I doubt they came looking for female company. The docks are crawling with eager ones."

Tori blushed at his bluntness and continued to press the sheet to his shoulder to avoid looking up at him.

A shout sounded from the upper deck. "Nicholas, you'd best come up!"

With an impatient side-step, he brushed off her assistance. "It seems, we were both fortunate—this time."

As Nicholas entered the passageway, he spoke to the crewmen still milling about outside the door. "Send Hobbs down to stay with Miss Haverwood. The rest of you get back to your duties."

"Aye, sir," came the replies.

"Captain?" Tori straightened her gown and patted a stray curl back into her chignon. In all fairness, she needed to set him straight before this went any further. "I am not really a princess, you know."

"I beg your pardon." Nicholas grinned from the doorway and tipped his head. "Maybe this knocked some pretentious air out of your pretty little sails."

"I am a merely a lady of the elite class," she announced, clasping her hands in front of her. "My father is an earl, you see."

He shook his head before disappearing from view.

The upper deck was in a whirl of activity. A crowd of sailors gathered near the stern railings. Everyone was wildly discussing and gesturing at the same time.

"Who is the dupe?"

"Ain't never seen him before."

Nicholas pushed through the horde to stand directly over the plump corpse of the freakish man who'd shot him.

Zach stood directly across from him.

"One of your men?" Nicholas addressed his brother.

"No." Zach was quick to respond. "Apparently a freebooter. Ever seen him before?"

"Just long enough to sample his poor hand." Nicholas indicated to where his white shirt was torn and bloody. "There were two of them. Where's the other one?"

Zach turned to the burly bondsman at his side. "What happened, Amos?"

"We heard screamin' from down below, and wasn't long before a shot rang out." Nods of agreement spurred him on. "So me and Simon and Hobbs went down. Cap'n told us to bring this one here up to the magistrate. I latched on to the other fella but when I got him up on deck, he pulled a knife and run his partner clean through. Killed him dead. Then he took off lightning fast down that ramp and ain't nobody could stop him."

"All right. Get him off of the ship." As Zach barked orders the crew scattered. "Rawlings, go inform the dockmaster. He can inform the magistrate. You others get this mess cleaned up."

Nicholas moved to the rail and scanned the harbor for any sign of the intruder. These two were likely no more than insignificant lackeys. If he could follow the one who got away back to his source, he'd find the real culprit.

"I'll get Tibbs up here to bind that for you. Did you get a good look at the other one?" Zach skimmed the area as well.

"No. But they weren't freebooters."

Zach frowned. "What then?"

"They were in Victoria's quarters passing off as a couple of your men." Nicholas's jaw tensed. "They had her at knifepoint, Zach, before I interrupted. And I'd wager I was just in time." He turned a hard focus on his brother. "How did they get on this ship?"

"I wasn't here. I was with McGinnis, remember?"

"You are responsible, Zach!" Nicholas raised his voice and all activity on deck stopped. "Everyone on this vessel is your responsibility. Make it your business to know every move that's made on this ship or be prepared to swab the deck." He pushed off from the rail and took long strides toward the ramp.

Zach rushed to catch up with him. "I'm going with

34

you."

"You're needed here. Have Amos install a new bolt on Victoria's door. And check the earl's door, too. I want guards posted at all times. No point in taking any more chances until the other one is caught."

"Was Lady Victoria hurt?" Zach's question resonated with shame.

A fitting response considering the enormity of what just happened. Though Zach was fully capable of handling his own ship, he needed to feel the weight of his responsibility. Had Victoria been truly hurt, the consequences would likely crush even a seasoned commander.

"Not badly, but she was definitely shaken up." Nicholas took a piece of cloth offered by the boatswain and wrapped it around the wound, briskly tugging it into a knot.

"I never considered the possibility that the earl or his daughter might be threatened aboard this ship." Zach's shoulders sagged, the sincerity of his words was unmistakable. "We've known this crew for a good many years. Both of us have. There isn't one of them that would hesitate to protect the girl. With their life if need be."

"I don't know who they were, or how they got on here, but they weren't out to rob or put a scare into her. That skinny one, especially, was out for murder."

Nicholas paused to look out over the rabble. If the man was out there, he would find him before leaving shore. "And there's no doubt Victoria was targeted."

Catching a glimpse of Zach's serious nod, Nicholas

took a deep breath. He'd been hard on him, when he was every bit as angry at himself. After all, he'd given his word to keep Victoria safe.

"Look, Zach, you usually run a tight ship. You can't afford to let something like this get by. Do whatever it takes to make sure the Haverwoods are safe for the remainder of this passage."

Zach nodded. "We might not be so lucky next time."

"Make sure there isn't a next time." With that, Nicholas hurried down the ramp and onto the crowded wharf.

When I saw you, I fell in love
and you smiled because you knew.
~ Arrigo Boito

Four

For the better part of the afternoon, Tori had been forbidden to leave her quarters. A hulking, armed guard stood outside the shattered doorway. Twice, when she'd tried to venture out, he'd informed her that his orders were to keep her in her cabin until the ship was well underway.

Just after dusk, she was provided a tray of food and informed the captain had issued orders to sail at once. Pulling away from port on an earlier tide put them to sea at least twelve hours ahead of schedule.

Settling in, she had no other option but to wait to see her father.

Surely he was beside himself with worry by now. What with the attack and all that had transpired, she couldn't wait to tell him all about it.

As soon as she felt a steady roll of the ocean beneath her feet, she again approached the enormous man. "It appears, your orders are now fulfilled, sir." To his credit, the guard didn't lift a finger to stop her. Instead, he stepped aside and gave a tip of his brimmed straw hat.

Hurrying to the far end of the corridor, Tori tapped on the door of her father's cabin and found it partially open. "Father, may I come in?"

No response.

Cautiously, she entered the darkened room. Her eyes took a moment to adjust as she looked for some sign of her father. "Are you in here?"

Still no answer. Had he been attacked as well?

A low moan came from the direction of the narrow bunk, and Tori went rigid.

She rushed toward him. Searching out his face in the dim light, she gulped to hold back a whimper. "Father, who has done this to you?"

"Imbecile ... cook." He barely got the words out before another wave of nausea struck him." Teatime ... wretched ... crumpets." He groaned again, this time much louder.

Beads of perspiration dotted his forehead where Tori laid a careful hand. Thankfully, no fever warmed her palm. He was indeed suffering, but apparently from illness rather than an attack.

After pouring cool water from a pitcher into the washbowl, she carried it to where her father lay doubled over on his side. Dampening a cloth to bathe his face, she tried to interpret his delirious rantings.

"Must get her out …"

"Who, Father?" Tori smoothed a gray lock from where it had fallen across his high forehead. "Who must you get out?"

"Saberton … she must marry …"

Tori's hand stilled.

Strangely, her breath left her at the mention of Nicholas Saberton. She'd never met a man so fearless in the face of danger. He'd risked his life to protect her. But, instead of finding comfort in his gallantry, she found him all the more baffling.

She fully understood her father's appreciation for Captain Saberton. He was a fine specimen, as far as men go.

"Mustn't let … murder …"

Murder?

Her father was more delirious than she'd guessed. He was babbling nonsense. She was about to question him further when the earl threw the cloth to the side and made ill use of the washbowl.

Tori grabbed the cool cloth again and held it to his mouth. "Father, lie back. Don't try to talk anymore. I'll go for the captain."

Tori rose to get some fresh water, making him as comfortable as possible.

A light rap on the door, still ajar, caught her attention. "Lady Victoria, it's Zachery Saberton. May I speak with you for a moment?"

"Certainly. Come in, Captain." Tori put her finger to

her lips to hush him as he joined her at her father's bedside. "I was about to send for you."

The earl had slipped into a shallow slumber, but she figured it wouldn't be long before he underwent another bout. "I'm afraid my father is a bit under the weather. He seems to have an aversion to your cook's crumpets." Whispering, she folded her arms across her midriff to continue her watch.

"Crumpets?" Zach chuckled. "I'll wager Tibbs had more of an aversion to making them." He laughed louder this time. "I'd liked to have seen that. Tibbs, with his stub of a cigar clenched between his few good teeth, serving up tea and crumpets."

Zach's laughter turned into a smothered cough when Tori motioned for him to lower his voice. "Well, what he lacks in the galley, he more than makes up for as a medic. I'll have him blend up his concoction for seasickness." In a forced whisper, Zach continued with a shrug. "The taste is worse than the smell, but it works like a charm. Can you see that he takes it?"

"Father is seasick? I hadn't considered that."

"Definitely. I've seen that color of green before. But don't worry, it should pass after a few days at sea."

"Oh, dear. My father is not an easy one to keep down." She lifted a sheet to pull it across him and the earl flung it back as if to prove her point. "Well, I should say the next few days will be challenging if nothing else." Determination spurred her to lift the sheet once again, this time managing to keep it over him.

"Lady Victoria." Zach turned serious.

"Tori," she stated absently, her attention on her father. "You may call me Tori."

"Lady ... Tori," Zach rushed on. "I must apologize for your intolerable treatment at the hands of criminals while aboard my ship. I assure you those men were not a part of my crew. Furthermore, I want you to know the dockmaster is confident the perpetrator will be apprehended. And when he is, you may rest assured he will be prosecuted to the fullest extent of the law."

Zachery's fervent whispers sounded as if he'd practiced his speech several times before coming to speak with her. It was an honest gesture of amends and Tori could see he was anxiously awaiting her response.

"Why, thank you, Captain. Very much. And I certainly do appreciate your consideration of me. I feel much safer, knowing the matter is in your capable hands."

With an audible sigh, Zach relaxed his shoulders. "Please let me know if I can do anything to make the earl more comfortable. I'll send Tibbs up with his brew right away."

Tori welcomed the change in him. "Splendid." She barely smiled. "But, please, no more crumpets."

"No more crumpets." Zach crossed his heart and sent her a wink.

The next few days passed in a blur.

The earl continued his persistent retching while Tori

kept a constant vigil. He'd managed to swallow only a small portion of the cook's foul remedy. Day after day, the majority of the concoction remained in his cup as the battle to make him drink became greater than its benefit.

She prodded, pampered, pleaded, and pacified until he finally agreed to take a sip or two but holding it down was another matter.

When exhaustion made it impossible to stay awake, Tori dozed in a chair at her father's bedside. When she awoke, a quilt lay mysteriously about her shoulders.

Nicholas checked on them every couple of hours, usually with food in hand or a cup of tea for Tori. He stayed close throughout the week, never far should she need anything.

Mercifully, after the fifth morning the great Atlantic took pity. The high seas calmed to provide a smooth, steady course. The earl's illness abated, and he lapsed into a much needed rest.

Drained, Tori curled up on the wing chair and dozed in and out of a cloud of dreams. Believing that the strong arms carrying her to a soft, inviting pillow were all a part of her gentle sleep, Tori snuggled in closer.

Hours later, she roused and was surprised to find herself back in her own cabin. The same apricot day dress she'd worn the day before was now twisted about her in a frightful mess.

Deepening shadows of late afternoon told her she'd slept most of the day.

Slowly unfurling, Tori stretched, before leaving the

warm place she'd burrowed beneath the quilt. She'd spent nearly every moment of this voyage seeing to her patient, only briefly returning to her cabin to wash and change her dress.

New facings on the door frame caught her eye. A large metal lock and bolt now hung imposingly on the rebuilt door. She had been so absorbed with caring for her father, she hadn't had time to think about the horror of her first afternoon aboard ship. But here, in this room, the whole affair came rushing back to haunt her.

In the fleeting moments after the attack, Tori had come to realize how isolated she'd been for most of her life. Truthfully, she'd never given danger a second thought. No one in all of England would dare harm the daughter of an earl. The notion that she was untouchable had been crushed the moment she'd been thrown to the floor at knifepoint. She had been powerless to help herself. A jarring discovery at best.

Least to say, the attack humbled her, and still lingered like a faceless shadow following at every turn. Refusing to live in fear, she resolved instead to become much more aware of her surroundings. She couldn't live behind the safe walls of the Ladies Academy forever.

Still, something else bothered her about being here in this room. Turning her back to the door, she clutched a pillow to her chest, still deep in thought.

Nicholas Saberton. What was it about the man that made him impossible to ignore?

A tender recollection of brown eyes, alert and shining

with concern as he'd burst into this very space, made her heart skip a beat. She'd be lying to herself if she didn't admit he was a most unforgettable man.

To be certain, he was confident to the point of arrogant. He taunted her shamelessly until she forgot her manners most every time he was around. Yet, on scant occasions, she'd seen something more. Something deep inside of him. A genuine concern that in many ways was foreign to her. Most people cared for her out of obligation. But the captain had gone beyond the call of duty to see she was safe and warm and comfortable. His attention had been kind and completely sincere.

Her hand went to her midsection to still a small flutter brought on by her fanciful thoughts. An insistent growl rumbled beneath her hand to remind her she hadn't eaten and was actually quite hungry.

Yesterday, Zachery Saberton had stopped by her father's room and invited her to dine at the Captain's table. She'd missed last night's dinner, but perhaps tonight he might make room for one more.

Nearly a week had passed since she'd been above deck and she was anxious to take in a bit of fresh air. With that in mind, she fetched her cake of lilac-scented soap and set about making herself presentable. Choosing a gown of rich, iris blue, with silver brocade and a fitted waist, she secured her chestnut curls into combs above each temple, allowing the mass of it to cascade down her back. This was the best she could hope for without her lady's maid here to pin and tuck her hair into the latest style.

Tori stepped into the dimly lit hallway and nodded at the ever-present guard. A quick stop to check on her father found him sleeping comfortably.

Not at all sure which direction the captain's quarters might be, Tori relished the thought of exploring along the way. This was her first time aboard such a large ship and she was eager to look around.

The companionway was steep with slick narrow steps. Tori lifted her skirts to assure her careful footing as she began her ascent. The upper deck was quiet and deserted. Her first breath of moist, open sea air was revitalizing.

Looking out over the sides of the huge vessel, she was drawn to the rails by an entrancing sight. Warm shades of indigo purple splayed across the endless sky. The full moon looked as if it rested at the edge of the sea, gathering in the expansive waters, transforming them into shimmering liquid silver.

"Breathtaking." She spoke aloud to no one in particular.

"I was thinking the same thing," came a low, velvety reply.

Her heart nearly stopped. Without turning, she knew Nicholas had come up beside her. Keeping her gaze straight ahead, she was determined to maintain her poise.

"Glad to see you've come out of hiding." He casually leaned against the rail. "I take it the earl is feeling better?"

"Yes, thank goodness. He should be back to his wonderful, cantankerous self in no time." She passed a fingertip over her brow to catch a stray curl, before chancing a glimpse over at him.

Pressing her eyes shut again, she berated herself for not being better prepared for the sight of his broad, tanned form adorned in solid black evening clothes. A dove-gray ascot lay neatly against the high collar of his white shirt. Nonchalance tugged at his curved lips.

She'd always prided herself on her ability to show restraint and dignity in the face of adversity. Nicholas Saberton, however, was an adversity her gentle breeding could not possibly have prepared her for. His eyes showed a keen awareness of her that drew Tori closer.

Like a moth to a flame, she warned herself.

"How is your shoulder? No infection I hope." A change of thought was definitely in order.

"Healing nicely."

"I don't think I've had a chance to thank you, but I do appreciate your coming to my rescue the other afternoon. If you hadn't happened by, I'm afraid those barbarians might have pilfered more than my baggage."

He graced her with an engaging smile. She forced herself to keep talking before she lost her nerve.

"A—And though I didn't say much at the time, I am terribly grateful for your concern about me during my father's illness." Her appreciation was genuine as she reached over to touch his arm. "I wouldn't want you to think I hadn't noticed."

Nicholas's brow drew together as he glanced down at

her hand, before turning away. "If you'll remember, Miss Haverwood, that's what I'm here for. Looking out for you is all part of the package."

He was obviously trying to put her off, but she refused to be riled. The clear early twilight with its fresh glittering of stars, was too enchanting for argument.

"Please, you may call me Lady Tori. Almost everyone does."

She watched a muscle work in his jaw, and he didn't say anything for a long while. "What, shall I call you?" She tried to keep her tone light, although his silence was exasperating. "Since you're not really the captain of this ship, it hardly seems correct to address you as such. Perhaps, Mr. Saberton will do?"

Nicholas straightened and turned from the railing to face her.

Much too close.

His serious expression made her want to run away and get closer all at the same time.

"Or ... I suppose if you insist I could call you Nicholas." She took a nervous step back. "Only with your permission, of course."

Continuing his persistent gaze, he barely cocked a brow in answer.

It occurred to her that he was enjoying her unease, provoking it even. She lifted her own brow in response, and along with it, her chin.

Nicholas grinned.

Straightening her shoulders, she tapped a neatly

shaped fingernail at his chest to make her point. "Very well then. How about I call you Surly Knave?" She curved her lip, and gave a try at turning the tables. "Insolent swain? Loathsome toad? Onion-eyed loon?"

Nicholas reached down and played with an unrestrained curl on the back of her neck which made her shiver. "You read too much Shakespeare."

"I—I do." Tori felt a warm blush stain her cheeks. "And I often quote him when I'm flustered."

"Really?" Nicholas grinned and took another step to seal the gap between them. "Surely, I don't make you feel flustered."

"Well, certainly not." Tori observed the deck and his shining boots to keep from having to endure his warm gaze. Her bravery was rapidly waning. "I simply forgot my wrap, that's all. I'm beginning to need it. Perhaps I'll go—"

The roll of the ship pitched her forward and Nicholas wrapped an arm about her as he searched her features.

Closing her eyes to his intense inspection, Tori frantically grasped for a thread of proper restraint. She should never have come up unchaperoned. When her eyes fluttered open again, her focus centered on his mouth.

"Mr. Loon...er, Nicholas." She fought to keep her voice steady. "I do hope you aren't thinking of ...."

"I thought about it," he answered with a smile. "And so did you."

"I assure you, I did not." Though not entirely truthful, he'd best not know what she was truly thinking.

Taking her completely by surprise, Nicholas cupped her face and came excruciatingly close to brushing his mouth against hers. The mere anticipation of it sent Tori's world into a spiral. Closing her eyes, she made a pucker.

Nothing.

With a discreet peek, she opened one eye.

A smug grin spread across Nicholas's face as he looked down at her. "Mm hmm. I see it never crossed your mind at all." His teasing tone affected her like being doused with a bucket of ice water.

The deep rumble of his laughter went straight through her as he still held her close.

"I was merely enjoying the evening breeze." Tori pushed away from him. Heat rose in her cheeks and her pride stung terribly at her clumsy gaffe.

"Yes, I do believe the breeze is quite flustering." Once more, his laugh drew her attention to his lips. She knew she was staring, but Lord help her, that brief encounter had only left her curious about what it would be like to be kissed by this man.

"Come on, princess. I'll take you below to dinner." Amusement danced in his eyes. "I'm suddenly famished."

Tori remained silent. Partly to cover her embarrassment, and partly because she didn't trust herself to speak at the moment.

Nicholas offered his arm with a gallant flair.

A clatter from behind caught them off guard. Two large barrels reeled across the deck toward them. Nicholas immediately set her out of harm's way as he scanned the area.

The wind had picked up and the flapping of the sails was the only movement besides an occasional creaking of the high wooden masts.

Tori shuddered as apprehension prickled her senses.

Nicholas pulled her closer to his side. With one last glance over his shoulder, he led her down the stairway.

Neither were aware, a killer watched from the shadows.

Her very frowns are fairer far,
than the smiles of other maidens are.
~ Hartley Coleridge

Five

It was their last morning aboard *The Tempest,* and the ship was teeming with excitement.

"Leave it, Victoria." The earl was already out the door, calling back behind him. "Let the cabin boy tidy up. We mustn't miss landfall."

"On my way, Father." Tori took one last look around her quarters before joining her father in the hallway.

"Step lightly. The sun's been up a good hour." He checked his timepiece, as he'd done ten times in the past five minutes. "Our first order of business is getting off this rickety packet and setting foot on steady ground."

Her father couldn't possibly imagine how much she was ready to be done with this voyage. Since the evening on deck with Nicholas Saberton, her enthusiasm for this trip had taken a downward turn.

Convinced the stars had shone just for them, with the gentle roll of the sea adding a dreamlike quality to the evening, Tori had finally understood the romantic notions of her favorite poems.

Nicholas had been charming and daring. Tori had been utterly convinced he'd felt the magic between them as well.

Until the next morning when he'd avoided her like she had some sort of horrific disease. Every day since, he'd made himself scarce. On the rare occasion when they'd spoken, he'd dutifully asked as to her well-being yet treated her with cool reserve.

The sting of his indifference added to her shame at having been so brazenly curious that night.

Stepping up onto the deck, Tori opened her parasol with a snap and lifted its lace spindles to shield her face from the morning sun. Thoughts of Nicholas had her miffed more than she dared let on.

For her father's sake, she put on a carefree expression, one that had nothing to do with the ache in her heart. He was far too fragile these days.

"Good day to you, sir. Lady Tori." Zachery called to them from the other side of the deck.

"Ah, young Saberton." Lord Haverwood didn't bother to hide his disappointment at being greeted by Zach rather than his older brother. "Shouldn't you be minding the helm?"

Zach grinned. "I'm headed to do just that."

"I see land. Where are we exactly?" The earl lifted a

hand to shield his eyes against the glare reflecting off the waveless water.

"We've just entered the mouth of the Savannah River." Zach pointed to the lush banks on either side of the craft. "It won't be long now before we round that corner and you'll be able to see the grand city, herself."

"I say, it's a touch warmer than we are accustomed to. Wouldn't you agree, my dear?" The earl took a kerchief from his lapel pocket and dabbed his brow.

Tori smiled at the consideration he was showing this morning. The old rascal was up to something, although she had a feeling she didn't want to know what it was.

"Where's the captain?" Lord Haverwood looked past Zachery to search the deck for Nicholas.

Thankfully, Zachery had been blessed with an understanding nature. He appeared unaffected by her father's discourtesy. "Nicholas went ahead in the lifeboat to make arrangements for your transportation once we set aground. He'll be waiting for us when we make port.

The river came to a bend, and the distinctive outline of Savannah unfolded before her eyes. The sky was a brilliant blue and there wasn't a cloud in sight. Pink and yellow wildflowers scattered across lush grassy knolls and the tallest trees she'd ever seen stood in silent guard around the city. All in all, it was a beautiful welcome to the shores of America.

Her father had become solemn and exceptionally quiet. The faraway look on his face was hard to read. Whether an expression of immense sadness or one of fond remembrance she had no way of telling.

Placing her lace-gloved hand to cover his wrinkled one atop the polished brass handle of his cane. They stood silently for several moments taking in the view.

As if coming out of a trance, the earl suddenly cleared his throat. "Saberton, see that our baggage is brought up posthaste."

Tori directed an apologetic glance at Zachery and found him leaning against the rails, grinning with a good-natured shrug.

"I'll see to it right away, sir." Zach bellowed an order to prepare for landing and the deckhands swung into motion. They eased the mammoth ship into her berth with the fluid dexterity that must come with years of experience. Once secured, a roar of excitement went up as the ramp was slowly lowered.

"No more dallying. Come, Victoria, let's find the captain."

Barrels sectioned the quay into uniform tracts. Fashionable carriages were stationed in one portion, waiting for or dispensing passengers, and buckboards full of cargo were being unloaded in another. Orderly activity buzzed all around them as the ramp was set.

"That's Nicholas's carriage over there on the right." Zachery called from above, directing them to a glossy black brougham, drawn by beautifully matched grays. "I'll have your baggage sent over to Mrs. Charlotte's as soon as we get it unloaded." With a wave, he turned and rejoined his crew.

Tori had to hurry to catch up with her father, as he clopped along at an amazing pace. A gentleman with gleaming dark skin and steel gray hair waited for them, holding the carriage door open.

"Are you the Haverwood folks?" he asked in a low, gravelly voice.

"Where is the captain?" The earl scanned the area with an impatient glower.

"I'll be the one seeing you over to the Haverwood's residence. Mr. Nicholas has gone on to the office for the afternoon. He told me to see to your comfort and tell you he's mighty glad to have had the pleasure of servin' you. Especially the lady, he said."

Lord Haverwood sputtered while Tori closed her eyes and took in a deep, calming breath.

"What is your name, sir?" Tori inquired with an honest smile.

"Jonas, Ma'am."

"Thank you, Jonas, for seeing to our comfort. You are quite thoughtful." She was determined to disregard Nicholas's lack of consideration, ignoring the tweak it left on her pride.

"I must say your employer is quite resourceful if a bit spineless sending his valet to complete his obligations." Her annoyance escaped her lips before she could think better of it.

"'Scuse me, ma'am?" Jonas seemed truly astonished. "Cap'n Saberton? Cap'n Nicholas Saberton?"

"Victoria, remember yourself." Though the earl's reprimand was directed at her, Tori knew he was also irritated by Nicholas's disregard.

"I don't fault the man, Father. I believe he spent far too many days in the sun. I hear one can become completely addle-brained in excessive heat."

"Actually, my dear, I was under the impression the captain was quite taken with you. I spied him watching you last evening." The earl's remark drifted up as he climbed into the vehicle behind of her.

"Wearily watching me, perhaps. I believe I quite intimidate the man." Nibbling her lower lip, she lowered her parasol and nodded politely at Nicholas's driver thanking him for his help.

The coach lurched forward as the horses took lead onto the well-traveled road. It occurred to her that her association with Nicholas Saberton had finally come to an end. She'd likely never see him again. Never be drawn by his mesmerizing gaze one minute, or spurned by his cool indifference the next.

The top of the vehicle was folded down, and Jonas was a delight as he pointed out various landmarks along the way. Savannah was neatly laid out in prominent squares, each having a specific function for the city.

They passed Johnson Square, where Jonas said the important families participated in nightly promenades, mainly to see who was with whom. Market Square was where the ladies took their daily constitutional walk, exchanging gossip while the servants shopped for food. Chippewa Square, Jonas explained, held the theater and was lined with glittering carriages by night.

Twenty-four squares in all and Tori looked forward to exploring the individual personalities of each of them. By the time they turned onto the sandy drive of Habershire Street where the exquisite Haverwood home was poised in grand elegance, Tori was more excited than she'd been in weeks.

"Father, this trip was a marvelous idea. You always know what we need."

He tried his best to suppress a smile that threatened to crack his gruff exterior. His mustache wobbled with the effort.

"Whoa, there." Jonas secured the horses and climbed down from the driver's seat.

"Jonas, you've been most kind to show us about." Tori turned her best smile on their driver and he was quick to return it.

The large front door swung open and an elderly man tottered down the wide steps to receive the new arrivals.

A woman with in an outdated fuchsia gown stood in the doorway, spouting instructions in a loud voice. Fiftyish, with a rather wide girth, she waved a white handkerchief at each one that she addressed.

"Gabe, you be careful now and don't break anything. Help them down, Jonas. Tell Flossie to put on a kettle for tea. Edward likes his tea, you know. My, my, my, but look at you. What a beauty. Come on in here, honey. Hello, Edward!" She sang, flagging him with her tatted hankie, chattering in what Tori was beginning to recognize as a soft Georgian drawl.

"Charlotte," the earl grumbled in greeting.

"Aurora has been on pins and needles waitin' for you all to get here. This is her season, you know. Her comin' out party was earlier this month. Why, you girls have a whirlwind of social engagements comin' up. It'll make your head spin, yes it will."

Finally pausing to take a breath, she got a good look at the earl and lifted her skirts to meet him halfway. "Lord have mercy, Edward. You're lookin' so much older than the last time I saw you. A cane! Merciful heavens. Flossie, nevermind the tea, fix the earl a stout lemonade."

"I detest lemonade." Her father sloughed off his sister-in-law's assistance. "I do not need your help. And in case you haven't noticed, woman, walking sticks happen to be the thing this season. However, it would seem that you, Charlotte, have not changed in the least." He added something to that statement under his breath, as he came up the steps to join Tori.

"Why thank you, Edward. You're a dear to say so. You know, I've always tried to keep myself up. Believe it or not, it's not as easy as it used to be."

"So you are my Aunt Charlotte?" Tori spoke over her father's muted response. "I've so looked forward to meeting you."

"My manners, child. Of course I'm your Aunt Charlotte."

She caught Tori up in a crushing hug, calling out over her shoulder. "Aurora! Darlin', come on down here now.

Our guests have arrived." An overwhelming vapor of French perfume nearly stole Tori's breath.

Struggling to gain her release, Tori stepped into the grand foyer. "Your home is lovely, Aunt Charlotte." She looked up at the magnificent high ceilings.

"Why, thank you, sweet. It was a gift from my dear, dear, Percy. One of his many indulgences over the years." She took a moment to sniff into her kerchief before leading them on a tour. "It was built by Isaiah Davenport. He's famous, you know."

Tori didn't.

"Edward, you've never seen this house. I do believe we were still living over on Liberty Street when you last visited. Come on into the drawing room, you two. I want to hear all about your trip."

The ornate double doors leading into the parlor stood open, and as Tori followed her aunt into the room, she stopped short. Her jaw dropped at the sight looming before her as her father ran into her from behind.

Tori turned to see Lord Haverwood's bushy eyebrows shoot upward. "Dear heavens."

Not a piece in the room matched another. Yards of sheer yellow gauze crisscrossed over floor-length windows, tied in billowing festoons at each side.

On one wall, hung red-flocked wallpaper, while the other walls were painted in pumpkin stripe. A colorful blue rug covered the dark wood floor, and two purple paisley settees faced each other in the middle. A low wrought iron table completed the hideous ensemble.

"I see you're admiring the illustrious and well-known work of my decorator, Madame Dupree." Aunt Charlotte overflowed with pride as she sashayed over to sit on a settee.

"You see no such thing, I assure you." The earl chose an overstuffed floral side chair.

"I can't tell you the compliments I get over the wonderfully unique and different schemes that woman comes up with. Why, it just boggles the mind." She patted the seat for Tori to sit beside her. "She's straight from Paris." Her aunt leaned in to see if Tori was impressed. "In France."

Tori nodded, deliberately ignoring the earl's grunt.

"Those people over there have a knack for these sorts of things that you don't find anywhere else. She and her son Jean Pierre own the most fashionable shop in town. Jean Pierre designs all my hats and gowns for me. Exclusively. That means no one else has any like them."

"Simply ... fascinating, Aunt Charlotte." Tori tried to remain diplomatic. "I can truly say, I've never seen such a diverse application of color and pattern. Quite an original effect, to be sure."

The earl snorted, and Tori's teeth caught the edge of her lower lip.

"Mother?" A quiet summons came from the hallway.

"In here, precious. That's my Aurora. Oh, you two are going to be such friends." Aunt Charlotte tapped Tori on the knee with her fan, then rushed over to the double doors.

Be worthy of love and love will come.
~ Louisa May Alcott

Six

urora was just as Tori had pictured her. Her pale blond ringlets hung down past her small shoulders, and she had a fresh, milky complexion. Her eyes were as blue as Tori's own, and she wore a pleasant, shy smile.

Only a year and half separated them, yet Aurora stood at least two inches taller than Tori's five feet and five inches.

"I beg your pardon. I hope I didn't interrupt." Aurora joined her mother obviously uneasy as all eyes turned to her.

Charlotte took her daughter by the elbow and half dragged her to where Lord Haverwood was seated. "Edward, this is Aurora, your niece."

As the earl stood, Aurora greeted him with a sweet smile. "Uncle Edward, I'm happy to meet you."

"How do you do, my dear? I'm pleased to see you've

inherited your grandmother's eyes. Percival must have been delighted. Positively delighted."

He took her arm and brought her over to the settee. "Might I introduce your cousin, Lady Victoria."

"Hello, Victoria, I can't tell you how much I've looked forward to your arrival."

"Please, call me Tori."

It felt as if they already knew one another. They'd corresponded by long, detailed letters since they were old enough to hold a pen.

"I hope you'll have a chance to play the harp for us this evening, Aurora. I've so looked forward to hearing you play."

"Oh, my yes! Lordy, you have such a treat in store. Not a cherub in heaven can play as beautifully as my own little angel. Aurora, honey, you'll have to play that little sonata you've been practicing all week. Edward just wait'll you hear. I declare you'll think you've crossed on over into Glory." Aunt Charlotte was as puffed up as an excited peahen and Aurora's fair complexion was two shades darker than before.

It occurred to Tori that Aurora might not be as timid as she first appeared. Aunt Charlotte just never gave her an opportunity to speak.

"I shall look forward to it. Now, if you ladies will excuse me, I should like to freshen up. Which way to our chambers?" Lord Haverwood headed for the doors.

Charlotte raced him to the entrance. "Gabe! Come show his Lordship to the chartreuse guest room. You go on and rest now, Edward. You do look tired." She patted him on the back.

The earl glared at her but held his tongue. Instead he stamped his cane noisily as he followed the butler from the room.

"And you girls can go upstairs, too, if you'd like. Aurora, show Victoria to the room adjoining yours, darlin'. Y'all spend a little time getting to know one another before dinner. I'll have Flossie bring up some tea cakes to tide you over."

"Yes, Mama," Aurora's answer was quiet.

"Oh, and since we're having company for dinner, I'd like you all down here early to receive them. Be sure to wear something appropriate for an evening with guests, now. You'll be acting as hostess for plenty of social functions in the coming months, Aurora, so you must get in as much practice as you possibly can."

Aunt Charlotte turned toward the door again. "Not that those two Sabertons are the best guests to practice on, mind you. Still, we must show our gratitude to them for kindly lookin' out after Edward and Victoria these past few weeks." With that she disappeared around the corner, leaving a stunned silence in her wake.

Aurora stared straight ahead, looking petrified.

Tori found the edge of the settee with her hand and slowly lowered herself onto it. The very breath had been knocked from her lungs.

It had not occurred to her that she might encounter Nicholas socially once they'd set aground. A costly assumption. Savannah was his home after all, and it would only be reasonable to expect a man of his stature to move in the same circles as the Haverwoods.

Wealth, it appeared, dictated social status in America rather than birth. And, by all indications, Nicholas Saberton had plenty of wealth.

Surely Aunt Charlotte would understand if she explained she was too exhausted from traveling to come down for dinner. Her father, however, would insist she join them, or demand to know why.

From of the corner of her eye, she spied Aurora still affixed to the same spot as when her mother left the room. The girl nibbled on a thumbnail and a frown worried her brow.

Poor thing. She must be terrified of her new responsibilities. Tori had handled this sort of thing at Miss Mair's. It wasn't uncommon for a young lady to be nervous when first called upon to make her entertaining debut. All but forgetting her aversion to tonight's guest, Tori's focus now centered on her frightened cousin.

"There's really nothing to it." She spoke gently, as she came to Aurora's side. "I've done it dozens of times, and I shall be right here to help if you need me."

"Beg your pardon?"

"I know it can be overwhelming to suddenly carry the burden of entertaining, but you'll do just fine. And thank heavens it won't be as if we are having legitimate callers over this evening. From what I've seen neither one of them cares a fig about social graces." Tori tried her best to sound reassuring. "Although, Zachery, at least, can be quite charming when he takes a notion."

"Oh, Tori!" Aurora spun around and landed in a side chair. "That's the whole problem, don't you see?"

"I ... well, no. I'm afraid I don't. What is it? Surely Nicholas doesn't frighten you."

Tori watched her cousin continue to shake her head. "Well, it couldn't possibly be his brother."

"Yes!" Aurora's ringlets bounced as she nodded emphatically.

"Zachery? What could possibly be frightening about—" Tori stopped herself as understanding dawned like a beacon of light.

Aurora blushed profusely.

"Oh, I see." Tori smiled knowingly. "Does he suspect how you feel?"

"Oh, heaven's no. To tell you the truth, he barely knows I'm alive. Whenever he's near, I waste time trying to think up something clever to say. In the end, I never say much of anything. He must think I'm such a goose."

She covered her face with her hands and Tori thought for a moment that the poor girl had dissolved into tears. Just as she moved to comfort her, Aurora looked up with laughter shining brightly in her blue eyes.

"And it's no wonder. When he speaks to me, I freeze up and choke. I look like a chicken with an onion skin caught in its throat. I'm surprised he bothers to talk to me at all."

"I see." Rather an unorthodox description, but Tori

caught her meaning. "Well, at least you have the proper attitude, Aurora. I always say one can change an unpleasant circumstance as long as one keeps a good head and goes about it in the right way. And now that I am here, I shall help you."

"Would you? I mean if you could somehow get Zach to notice I'm a woman now, nearly eighteen. That would be a start. Don't you think?"

Tori nodded. "Certainly and we shall. Don't you worry, Aurora. Zachery will take notice. You're a lovely girl."

"You think so?"

"You have a quick mind and you're extremely talented. Why, we've simply to show him what it is he's been missing all this time. Zachery's a bright enough young man. He will soon be congratulating himself over his marvelous new find."

Tori folded her arms and walked over to look out of the tall window, taking in the beautiful panorama bathed in springtime. A couple of blue jays caught her attention as one pursued the other in a merry game of tag.

Giggling, Aurora sprang from her chair to look out of the other window before she wandered around the room. "Tori, I'm so glad you're here. Oh! Won't Viola Mae Jenkins be positively beside herself?"

"Who?" Tori asked absently, still not fully accustomed to the accent.

"Viola Mae Jenkins. She goes around telling everyone she's got Zach Saberton wrapped around her pinkie finger. As far as I can tell he doesn't give her the time of day. Her sister, Felicity, is the same way about Nicholas."

Tori was suddenly staring at the window instead of out of it, as Aurora's words became more than just chatter.

"...always fawning after him like a lovesick calf, telling everyone he's on the verge of proposing marriage. Pooh! Nicholas would never take up with that hussy."

Tori turned to face Aurora.

"She was married once, for about two years. The poor man drowned in a lake somewhere. But, she flirted shamelessly with Nicholas even before her husband was dead. Of course, he didn't pay her any mind. At least, I don't think he did."

Aurora frowned for a moment and brought her thumbnail to her mouth, then rushed on. "Mother says the Saberton brothers are too handsome for their own good." She sighed heavily. "Nicholas and Ian are well known for turning heads. They are the two oldest. But, I think Zach is every bit as attractive."

"There's more of them?" Tori returned to the settee to retrieve her reticule and parasol. "Heaven help Savannah."

It wasn't as if she hadn't been aware that Nicholas was an old hand in the art of flirtation. His skill had been more than apparent. It just galled her at how easily she had let him lead her down a path he'd obviously taken many, many times before.

"Ian goes to seminary up in New York somewhere.

But he comes home for holidays."

"A Saberton minister?" Try as she might, Tori couldn't imagine it.

"Not yet, but he's working on it. He's always been nice to me." Aurora came to Tori's side. "Do you suppose Zach might be persuaded to escort me to the Hermitage Soirée in August? It's the party of all parties during the season. The Hamiltons throw it every year over at their plantation out on Argyle Island. I'm dying to go, but it would be even better if I were to show up with Zach."

Her cousin's pained expression was all the encouragement Tori needed. "First things first. Let's get you upstairs and ready for this evening." Tori smiled and patted Aurora's hand. "Then, we shall go to work on the big soirée."

Tori was determined that Zachery would indeed notice her young cousin. And as for Nicholas ... she'd make certain he understood she wasn't interested in adding to his collection of discarded women.

The offices of Haverwood Shipping and Trade were quiet yet Nicholas had trouble concentrating on his records. Once again, the figures in front of him melded into deep azure pools until he tossed the pen to his desk.

He'd made an extreme effort to distance himself from Victoria. It had been a challenge while they were still on the ship because he'd pledged to guard her. He knew she considered his lack of attention an outright snub, but he could see in her eyes what Zach had warned him of. So he'd backed off.

It was better she understood from the start of their visit to Savannah that he was not available for long-term commitment. Nicholas had decided it was easier for all involved to leave them to themselves once they set down. From now on, he wanted a workable business relationship with the earl, but Victoria was on her own.

They were an ocean away from any danger now. No more mishaps since they'd pushed off from England's shore. Besides, once Mrs. Charlotte began circulating the earl and his daughter, she would forget all about him.

"Mr. Nicholas, I brought a note for you." Jonas appeared in the doorway, holding out an envelope.

"Bring it here, Jonas. Who's it from?" Nicholas came around to the front of the heavy oak desk and leaned on the edge. He took the message and broke the seal.

"Mrs. Charlotte Haverwood said to see you and Mr. Zachery both get one." He stood by, while Nicholas pulled the card from its pocket, scanning the contents. "Bad news, sir?"

"Dinner invitation." Nicholas reached for his pen and ink. "Take a note back with our regrets."

"I don't see as how I blame you. 'Specially after what all that pretty little gal stayin' over there done said about you."

Jonas turned to leave when Nicholas's voice stopped him in his tracks. "What exactly did the little gal say, Jonas?" He crossed his arms over his chest and waited for the answer.

"She, ah, she ... Well, sir, I believe she said you was weak in the head."

Nicholas's mouth fell open before curling into a slow grin. "Go on."

"And I believe she also said you was a coward, too."

Nicholas's brow rose as amazement brightened his spirits. He fought to keep from laughing out loud.

"For some reason, she thinks you are scared of her. I ain't never seen you scared of nothin'. Surely not of no little snip of a girl like that."

"Afraid of her?" Nicholas roared in amusement.

Jonas nodded, then shook his gray head all in one motion.

Zach came up the stairs, catching the tail end of the exchange. "Who's scared of what?" "No one." Nicholas started for the door, turning Zach around by the arm as he passed. "Come on. We have to change."

"Where are we going?" Zach hurried to keep up with Nicholas.

"To dinner. At the Haverwood's."

Saying nothing, sometimes says the most.
~ Emily Dickenson

Seven

"Girls!" Tori startled at the shrill summons that came from the stairway. "Our guests have arrived. Mustn't keep them waiting."

"Oh my." Aurora's hand flew to her small bosom. "I don't know if I can do this. Look, my palms are wringing wet and my stomach just flip-flopped." Her eyes pressed shut, then opened. "What if I can't think of anything to say? What if I turn mute again?"

"Then say nothing until it passes." Tori handed Aurora her shawl with a confident nod. "Smile that adorable smile of yours. When you feel ready, you'll contribute just fine. If you begin to feel overwhelmed, simply catch my attention and I shall try to cover for you."

"I suppose I could do that." Aurora placed the wrap around her shoulders.

The two had spent all afternoon poring over Godey's

latest fashion plates, delving into Aurora's wardrobe trying to find the right look for her. Gowns were considered, then discarded until every available space was strewn with the samplings.

After much deliberation, Aurora finally settled on a dusky pink gown of sateen, high-necked and bordered with white lace. Tiny rosebuds were woven throughout her pale locks which were carefully pinned atop her head. The final effect was stunning.

Tori guided the younger girl down the hallway. "Let's just consider this your first step toward an invitation to the Hermitage Soirée."

Aurora nodded, nibbling on a nail.

Reaching for the girl's hand, Tori brought it down to her side. "How can we impress our dear Mr. Saberton with your musical talents, if your fingers are nibbled to the bone?"

As they started down the winding stairway, Tori smoothed her own gown with a careful hand. She had chosen an elegant silk of shimmering gold, with deep blue laurel leaves embroidered across the scoop-necked bodice. The wide hem flowed lightly over her blue slippers.

The Saberton brothers stood near the open windows. Nicholas moved when the cousins entered the room, offering each one an arm.

"Might I say you ladies look lovely this evening?" His low, smooth voice never failed to take her breath. She chose to forgo taking his arm for the sake of her composure.

"You might," Tori smiled but just barely, deciding to disregard his dismissal of them earlier.

Nicholas smiled back at her as he seated Aurora on the garish settee. Something about the gleam in his eye caused Tori to believe he was enjoying this entirely too much.

"A pleasure to see you again, Victoria. I'm glad you were able to get along without me this afternoon."

Jonas had apparently filled him in on her remarks. Good. It still irked her that he had all but dumped them the minute the ship set ground. "The ride was extremely pleasant. Jonas was a wonderful guide."

Nicholas made a comment to his brother over his shoulder, yet loud enough for all to hear. "Exquisite beauty. And so clever, don't you think? Indeed a rare find."

Zach held up a hand to show a neutral position.

"Enough to frighten an average man half to death." His eyes met hers and his voice dropped to a velvet huskiness. "However, never make the mistake of confusing me with your average man."

Tori tried to appear unaffected by his bold assertion as she settled into the seat next to her cousin. Her heart beat loudly in her ears as she made a concentrated effort to smooth her skirts around her.

Nicholas chuckled as he took a chair. "How fortunate we are, Zach, to have the honor of dining with three of the fairest flowers in all Savannah." He flashed a handsome grin as Tori rolled her eyes at his trite compliment.

Charlotte Haverwood squealed with delight and dissolved into a flurry of fan waving. "Nicholas Saberton, behave yourself, you scamp. You oughtn't fill these girls' heads with all that nonsense of yours. You always were the charmer. Why, you got yourself out of more trouble when you were a boy with that silver-edged tongue of yours. Gabe, go and tell Edward he's holding up dinner. I can't imagine for the life of me what could be taking him so long."

Aunt Charlotte was barely finished when the earl entered the room.

"Can't one see to his dress in peace and quiet without you chirping about it? For goodness sake, Charlotte, calm yourself."

Apparently her father had not finished his nap and Charlotte was the closest to take it out on. He twitched his mustache as he passed her by.

Aunt Charlotte made a face at his testiness and continued to wave her fan.

Zach turned the conversation to Aurora. "I understand you made your big social debut this month." He smiled as a blush glowed in her cheeks. "I'm sorry I missed it. It's hard to believe that the same scrawny brat who used to throw pecans at me from the top of a tree is now about to take society by storm."

"Indeed, she has grown up, Zachery. Quite nicely, wouldn't you say?" Tori answered for her when she saw Aurora's mouth moving, yet no words were coming out. "Did you know that she is an accomplished musician as well?"

Nicholas raised a brow at her, which she chose to ignore. Let him think what he would. She was determined to have this evening go well for Aurora.

"Well, now that you mention it, I do recall that you play an instrument. Harp, isn't it? Could we persuade you to play something for us later?" Zach smiled at her and by all indications he seemed genuinely interested.

Aurora nodded, while Tori and Aunt Charlotte watched the exchange with a sense of accomplishment.

"Mrs. Charlotte, dinner is all set whenever you all is ready," Gabe announced from the doorway.

"Wonderful. Aurora, sweet, see that your guests are properly seated. Come along now, Edward, let's get you fed. You'll feel more like yourself once you've tasted Flossie's round of beef." Aunt Charlotte took her brother-in-law by the arm and led him to the dining area.

"How about a truce, princess, before you skewer me with that sharp look?" Nicholas held out his hand to Tori.

Aurora had already latched on to Zachery and silently implored her cousin to relent.

Tori didn't have the heart to spoil the evening for Aurora. She had no choice but to concede. She took Nicholas's arm instead of the hand he offered and gave a look that promised it was far from over between them.

He lifted her hand from off his arm and up to his smiling lips to promise the same.

Aurora seated Zachery next to herself. Nicholas and

Tori sat directly across from them, with Aunt Charlotte and the earl at each end.

"Mmm. Smells delicious, Mrs. Charlotte." Zach looked over the steaming dishes.

"As much as I'd love to take credit, Zach darlin', this was after all Aurora's menu. She makes a fine little hostess, don't you think?"

"Well, then, Miss Aurora, I have you to thank. I haven't seen a meal like this in months. Tibbs keeps us alive, but that's about the extent of it."

"Humph! If the man had his way, we'd all be dead." The earl sniffed.

Placing her napkin on her lap, Tori admonished herself to get through the evening with grace and dignity. Then she caught Nicholas smiling down at her with a genuinely sweet expression and her resolve went out the window. She smiled back in spite of herself and he held her gaze for a moment longer than was considered proper.

The two of them received questioning glances all around.

"Shall we say grace?" Aunt Charlotte bowed her head.

The earl's voice interrupted. "Isn't it the custom, if I recall correctly, that you people normally clasp the hand next to you while offering grace?"

Tori closed her eyes as Nicholas took her hand.

The prayer went on and on until Tori was sure the woman had thanked the Good Lord and all twelve of His disciples for every blessing known to man. Chancing a peek at Nicholas, she found him still smiling at her.

Finally, when everyone said their amens, Tori tried to retrieve her fingers from his grasp, but he continued to hold them tight.

She decided she must go about this differently. There was more than one way around a headstrong male. "Nicholas, I rather need my hand, just now. It makes it easier to eat, you understand. You may hold it again later, if you wish."

He narrowed his eyes for a moment before releasing her hand.

"Thank you, Nicholas." She smiled at him demurely, lifting her fork and knife.

"You shouldn't play coy." He took the serving fork from a platter offered at his right and placed a large slice of beef onto his plate. "You're no good at it."

"I most certainly am." Tori was grateful that everyone else at the table seemed to be involved in their own conversations. "Besides, I don't know what you are referring to."

"What I am referring to, Victoria, is that you are as transparent as glass. You're no good at hiding your opinion, but insist on trying to anyway."

Tori blinked as she considered his words.

"What would be so hard about telling me to shove off if that's what you mean?" His voice was quiet. "Believe it or not, you've already said as much with your eyes, so it doesn't matter whether you say it aloud or not."

"A lady would never express such rudeness. Thinking

and saying are two very different matters. It's what keeps
this world civilized, after all." Silence fell between them
for a brief moment until Tori cocked her head and asked
what she had been wanting to ask him all evening. "Why
must you challenge me at every turn?"

When she caught Aunt Charlotte's questioning
glimpse, she took a bite to show appreciation for the fine
meal.

"Because, if you remember, I've seen you 'flustered.' It
was highly entertaining."

Her fork froze halfway to her lips.

"Now, which of the two of us is a coward?" He casually cut his food with a knife, as if they were discussing
the weather. "I'd say, sweetheart, I'm daring enough to
say what I mean. And at the moment that has you
terrified."

Tori nearly choked.

"Here now! Take a drink, my dear. She's forgotten
one must chew real meat." Lord Haverwood motioned
for Tori's water goblet to be refilled.

"Oh! I'm terribly sorry." Tori dabbed at her mouth
with a napkin. "I'm afraid I must pay more attention to
what I am doing and less to the conversation." She
avoided Nicholas's grin and gave her cousin a weak smile.

Tori pushed the food around her plate, hoping to give
the appearance of having an appetite and thankful
Nicholas let the matter drop.

After dinner, the men adjourned to the library, while
the ladies went to the drawing room to wait for them.

Nicholas's advice lingered in Tori's thoughts and she had difficulty concentrating on her needlepoint. The things he suggested were completely foreign to her.

Didn't he realize that in restraining herself, she was only practicing the most polished of manners? Proper ladies of good breeding always did so. Why, to do otherwise, would be exceedingly brash.

Though it hardly seemed fair, women had to find other, more discriminating, ways of expressing themselves.

Poking her finger for the third time with her sewing needle, Tori put the piece aside and quietly sipped her sweet apple cider. She couldn't understand what Nicholas expected of her. He couldn't possibly be familiar with the ways of the gentry, being American and all. Nevertheless, he felt at ease offering her advice on how she should behave. He was most exasperating.

"What should I do now, Tori? I think Zach has finally noticed I'm more than a silly child" Aurora was on the edge of her seat, too enthused to work on her quilting square. "I've got to somehow win him over and show I'm interested in him."

Aunt Charlotte clapped her hands together. "I knew it! I knew it! I was sure there was some sparking goin' on between you two. Oh goodness gracious me, my sweet, sweet baby has her very first beau." She made a flagrant display of pulling the lace hanky from her sleeve and swiping at her eyes, before resting the wrinkled cloth to her trembling mouth.

"Mother, please." Aurora rewarded her mother's

dramatic show with an impatient roll of her eyes. "I'll never get him to ask me to the Hermitage Soirée if we scare him off. Tori says we need to be subtle about these things. Isn't that right, Tori?"

"Well, yes, actually. I imagine the less you say on the subject, the better off you'll be."

"What do you mean?" Aurora asked.

Aunt Charlotte nodded, setting her own patchwork aside.

"I mean you must use indirect actions to show Zachery you find him fascinating. Once you've engaged his interest, gently lead him toward the subject of the soirée. He will think it was all his own idea, mind you, and you won't appear as having been too forward."

Thank goodness Zachery was the more predictable brother. Such a plan would never work on Nicholas.

"I still don't understand what you mean about indirect actions." Aurora stood and came to sit next to Tori. "Can you give me an example?"

Aunt Charlotte chimed in, "Well, she means like propping pillows up behind him and kneeling adoringly at his feet. Hanging on dearly to every word he says. Don't you, sugar?"

"Heaven's, no! He is a grown man, after all. What I'm suggesting is more of a fine flirtation. Perhaps a faint fluttering of the eyelashes. And, if he says something amusing, give him a tender smile. Nothing too eager and certainly nothing too provocative."

Seeing that they were still perplexed, Tori chose another example.

"Picture the Mona Lisa. Men have found her most intriguing for hundreds of years, and all she really does is just sit there and sort of…smile. Like this." Tori illustrated with a quaint imitation of da Vinci's masterpiece. "That's all a man wants. An ear to listen and a smile showing your approval."

"Oh, Tori, that's brilliant!" Aurora jumped up and spun around. "It isn't what I say at all. It's all in the way I react to what he says."

"Exactly." Tori folded her hands in her lap, pleased they finally seemed to be getting somewhere.

"Shh. They're coming. Aurora, honey, do sit down. Mercy sakes." Aunt Charlotte nervously wound her embroidery floss into a mess.

Tori was glad for the chance to tutor her cousin in the fine art of flirtation. She'd been anxious to try it out since reading all about it in her favorite magazine. It couldn't possibly go wrong.

Mary had a little lamb whose fleece
was white as snow.
~ Sarah Josepha Hale

Eight

"May we join you, ladies?" Zach came directly over to stand beside Aurora and she flushed.

Nicholas and Lord Haverwood entered the room pre-occupied in conversation. Something about labor costs and embargo taxes or some such drivel. They barely acknowledged the presence of anyone else in the room.

"I believe you promised us a musical treat, Aurora. Would you mind playing something?" Zach leaned over her to make his request.

Aurora looked like she was prepared to stand on her head—anything to keep him looking at her that way. With a gentle nudge, Tori reminded the smitten girl to stay within the plan.

Aurora sat up straight. Adopting her best coquettish expression, she tilted her head ever-so-slightly toward

Zach. "Why certainly Zachery, if that's what you wish."

All was going splendidly until Aurora turned skittish under Zach's warm gaze. Her eyelash flutters became increasingly exaggerated until her eyes resembled canvas flapping in the wind, her head nodding perceptibly with each ridiculous blink.

"Aurora?" Zach straightened and appeared at a loss. "Have you something in your eye?"

Aurora's Mona Lisa smile fared no better. Actually, it gave her the unfortunate appearance of one who had eaten too many green apples.

"Good heavens!" The earl motioned for the butler. "She's ill. Grab a vase."

"Father." Tori was up in an instant. She couldn't fathom how things were going so awry, but she did know her father was only going to make matters worse.

"Has the girl got bowel trouble?" he asked Charlotte who was lying back against the settee with her eyes closed.

"Our Father, which art in heaven …" Aunt Charlotte furiously fanned herself.

"Aurora please, let me help you lie down. Should we call the doctor?" Zach's concern was more evident by the second.

Aurora ceased her bumbling flirtation. Looking around the room, she took in the odd stares of the others. She appeared mortified.

With nervous hands, she reached up to smooth her hair, but caught her bracelet in one side of the upswept locks. Tiny rosebuds rained across her lap as an entire section of her hair came tumbling down.

Zach's look of unmasked pity proved her final unraveling. Aurora pushed past him and ran from the room.

Tori, on the other hand, fumed. She started to go after her cousin, but Nicholas stepped in front of her, refusing to let her pass. "Why do I get the feeling this fiasco is somehow of your making?"

"Let me by!" She pushed against his wide chest.

"Aurora doesn't need any more of your help. Why don't you just tell Zach the truth? She was attempting to flatter him. Let them work it out themselves."

This was her fault.

With a groan, Tori bit her lower lip and stole an irritated look at him. Why must he be so sure of himself all the time?

Turning her back to him, she addressed his brother. "Zachery, did it ever occur to you that Aurora might have been trying to gain your attention?"

"Well, she got it. What was that all about?"

Tori sighed before going on. "For some reason, she is a bit infatuated with you. What you and Father mistook for queasiness, was her innocent attempt at wooing you."

The earl took a seat and opened a periodical with a brisk shake.

Aunt Charlotte sniffed loudly into her hanky.

"What? Why didn't she just say so?" Zach went to the mantle and rested both hands on it, gazing down into the empty hearth.

"That would have been too easy." A muscle flicked in Nicholas's jaw, and he crossed his arms over his chest.

"Zachery, you must listen carefully to what I'm telling you." Tori caught up her skirts and went to stand next to him. "It's quite possible you've broken the poor girl's heart."

Zach provided the exact look Tori was going for. Astonishment with just a smidgeon of guilt.

"Well, you'll simply have to make it up to her. That's all there is to it."

"I never meant to embarrass her. I thought she was in pain." The young captain was nearly beside himself. "What should I do now?"

"Well, there is only one thing you can do, I suppose." Tori glanced at Aunt Charlotte, who ceased her fan in mid-flutter, sitting forward with a nod of understanding as it finally dawned on her what her niece was up to. "It seems to me she mentioned a certain event coming up. Heritage, is it?"

Tori strolled to where a vase of colorful tulips adorned a rosewood side table, carefully avoiding Nicholas. He wouldn't approve of her tactics.

Zach mouthed the word, without recognition.

Tori brought her finger to her chin. "Herman's Ball? No, no that's not it."

Nicholas cleared his throat and rolled his eyes.

"Hermitage?" Zach provided.

"Yes!" Tori pointed at him to indicate he'd guessed correctly. "The Hermitage Soirée"

"What about it?" The look of confusion on Zach's face told her she was going to have to spell it out for him.

"Aurora would like to go." She paused for effect. "With you as her escort."

"Well, why didn't she just say so?" Zach settled a hand on his hip and turned back to the hearth.

This time Tori did chance a look at Nicholas. Though he shook his head, he was grinning.

"Do you think you can get her to come back down? I'd like to apologize. I'll invite her then," Zach spoke over his shoulder.

"I'll be right back!" Charlotte Haverwood's skirts billowed as she bounded from the room.

"I say, Zachery, you're a noble chap, if nothing else." The earl turned the page of his newspaper with a bored tone. "However, don't go overboard with it. Women should be kept in their place, you know. They actually prefer it that way."

Tori winced at her father's careless remark. He couldn't possibly understand the makings of a woman's heart.

"You look perturbed, Victoria." All eyes turned to her, as Nicholas called her out. "You wouldn't by chance, have something to say about your father's comment, would you?"

Tori froze.

Gathering her wits, she faced them both. "My father has every right to his opinion."

"Yes, but, what is your opinion on the matter?" He

persisted in a low voice.

"I don't remember offering one," she ground out.

"There you see?" The earl snapped his paper shut and motioned for Gabe. "Go find your mistress. Rather rude to leave us here to ourselves."

Tori glared at Nicholas as she settled on the edge of a side chair. Zach remained at the door, peering anxiously down the hallway.

Footsteps sounded in the marble corridor.

"Here we are." Charlotte warbled cheerily, reentering the room with Aurora in tow. "Good as new. Edward, I'll have Flossie bring in some spearmint tea, with honey." With that she traipsed back out again.

Tori carefully moved to her cousin's side. "Aurora, I'm delighted to see you're feeling better. Come and sit with me."

Zach joined Tori at Aurora's side. "Your color has returned. You look lovely as ever."

"Thank you, Zach, but you don't have to pretend. You know I wasn't really sick. I just wanted you to notice me. I guess I tried a little too hard." She shrugged and gave a timid smile to her cousin. "I'm sorry, Tori. I'm not good at being subtle."

That wasn't at all how it was done., although Tori had to admit she almost envied Aurora's forthright confession.

"Then, I suppose that you also know I'd like you to go with me to the social out on Argyle Island." Zach smiled easily and Aurora responded in kind.

"I believe Mother did mention something about it. But I won't hear of it if you're just feeling sorry for me."

"Never." Zach laughed lightheartedly. "It's all the other young men that never got a chance to ask that I feel sorry for."

"Really, Zach?" Aurora sighed.

Zach nodded.

The earl snorted.

Tori stood and turned her back to the group, making a pretense of studying the odd lines of the pumpkin-colored wallpaper. Tears stung the back of her eyes and she blinked to collect herself. Aurora had gotten the invitation she'd hoped for and Tori was overjoyed for her cousin.

It was the ache in her own heart that took her by surprise.

"I hadn't planned on going, myself." Nicholas spoke softly at her back, interrupting her quiet reflection. "But someone needs to look after you. Will you allow me to once again play your escort, princess?"

Tori swiveled just enough to meet his gaze. As usual, she found an odd comfort in the midnight depths.

"Oh, please say you'll go, Tori." Aurora came up next to her and took her hand. "For me."

Of course, Aurora did need her. Before her mind could fully reason it out, she accepted his invitation.

"Wonderful! Shall we adjourn to the music room? I've had Flossie lay out tea and cakes. Aurora always feels much better when she's playin' her music." Aunt Charlotte went straight over to Lord Haverwood. "Edward, let me give you a hand."

He tried to stand, but had a hard time as her aunt was tugging at his arm. "I'd thank you to remove your hands from my person, Charlotte. I am perfectly capable of seeing to myself." He snatched his arm back, took up his cane, and smoothed his rumpled waistcoat before sidestepping her without another glance.

Across the entryway, a long narrow room was sparsely furnished with little other than six wingback chairs set in pairs around English oak tea tables. As promised, tea cakes and pots steeping with tea were laid out on silver trays. Rich, golden-framed paintings of Biblical characters hung above the wainscoting on each wall and a cool night breeze wafted in through the open French doors, ruffling the tasseled swag above.

Moving to the head of the room, Aurora bore no signs of her earlier bashfulness. Gabe pulled a tapestry-covered stool in front of the exquisite gilded harp. She swept her dusky pink skirts around her, and pulled the instrument back to rest against her shoulder.

Everyone was seated and Aunt Charlotte took up her fan.

Music filled the room as Aurora began with Beethoven's *Sonata No. 2, Moonlight.* The composition was enchanting. Her fingertips alternately strummed and plucked at the long vibrating strings, performing a melody that had endured for ages. Mesmerizing chords, played in bass minors, silenced the audience into awed appreciation.

Upon the last run of the sonata, Tori slipped through the tall French doors leading out onto the verandah. The others listened as Aurora began a second piece, this one a familiar hymn.

The sweet performance had only contributed to her melancholy mood. Lifting her face to the breeze, she let the night air cool the warmth in her cheeks.

She didn't have to turn to know Nicholas had followed her outside.

Running her hand along the rail of the wooden verandah, she stopped to lean against a Roman column. "You needn't gloat so."

A chuckle rumbled from his chest as he came to stand behind her. "Why would I care to gloat, Victoria? I should thank you. You've once again provided an entertaining evening." Nicholas rested his forearm on the pillar above her head and she turned to face him.

"Why must you believe the worst of me? Like it or not, Aurora needs me."

"Like she needs the plague," Nicholas commented with a casual air as he looked over the top of her head, at the manicured gardens. "You know, if you share any more of your expert advice, she'll never survive it."

"According to Miss Sarah Hale—"

"Who?" Nicholas quirked an eyebrow, looking down at her.

"Sarah Hale. The utmost authority on goodness and virtue. She has a regular commentary in Godey's Lady's

Book, a model for the perfect lady."

"Victoria, you don't need anyone to tell you how to be a lady. It comes naturally. The Good Book is the only authority you need to live by."

"Miss Hale abides by the Good Book as well."

"Believe it or not, I've read that Book a time or two. Nowhere does it say that you should apologize for being you—that your unique ideas and opinions are any less valuable than anyone else's."

He twirled a curl at the base of her neck and any reasonable argument left her head. Tracing her jaw with his thumb, he tilted her chin up to force her gaze to meet his own.

Nicholas looked down at her and the message in his eyes spoke of safety and security. When his gaze dropped to her mouth, however, she got another message altogether.

Tori shivered from both the breeze and the intensity of the moment.

He cradled her face in his hand and her eyes drifted shut. When his lips met hers, Tori's breath caught in her throat. He tasted of spearmint and the effect of his kiss was heady. Leaning into his solid chest, she felt as if she couldn't get close enough.

"Captain? Victoria? I say, can't see a blooming thing out there." The earl's voice put an abrupt end to Nicholas's kiss.

Tori ducked under his arm and stepped around him to go to her father.

Nicholas clasped her arm as she passed but she kept her head down, refusing to let him see the desire in her eyes.

"Hold up, princess. We can't have your father thinking anything improper is going on out here." With that, she did look up at him, and he flashed a facetious grin.

"Are you mocking me?" she half whispered.

"I am." He had the most disarming way about him. "But we go back inside together. Otherwise, you'd be here all night trying to concoct a suitable alibi."

Nicholas took her hand and started back toward the house, pulling her along.

Tori spoke again, quietly. Barely audible.

"Did you say something?" Nicholas glanced down at her.

Tori stopped and lifted her chin, meeting his questioning gaze straight on. "Yes, Nicholas, I did." Taking her hand back, she lifted her skirts with a swoosh, "I said, shove off!"

Brushing past, she left him to enjoy his laugh alone, glad he couldn't see her satisfied grin.

Strength and honour are her clothing.
~ Proverbs 31:25

Nine

Three weeks passed since their arrival in Savannah. As July wound slowly to a close, Tori missed the cool afternoon breezes she was accustomed to back home.

Teas and luncheons took up most of their days. As word spread about town of the earl's arrival from England, she and her father became the main attraction at countless social engagements.

The Ladies Academy had trained her well for this sort of thing, barring one minor detail. Georgia had a style all its own. Women here were no demure misses, nor did they hesitate to say and—for the most part—do exactly as they pleased. They were allowed to speak freely. Not that they weren't submissive to their husbands, but it was a different sort of submission. A mutual respect existed between genders that Tori found utterly refreshing.

During their many garden get-togethers, the ladies

discussed fundraising for a good cause, such as quilting blankets for the orphanage or raising monuments to heroes of the Revolution. Back in England, these decisions were always made by men. As far as Tori knew, ladies were never even consulted. This land of liberty apparently was designed to include the female population as well.

Tori had watched her father carefully over the past few weeks, curious to take in his reaction to this generous concept. As long as these Savannians fawned after him as if he were Prince Albert himself, he appeared happy to extend whatever tolerance was needed on their behalf.

With concealed amusement, she'd observed lady after lady greet him with, "so nice to meet you, Your Royal Eminence," or "are you enjoying your visit, Your Graciousness?" As it was, his invitations extended through most of August.

Most days, however, Lord Haverwood indicated that he preferred the familiar atmosphere of the Savannah Gentlemen's Club. The camaraderie among the other gents, along with his genuine liking for the natural southern wit, kept him occupied well into the evening most days.

Without a doubt, Tori found dusk in this American South utterly fascinating. High society folk migrated toward Bull Street to promenade around the plaza until dark. Everyone nodded in passing. Babies in carriages were proudly strolled about while ladies and gentlemen of all ages donned their finest to come out and exchange pleasantries. With every turn around the square, Tori fell in love with the unique charm of this city.

By the time the oil lamps were lit at all the major intersections, stately carriages made their way to the magnificent theater on Chippewa Square.

Aunt Charlotte was in a virtual euphoria, or as Aurora so aptly put it—she was in a "tizzy."

Her aunt's outlandish fashion sense stemmed directly from Madame Dupree's flair for the absurd. The first time Tori laid eyes upon Aunt Charlotte's round little form bedecked in one of her truly outrageous hats, Tori didn't know whether to compliment her aunt or rescue her from the ghastly contraption.

No one for three rows behind her could see the pulpit, yet none at First Christian Church gave her or her hat a second glance, except to rave about the skills of the popular French designers. Charlotte Haverwood was one of the city's most prominent matrons, therefore much was overlooked.

Such was the case this morning, as Tori and Aurora waited for Aunt Charlotte to join them in the family's plum-colored barouche. The day promised to provide the most elaborate affair yet.

A parade was scheduled in her father's honor, followed by a speech and presentation from the Ladies Historical Society. A picnic luncheon on the square would be served directly afterward by wives of the Chatham Artillery. Lord Haverwood was immensely flattered by all the attention and had gone ahead of the Haverwood ladies to meet early with the parade committee.

Tori suspected it didn't take much of an event to set these Georgians in a whirl. Any excuse could be turned into a perfectly justifiable reason to socialize. The city's newspaper devoted entire sections to who was where, with whom, wearing what.

These Americans had their own provincial version of the English ton.

Aurora chattered excitedly, wondering at the chances of Zach Saberton making an appearance at the parade. Tori's thoughts turned to Nicholas.

She had not seen him since they'd come to dinner. Zach had sent a note saying they would be traveling to Boston on business for a couple of weeks and poor Aurora had been quite disheartened.

"I'm positive that Viola Mae Jenkins and her mother sent him an announcement. She's obvious when it comes to Zach." Aurora shook open her fan with a flap and smiled mischievously. "We'll just make sure to see him first, won't we?"

Tori returned her cousin's smile. Aurora was emerging from her bashful cocoon like a rare butterfly.

Tori had met Viola Mae at the church's Springtime Bazaar and immediately recognized her type. Flighty and self-centered girls like Viola Mae were easily disarmed. Their sting only hurt if allowed to get under one's skin.

The Jenkins girl, taken with the notion of befriending an English heiress, had pushed herself to Tori's side at every opportunity. But, after Tori's casual mention that Aurora was going to make Zachery a lovely date for the upcoming soirée, Viola Mae sulked quite unbecomingly.

At any rate, that particular Jenkins sister was annoying but certainly no menace. Tori had yet to meet the other one.

"Here comes Mother. I can't wait to get there." Aurora clapped and Tori laughed aloud. That's when she caught a glimpse of the apparatus angled precariously atop her aunt's red head.

It was alive.

Upon closer inspection, Tori found the small bamboo cage housed a tiny yellow bird on a swing. It chirped cheerfully in duet with Aunt Charlotte's constant chatter.

"Oh, how I wish Edward would have joined us instead of going on early. He's the most stubborn man. Percy wasn't nearly half so pig-headed." Despite Gabe's awkward assistance, she struggled to heave herself into the carriage seat opposite her daughter and niece, continuing to babble though quite out of breath. "If I thought for one minute ... My heavens, don't you two look sweet! Aurora, honey, that new dress brightens you up. I don't believe I've ever seen you wear anything that peachy before. But you know, it flatters your coloring. It most certainly does."

Aurora blushed and pinched at the pleats in her skirt.

"Now, hold that parasol so the sun can't get to your face." Aunt Charlotte turned to her niece. "Good gracious! Are those your mama's pearls?"

Tori nodded.

"My word, they're the size of marbles! Lean over here,

honey. Look, Aurora, there's sapphires stuck in the midst of it all."

"I don't usually wear them before dinner, but I thought today was a bit special. And they do go with the dress." Tori was having a hard time staying seated between the jostle of the carriage as it rolled onto the shell lane and Aunt Charlotte pulling her across the seat by the necklace.

"And earbobs to match?" With a quick release, she hurried on. "Not just anyone could wear that cream color all over, but you've got just enough copper in your hair to keep it from overwhelmin' you. Now you all leave those bonnets on while you're out of doors, you hear? That horrid sun can turn you redder than a beet and you'll end up with a rash."

Tori watched the little bird swing unsteadily as her aunt jumped from topic to topic. It moved from one side of its perch to the other, as if looking for a place to escape the constant motion.

Aunt Charlotte turned quickly to wave at a passerby and the little bird was jostled completely off balance, disappearing somewhere in the bottom of the hat.

"Yes, indeed. The good Lord blessed you both. Straight from the streets of gold. That's all I have to say on the matter."

It wasn't by any means. The dear lady continued to babble until they reached their destination. The stifling heat and humidity made breathing a challenge, and Tori soon discovered the elaborate fans waving were actually a necessity.

They were met with music and laughter as a gentleman in a top hat ushered them to a platform covered by a striped canopy. The earl waited for them, seated in a place of honor.

Beautiful Johnson Square had been transformed into a carnival. Performers were doing acrobatics and magic shows, trained animals entertained the children, and peddlers hawked their trinkets on every corner.

"By Jove, these colonials know how to throw quite a hullabaloo." Lord Haverwood came as close to smiling as Tori had seen in months. "Glad to see you've finally made it, my dear. Now things can get rolling. Quite a show I'd say."

"Oh, *your majesty*." An ancient lady with an ear horn was trying to get the earl's attention. "With your permission, we'll begin."

He nodded, though his bushy mustache gave a quick twitch. She in turn nodded to the conductor and the trumpet blared a loud fanfare.

"Oh, my goodness." Aurora tugged Tori's sleeve. "There he is. Look, over there under that cypress tree across the road. In the back." She pointed with a gloved finger. "Should I wave or something?"

"I should think so, yes. People are beginning to turn to see what we are gawking at."

Aurora waved her program and Zach returned the gesture. Tori noted with odd disappointment that Nicholas was nowhere to be seen.

The parade began moving down Bay Street, separating them from Zach. He became increasingly difficult to make out, and Aurora squirmed in her seat trying to keep him in her sights. More than once, Tori lightly yanked at Aurora's skirt to remind her to stay seated.

With the end of the procession in sight, the crowd gathered noisily around the platform to hear the various speakers and presentations.

Aurora gasped.

Tori followed her cousin's horrified gaze to the culprit. A voluptuous female dressed in torrid red stood next to Zach.

Tori's eyes narrowed as the woman grabbed Zachery by the arm and made a show of planting a kiss on his cheek. To his credit, he barely acknowledged her and immediately made his way across the street toward them.

"Who is that?"

"That's the one I've been telling you about. Viola Mae's sister, Felicity Jenkins Duff. The one who has her claws set for Nicholas. She'll do anything to get him to notice her. Even using Zach to get his attention."

The woman turned and disappeared into the crowd.

"I'd say that one's intentions run deeper than merely getting Nicholas's attention."

The crowd clapped and cheered, but Tori had no idea why. A sudden heaviness settled in her chest and a lump formed in her throat. It must be the heat.

"I say! My daughter doesn't seem to be with us." The earl was standing at the podium addressing Tori. The gathering of people roared with laughter. "Victoria, my dear, I shall ask you once more. Please stand, so these good citizens might be presented to you."

Tori lowered her parasol and glanced about. All eyes were upon her as she slowly rose. Applause and whistles filled the air. From the far-left corner a group of young men made whooping sounds and called out offers of marriage amidst other even less appropriate proposals.

Tori smiled graciously and waved.

The rest of the speeches came to a close and the crowd dispersed to the square to enjoy some refreshment. Huge white clouds moved in, and a breeze gave relief from the heat. Delicious whiffs of magnolias and gardenias mingled with the mouth-watering aroma of freshly baked goods.

Zach appeared at the edge of the grandstand with a hand to help them down. "Good afternoon, ladies. That was some parade, wasn't it?"

"Hi, Zach." Aurora beamed.

"Hello, Zachery." Tori greeted him with a smile. A bright red lip print still blazed on his cheek. "What a lovely shade of red."

Aurora handed him a handkerchief and pointed to his cheek.

Zach blushed profusely. "Felicity's in town."

"You look funny with lip rouge on." Aurora nudged him with her elbow.

Tori was pleased to see Aurora effortlessly chatting, not stuttering even once.

"I've spread a blanket for us under that big oak."

Zach pointed to a large tree on the fringe of the activity. "I'll get us some punch and meet you two over there."

They watched him head toward the refreshment tables set under the gazebo in the center of the square.

People strolled past, greeting them with friendly smiles, introducing themselves and welcoming Tori to Savannah. She scanned the square and found her father involved in a lively discussion at the gazebo with some gentlemen from the club. Marveling at his improved condition, she reflected on what a difference this trip had made in him. The lines around his eyes had softened, and he acted years younger. The respite from his responsibilities had been good for him.

They found the quilted spread and settled down to relax under the shade of the enormous tree. Tori was soon caught up in the jovial spirit of the day. To the delight of a group of children, a tiny dancing monkey on a leash did backward flips while his master turned the crank of a music box. Other children ran behind a rolling hoop, keeping it upright with large sticks.

"I don't believe I've had the pleasure of an introduction." A low female voice purred above them.

Tori shielded her eyes from the sun to see who was speaking. Her eyes widened in recognition.

"Felicity Jenkins Duff. And you are?"

"Felicity meet Lady Victoria Haverwood," Zach joined them with drinks in his hands. "Of course, you already know Aurora."

Felicity moved to stand in front of Tori and made a

show of looking the younger woman over. A feline grin curled her painted lips.

"How do you do?" Tori adopted a guarded tone out of sheer instinct.

"I do exceptionally well, thank you. I've certainly never had any complaints, anyway." She turned her whole body toward Zach. "Darling, where is your brother? He promised to see me later."

Tori gritted her teeth. Something about the woman set her on edge.

"I can't say, Felicity. But if I know Nicholas, he's probably gone up to the offices for a while." He tipped his head toward the building on Commerce Row. "We got back from business in Boston yesterday, so I imagine he's catching up on a few things."

"Well, he and I have a few things to catch up on as well." Felicity fluttered her eyes over to Tori. "I hear you've just arrived from overseas somewhere." She tilted her head to the side and looked at Tori through slanted eyes, untying the thick red ribbons of her sun hat. "Did you make the trip aboard a Saberton vessel?"

Felicity more than likely knew they had come over under Nicholas's escort. Until it became clearer why she was asking, Tori chose to exercise caution.

"We did indeed."

"I must speak to Nicholas about taking on passengers. Once we are married I intend to see the entire fleet is limited to cargo only. Much more money to be made than having to cater to a bunch of spoiled world travelers. No offense to you, of course."

"Am I missing something?" A tall, attractive woman stepped up to join the group. "I wasn't aware Nicholas had asked you to marry him."

Felicity, obviously taken by surprise, drew in a sharp breath that threatened to spill the contents of her strained bodice.

"As a matter of fact, I wasn't aware that he had any serious intentions toward you at all." The lady directed a look at Felicity who mumbled something incoherent then turned to leave.

Tori's admiration for the new arrival soared. She wasn't used to witnessing a lady speak her mind and in such a pleasant tone, as if they'd been simply discussing the weather. True finesse.

"I'm glad you're here." Zach slipped an arm around the lady's shoulder. "There's someone I want you to meet."

Tori saw the resemblance between them immediately.

Before Zach could make the introduction, the lady offered her hand to Tori with a genuine smile. "Hello, I'm Zach's mother. Dottie Saberton."

"Lady Victoria Haverwood." Taking her hand, Tori was impressed by the butter-soft kid gloves that stretched over her fingers. "A pleasure to meet you."

"Hello, Aurora. How's Charlotte?" Dottie Saberton knelt next to Aurora and folded her parasol. "Zach, would you mind getting me something to drink, love? The ride down left me completely parched."

"Mama is fine." Aurora scanned the grounds for some sign of the birdcage. "She's around here somewhere."

"No doubt sporting some hideous millinery creation as usual." Dottie Saberton wore a half smile that was so very familiar.

Aurora clapped her hands together with glee. "She is, Mrs. Dottie. But you're the only one I know who can get away with saying that to her. Mother adores you."

"It's mutual I assure you. Charlotte and I took our lessons together as girls, longer ago than either of us care to remember."

"Did you happen to know my father?" Tori asked. "He visited Savannah when Uncle Percy and Aunt Charlotte were married."

"We met. Must have been some twenty years ago."

"Twenty-five," Aurora provided.

"It seems he was quite taken with Savannah. I can't imagine why he's waited so long to come back to visit." Tori moved over to make room for Zach returning with his mother's punch.

"Perhaps the memory was too painful. Thank you, Zach." Mrs. Saberton took the glass and brought it to her lips.

Too painful?

There was more Mrs. Saberton wasn't saying, but Tori resisted the urge to ply her with questions. Perhaps she could find out more when they became better acquainted.

I am not afraid of storms,
for I am learning how to sail my ship.
~ Louisa May Alcott

Ten

As the afternoon progressed, Tori was taken with the easy way Dottie Saberton handled herself. Though she was the epitome of elegance, she said and did exactly as she pleased. And everyone seemed to love her for it.

Nicholas's mother reminded Tori of country gentry she'd known in England, highborn yet approachable. From the way the townspeople strolled by to greet her, all with open respect and admiration, it was apparent they held her in high esteem.

"You two must come up to Brechenridge sometime to have a look at our new Arabians." Mrs. Saberton had removed her wide-brimmed hat and Tori admired the healthy pink in her cheeks. Obviously she wasn't as concerned about the ill effects of the sun as Aunt Charlotte.

"Mama's acquired an impressive stable." Zach lay stretched out on his side, tossing blades of grass at Aurora. "And we have the tastiest Peach Buckle this side of Atlanta."

"I'd like that very much." The thought of visiting Nicholas's childhood home was intriguing. "So, your estate is named for your great uncle? Quite a gallant name, indeed."

"Oh you should see it, Tori." Aurora swept a blade of grass from her skirt as Zach tossed another in its place. "Twice the size of Hermitage plantation. And there's a gazebo with a white swing looking out over the most beautiful lake.

"It sounds lovely." Tori nodded toward a white mare tethered to a tree. "Is that one of your Arabians, by chance?"

"Yes, indeed. Her name's Liberty. I recently picked her up from out near Richmond." Mrs. Saberton spoke with obvious pride. "Would you like to have a closer look?"

"She's magnificent." Tori rose easily to her feet and brushed at her skirt. "I've missed my own mare terribly while we've been away."

"Have you a large stable?" Mrs. Saberton took purposeful strides.

"Not overly. Three geldings, and two mares. One is my personal mount."

Nearing the beautiful creature, Tori picked up her pace. The horse was not at all skittish and held her head high. "There, now. That's a good girl." Tori stroked the white horse, speaking to her in a soft voice. Liberty nudged her hand as Tori stroked her forelock. "Hungry, eh? Let's see if we can't find you a nice treat."

Mrs. Saberton handed Tori an apple from her skirt pocket, and patted the mare's flank. Tori felt the elder lady watching her closely, seemingly taking in every feature.

"She trusts you, Victoria. She doesn't take to just anyone." Mrs. Saberton's gaze didn't waiver.

"I'd like to think she understands my appreciation for her. She is exquisite." Tori laughed when the horse nodded in apparent agreement. "Ah, and she's modest as well. Yes, you are."

"Good." The lady smiled kindly. "Then I'll speak to my son and have him make plans to bring you riding in the near future. I'm proud of our horses." Mrs. Saberton had a pleasant Georgian lilt in her voice. "Would you enjoy a day spent riding her?"

"That would be glorious." Riding was one activity Tori dearly missed.

"Good, you can plan on spending the weekend. I'll have Nicholas contact you as to which weekend would be most convenient."

"Nicholas?"

"Is that a problem?" Mrs. Saberton asked lifting a brow.

A fluttering sensation washed over Tori just thinking about spending a weekend in the country with Nicholas.

"Well, no, not exactly. That is, I rather expect that Nicholas is far too busy for such an outing. Perhaps Zachery could find the time."

"Nonsense. Nicholas is due a visit. Besides, if Nicholas comes, Zach will come, too." Mrs. Saberton placed a gloved hand over Tori's. "Whatever it is he's done to offend you, dear, I'm sure he didn't do it intentionally."

"I'm afraid I must disagree." Tori was shocked at the surge of emotion brought on by the mere mention of him. "Nicholas is quite intentional when it comes to provoking me. I'm certain he's made a sport of it."

Embarrassment finally caught up with her and she nibbled her lip. Perhaps she'd spoken too freely.

Mrs. Saberton tilted her head. "Most young ladies are more than happy to overlook a little teasing now and then, just to have the chance to be with him. I'm glad to see you aren't one of them."

"I most certainly am not," Tori said with conviction, then sighed after giving it more thought. "Truthfully, Nicholas baffles me. I don't understand him most of the time."

"He doesn't want to be understood." Mrs. Saberton replied flatly.

Tori frowned. "Why on earth?"

"He protects himself that way. From having to feel anything." Mrs. Saberton paused, carefully considering Tori before going on. "I'm going to tell you something, Victoria, that I don't normally make known."

Tori stopped petting the horse to listen intently.

"Nicholas did allow himself to care once. Very deeply, as a matter of fact. But just before the marriage was to take place, Celine decided a naval cadet wasn't good enough for the daughter of a ten-year admiral. Instead of telling anyone how she felt, she ran off with some first classman a month before she and Nicholas were to wed." Dottie Saberton gave a deliberate look. "I never want to see my son hurt like that again."

This was a mother who had seen her son's heart shattered and was bold enough say what needed to be said to make certain it wouldn't happen again.

Tori was silent, filled with compassion for the young cadet. No one, not even Nicholas, should have to live through such pain and humiliation.

She knew Mrs. Saberton was waiting for her to respond, but she felt inadequate in offering such assurance. She was no threat to Nicholas's heart. Instead, Tori looked away.

"My son has much love to give, but he must allow the Lord to rid his heart of the bitterness that has taken root there." Mrs. Saberton shook her head and the horse turned toward her. "Only the healing touch of grace can break down the walls he's put up to guard himself."

Felicity's red-clad curves flashed through Tori's mind and she spoke before thinking it through. "Well, he will never find the kind of love he needs in the places he's been looking."

Mrs. Saberton smiled with a wise nod of her head. "Very true. I believe he's coddled that broken heart long enough. Let's pray he finds love again."

Tori remained quiet.

Nicholas was infinitely obstinate, and more than annoying at times. But there had been times—precious few times—when she'd seen something else, a tenderness toward her that had drawn her to him from the beginning.

"So if it seems he occasionally distances himself from you, dear, it's only because you do make him feel something." Mrs. Saberton grinned and retethered her horse's reins. "Though he'd rather have you detest him than admit it."

"Thank you for telling me, Mrs. Saberton." Tori gave a weak smile and sighed, remembering Nicholas's constant impatience with her. "This explains much. But I'm afraid his lack of interest is quite real."

"Lack of interest? I don't think so." Mrs. Saberton drew Tori's attention to the second story window of a building across the street on Commerce Row. High above the crowd, Nicholas stood looking down at them in full view from where they stood.

His mother raised her gloved hand in greeting and he returned the gesture before pulling the shade.

"I daresay I've not seen him as interested in anyone in quite a long while." Mrs. Saberton grinned at her with a wink and a nod.

"Help! Someone help!"

Tori looked over the top of the horse toward the pond where a crowd was gathering.

Mrs. Saberton hitched her skirt with one hand and headed for the commotion.

Looking around for Aurora, Tori found the blanket empty under the tree. From across the park she spotted Zach coming from underneath the gazebo. He, too, appeared to be looking for someone.

"Tori!" The voice sounded oddly like her cousin. Tori didn't waste a moment. She lifted the hem of her skirt and ran toward the panicked cry.

Pushing through the crowd, Tori stood at the edge of the murky water. Just on the other side, Aurora hung for dear life onto a low limb of a scrub oak that snaked out over the pond. Viola Mae Jenkins stood shrieking on the bank while her sister, Felicity slowly stood up from the center of the pond where she'd apparently fallen in.

Ripples of laughter followed her slow trudge from the mire.

Crisscrossing between the onlookers Tori made her way to where Aurora hung precariously from the tree limb. By the time she got to her, Zach was already helping her down and Viola Mae had dissolved into an unladylike wail.

A group of children were highly amused and their laughter filled the air.

"What on earth happened?" Tori took Aurora's hands and dusted the bark from her palms.

Dottie Saberton came to stand on the other side of Zach.

"Felicity said she lost her wedding ring." Aurora said.

"Viola Mae's afraid of water, so she asked if I could see it."

Tori slipped a protective arm around her cousin.

A little girl stepped forward to provide more information. "We saw the whole thing. We were playing jacks on that stump over there. That lady there tried to push her in, but Miss Aurora grabbed a limb and hung on. The lady went splash!" She motioned big with her arms to the delight of the other children.

"Lies! You m-miserable little brat." Felicity stood dripping, with chattering teeth, looking every bit like she wanted to throttle the child. "I was trying to help and l-lost my balance."

"Felicity, you've ruined everything." Viola Mae stomped her foot. "Zach's standing there with his arm around Aurora, not me."

Tori's hand went to her bosom, to the cross she wore next to her heart. "Sweet merciful heavens."

With slow progress, Felicity sloshed noisily out of the water while her heavy red gown threatened to remain. She jerked at the low bodice with an irritable tug, glaring at the twittering crowd as she made her way back to her carriage.

Tori took her cousin by the hand, salvaging as much decorum as she possibly could. "Collect Aunt Charlotte, will you please, Zach? I do believe it's time we went home."

~

High above Forsyth Park, Nicholas looked down at the scene below from the second-story window of his offices. His building on Commerce Row faced the square with full view of the fish pond. No doubt all a part of Felicity's scheme.

It didn't take much to piece together the facts. Felicity had clearly planned on it being Aurora who was fished from the pond, and she was mad as a hornet that her trap had gone awry.

He had no interest in Felicity. She'd set her talons for him ages ago. There was no room in his life for any female, and certainly not for one the likes of Felicity. He'd escorted her to a couple of social events but had maintained that there was nothing between them, nor would there ever be.

As the throng scattered, Nicholas watched Tori and Felicity flounce off in opposite directions.

He had watched his mother and Tori talk earlier over by the new mare. Dottie Saberton was taking a personal interest in Haverwood's daughter and Nicholas couldn't help but wonder why.

Ever since Celine had run off, his mother made no secret that she believed his heart was in no shape to become entangled again.

Nicholas blew a heavy breath. On that account, his mother was right. He'd given his heart once, for all the good that had done. He never saw the blatant betrayal to come. All without remorse. Celine had made him the laughingstock of the Naval Academy.

He had his business. Haverwood Shipping and Trade was as vital and energizing as any human mistress could be. And for now, it was the love of his life. He'd spend every waking moment making certain it was thriving.

Studying the familiar advertisement hanging on the wall of his office, he was again filled with anticipation. With the new steam engines that were just rolling out, expeditions abroad could be made in half the time. It was an exciting time to be in the merchant business and he'd gotten in on the ground floor.

Commerce was a faithful companion. If cultivated with determination and perseverance, he had made the connections to be a world runner one day. Hopefully soon. He was already the largest transporter in the southern states for cotton, iron and textiles. It was a pivotal time for the country—the south in particular—and they were making great strides in finding innovative solutions to farming, processing, and transport. All with new, more efficient machinery. He planned to be an integral part of the "New South." His dream went beyond business with the big conglomerates of the northern Union. He wanted an international trade port based right here in Savannah.

Just thinking about it improved his mood.

Turning back to the window, he was able to smile when he caught sight of Victoria Haverwood. Without so much as a glance behind her, she marched off with her back stiff as a board and head held high, with a dazed Aurora in tow.

Victoria Haverwood was quite a catch. But for someone else. They were all wrong for each other. Anyone could see that.

Chuckling, he saw Felicity slapping away the hands of onlookers reaching out to touch her soggy dress as she passed them by. Trudging none-too-lady-like toward her carriage on the opposite side of the square, she looked fit to be tied.

Victoria was another story. She greeted everyone with a cordial nod, and no one who hadn't witnessed the ridiculous ordeal at the pond would ever guess she wasn't having a lovely afternoon.

"Princess, I can't leave you alone for a minute, can I? For someone so painfully proper, you draw trouble like a bull in a china shop."

With a shake of his head, he pulled the shade.

Casting all your care upon Him;
for He careth for you.
~ 1 Peter 5:7

Eleven

Miss Aurora Haverwood
The pleasure of your
Company is respectfully requested at
The Hermitage Soirée on Argyle Island
Friday 10ᵗʰ of August
Music will commence at 8 PM
Dinner promptly at midnight
MISTER ZACHERY L. SABERTON

Tori watched as Aurora reread the invitation for the tenth time since it had been hand-delivered by messenger half an hour past. An identical one had come for Tori, set with Nicholas's personal seal in royal blue wax.

"I hope my dress is ready in time." Aurora set a small glass of orange juice next to her plate. "Mr. Jean-Pierre will never forgive us turning down his design." Her cousin was excitable on any given day, but this morning she was especially animated. "I thought his eyes would pop right out of his head when you showed him the pattern we want from Graham's Book of Fashions. It's a good thing we don't know French. I have a feeling we would have suffered in the translation."

"I do speak French." Tori made a face as she spread a generous spoonful of apple butter on her toast. "And we did."

"Oh, but that frightful gown he had drawn up for me, trimmed in a solid mass of daisies. No discernable shape at all, just hundreds of white daisies tacked about from head to foot." Dissolving into giggles, she licked a spot of orange marmalade from the corner of her mouth. "I want to attract Zach, not a horde of bumblebees."

Tori couldn't help but laugh, too. The dress was hideous. "I do love the material you picked instead though. You will look glorious in ivory taffeta."

"This is fun! Kind of like preparing for a wedding." She tasted marmalade from the tip of her finger, then caught Tori's eye. "I mean ... because of the dress. Being white and all. Debutantes always wear white ..." Aurora blushed.

"Of course." Tori took on a somber expression. "The thought of marriage to someone like Zachery Saberton would never cross your mind."

"It most certainly would, too." Aurora gave a fervent nod. "And Zach will marry me someday. He just doesn't know it yet."

"Oh, I see." Tori smiled and lifted her water goblet in salute. "Well, congratulations to you both. Zachery is a fine young man and I wish the two of you many happy years together."

"What about you and Nicholas?"

"Hmm?" Tori lowered her glass. "That's hardly a fair comparison. There is no Nicholas and me."

Aurora looked doubtful.

"Aurora, really. You come up with the silliest ideas." Tori took a bite of warm cheese grits and swallowed with concentrated effort. "Zachery asked you to the ball, and Nicholas felt an obligation to see I was invited as well. He was merely being polite."

Her reasoning sounded hollow in her own ears. Nicholas didn't do a thing he didn't want to do, and they both knew it.

"I think he fancies you." Aurora took a sip of her juice and peered at Tori over the rim of her glass.

"I can't hold another bite." Removing the napkin from her lap, Tori placed it next to her plate. "We'd best get dressed if we are going to make Mrs. Merriweather's luncheon by noon."

"There's plenty of time. Mother's not even up yet. Tori, don't you like Nicholas?"

On a heavy sigh of resignation, Tori sat back in her seat. "It's not a matter of whether I like him or not, Aurora. We are from completely different worlds. He would never be accepted in mine and I don't belong in his." The truth in her words caused her heart to ache.

"Why not? Uncle Edward accepts him. As a matter of fact, I think he secretly wishes you two would get on with it."

"Yes, he made that quite clear. But, it's not as simple as all that." Voicing her doubts was proving much harder than she would have expected. "I was born into a class of people that frown upon marriage outside of their class. Father believes that if Nicholas married me, he would reclaim his rightful place. But, Father doesn't know him as well as I do. Nicholas would never leave his home here, nor should he. He's not had a suitable upbringing, and the peerage would eat him alive."

"Mrs. Dottie is very suitable!"

"No, I mean as far as the peers are concerned." Tori forged ahead quickly to ease Aurora's pout, reaching her hand across the table to rest upon her cousin's arm. "An upbringing suitable for titled persons."

"Sounds like plain ol' snobbery to me." Aurora moved her arm and folded it with her other one across her chest. "Remind me never to go to England."

"It's not just in England. Snobbery exists everywhere, I'm afraid. We of the nobility have simply perfected it, that's all." Her admission brought heat to Tori's cheeks. Things were so different here. Everything was cut-and-dried at home. Commoners never questioned the lot into which they were born. Did they?

"How is it that we have the very same amount of Haverwood blood running through our veins, but you see yourself as so much better?" Aurora tilted her head slightly. "Are you ashamed of mother and me?"

"Oh, Aurora, no. You have it all wrong. I'm proud of you and am happy to be with you any time, anywhere." Tori left her seat to go to her cousin's side. "You are my family. I love you dearly."

"Really?" Aurora pinned Tori with a serious look for a long moment. "So love does make a difference."

Try as she might, Tori could come up with no reasonable response.

The days flew by and Tori became as eager as her cousin to attend the biggest event of the season. Aurora's excitement was contagious. When the evening of the ball was finally upon them, neither could stand still long enough to have their corsets laced.

Gabe had heralded the arrival of the Sabertons a short time earlier and had indicated that they would be waiting in the parlor with the earl.

Finally, Aunt Charlotte stepped out ahead of them from the door of Aurora's bedroom and lowered her voice, as if anyone else could hear. "Let me go down first. I'll make sure y'all make a memorable entrance.

Aurora nodded and brought her hand to her mouth to chew on a fingernail.

Her mother scurried down the stairs as fast as her small feet would allow. Tori and Aurora watched from the top of the stairway as she made it to the doorway of the drawing room and waved the men onto their feet.

"Gentle ...men. Up!" It was all she could manage having run completely out of breath.

Aurora entered the room with a shy smile. Her ivory gown, with its high waist and lacy collar, swished with each step. A matching bow caught up her blond hair and simple pearl earrings were her only jewelry.

Zachery brought over a small nosegay and placed it in her hand.

"Edward, aren't they pretty?" Charlotte took a small hankie from her sleeve and held it to her mouth.

"Quite." He checked his timepiece without even glancing at his niece. "Where is Victoria? It's nearly a quarter past seven and we've a good hour's drive."

Charlotte Haverwood tapped his sleeve, directing his attention to Tori, who still stood in the doorway.

She'd been so taken with watching Aurora blossom under Zach's warm gaze that she forgot about making her own entrance.

"You look especially lovely tonight." Nicholas came to meet her, offering his arm. "I hope you'll make room for me on your dance card."

"Maybe just one," Tori conceded with a playful grin.

"I'll have the first dance, princess." He smiled. "And the last, too—if you behave."

"Enough gibberish." The earl grabbed up his cane and hastened to the doorway. He had been invited to act as an honorary chaperone for the evening and was anxious to begin his duties.

Tori turned so that Nicholas could help her with her

white ermine cape. Holding her loose curls, she was careful with the sapphire combs on either side of her temples. Her pale blue gown was fitted with a wide sash at her waist. White mitt sleeves hugged her arms to the wrist, hooking over her thumbs. A three-strand choker of pearls lay against her throat.

"Men shall sit on one side of the carriage. Ladies on the other." Lord Haverwood donned his top hat and pulled on his white gloves. "Let's be off."

Nicholas and Zach exchanged glances suggesting the earl had lost his proverbial marbles.

Her father remained undaunted. "It's a good hour's drive and I'll not tolerate any dallying behind my back." With an emphatic thump of his cane, he motioned for Gabe to open the door.

The ride to Argyle Island was uneventful, save the ferry ride which Tori thought was quite unique. Her father conceded somewhat, yet still insisted on depositing himself directly in between Nicholas and Tori. He had seen to it that Zach and Aurora sat at opposite ends of the seat across from them. Awkward silence hung in the air of the coach until they pulled into the drive of the Hermitage plantation.

Nicholas alighted and threw his cape off to the side of one large shoulder before reaching for Tori's hand. He looked dashing in his formal Navy attire of dark blue, which of course, he wore with his usual air of self-assurance. Brass buttons gleamed in rows down each side of the tailed jacket and his black Hessians were polished to a high shine.

Tori took his hand and set foot lightly from the step, taking in the marvelous view of the lit-up grounds. Strains from the orchestra filtered out, filling the courtyard with a rich melody. Well-dressed ladies on the arms of proud gentlemen strolled past, smiling in greeting.

"Tori," Aurora whispered beside her. "I declare, I have never been so excited in all my life. This feels like a dream, and I hope I never wake up."

Tori was amazed at the opulent surroundings. She had imagined a working plantation would be rather plain. Nothing was farther from the truth.

Swags of white material hung from the ceilings of the grand ballroom and hundreds of candles glistened from an enormous chandelier, reflecting brightly in a wall of windows on the opposite side. A lush garden, equally as brilliantly lit, could be seen through several pairs of open French doors.

Off to one end, on a small platform, the musicians moved their bows in unison. Several maids in uniform attended the refreshment tables on the other side. A row of chairs lined the outer walls where older matrons admired various couples as they swayed, dipped, and swirled past.

Lord Haverwood twirled his walking stick before proceeding down the steps in a stately posture. Two Naval widows waited for him at the bottom step and propelled him over to their cluster of friends gathered in a far corner. Her father stood tall, only slightly leaning on his cane.

Dozens of couples filled the dance floor, all moving gracefully with the music.

Tori glanced up at Nicholas. "It's been such a long time since I've attended a ball." She could barely think straight with him standing so near—and looking so handsome. "We were taught the steps in school, but rarely had a chance to practice them in mixed company. Do you suppose we could take a turn at the next go around?"

"There's plenty of time for that. How about I get us some refreshments?"

"Could it be that you don't know how?" She couldn't help herself. The festive atmosphere had her feeling cheerful, if not a tad daring. "Well, not to worry, sir. I shall teach you. There's nothing to it once you learn the basics."

"Do be gentle." He gave her a bright smile. "I'll try my best not to get flustered."

Tori bit her lip to keep from laughing. "You're quite impossible, you know."

When he laughed, dozens of eyes turned to them. "If truth be known, princess, you'd be downright broken-hearted if I didn't tease you at least once in a while."

"Well, now." She lifted her head. "It appears you don't know me well at all."

He chucked her defiant chin. "I can fix that, too. For now, though, I'll go find us some punch."

Starting in the direction of the tables, he was soon

intercepted by three giggling young women. One toyed with her ringlets as she spoke to him. Another tapped his arm with her fan with every other word. He nodded graciously and attempted to step around them, only to have another come up to keep him from his task.

Tori watched with a grin. His tall, broad shoulders commanded attention. Eyes from all over the room followed his every movement. Splendidly garbed in his captain's uniform he was an impressive figure. Even Tori had stolen more than a second glance.

Aurora attempted to gain her attention from across the room. Frowning slightly, she tried to comprehend her cousin's gestures.

Following the girl's pointed direction, Tori suppressed a chuckle. Viola Mae Jenkins walked through the door with a young man, inches shorter than herself. And Lord help her if she wasn't looking particularly daisy-like this evening.

The very same dress Jean-Pierre Dupree had created for Aurora now hung on Viola Mae Jenkins, and from the looks of things, she was quite pleased with herself as she tugged her harried suitor along beside her. Tori and Aurora smiled knowingly at each other.

"Might I have this dance, Lady Victoria?" A well-dressed young gentleman stood next to Tori, with several others hovering nearby.

"Thank you, but no. I've come with an escort, and I promised the first dance to him."

"My apologies. I thought since Captain Saberton was

already dancing, you would be free to accept an offer."
He started to return to the eager group, but Tori stopped
him.

"I'm afraid you're mistaken. Captain Saberton is my
designated partner for this first dance." She searched her
reticule for her card. Lifting it she pointed to the space
where Nicholas's name had been crossed out. This dance
was indeed open.

"No, ma'am. Nicholas assured me you were free to
dance if it pleased you to do so. May I be so bold as to
say we were hoping he would give the rest of us a
chance."

Confusion marred her brow for just a moment until
she remembered her manners. Turning a forced smile
toward the bewildered young man, she politely accepted
his offer. The conductor had announced a Virginia Reel
and though the dance was new to her, she soon found
herself enjoying it immensely. She hadn't realized how
much she missed the excitement of dancing and being the
center of attention.

Every now and again, she tried to spot Nicholas
amidst the magnificent array of colors swirling past, but
to no avail. She refused to let the thought of him ruin
what was becoming a pleasant evening.

The orchestra called a brief intermission, giving Tori a
welcome chance to catch her breath. Accepting a glass of
punch offered from a silver tray, Tori savored the cool
melon drink while looking over the animated guests.

She glanced up to see Nicholas watching her in a wide

mirror above the food tables. Turning her back to his indiscreet inspection, she tried to focus on the young man hovering over her. He was quite the chatterbox, yet Tori hadn't heard a word he'd said.

The orchestra resumed with the soft flow of a waltz. Nicholas made his way toward her and her pulse quickened as he drew near.

"Excuse us, won't you Jackson?" Nicholas approached and the young man stepped aside. With an offer of his hand, she didn't hesitate to accept. Neither did she give resistance when he pulled her into the circle of his arms once they reached the dance floor.

"You are quite horrid." Tori spoke though a forced smile for the benefit of those who watched them on every side. "You've behaved quite unbecomingly this evening—even for you."

Nicholas smiled in response, tightening his arm around her waist.

"I expect I shall be angry about this for quite some time."

"I've seen how it's kept you from enjoying yourself so far." Nicholas caught her in a full turn that left her breathless. "If you'd notice, princess, I traded my name on your dance card from the first Virginia Reel to this waltz. It's much cozier."

She'd been so dejected at seeing his name crossed out on the first dance that she hadn't bothered to look to see if he'd added it elsewhere.

"What must I do to earn your forgiveness? Name it

and it's yours." Nicholas caressed the small of her back, and Tori to leaned into his warm embrace.

"Well, now that you mention it, I would like to visit your mother's home some weekend. She invited me to come riding."

"It would be my pleasure." The sincerity she heard in his voice made her look up into his eyes to make sure she'd heard him right. Once more, she was taken unaware by his thoughtfulness. No teasing. His offer appeared genuine.

Unable to tear her eyes from his warm gaze, she was absorbed by his nearness, enchanted by the dance they shared.

"Princess?" The corner of his mouth ticked with the beginnings of a smile.

"Yes, Nicholas?"

He smiled down into her eyes. "The music stopped a good bit ago, but we can continue dancing if it makes you happy."

Dreamily, she smiled back.

When his words finally pierced her daze, Tori came to an abrupt halt. She scanned the questioning faces now openly staring as they swayed together in the center of the dance floor. A clap sounded from somewhere in the back and soon others joined in to offer polite applause.

Heat burned her cheeks as Nicholas took her hand to lead her through the pleased crowd. He paused only to pull her up beside him and tuck her hand into the crook of his arm. Several people spoke to them along the way, but Tori had no idea what they were saying.

Nicholas headed for the large French doors. She welcomed the cool breeze on her face and the chance to breathe again.

Swelling clouds now covered the moon and distant thunder rolled in from the sea. The air, heavy with moisture, smelled of the rain to come. The night breeze ruffled Tori's curls as she looked around at the couples who had paired off all around them. Some were seated on the white wrought iron benches placed in the lawn, while some sat on a low wall surrounding the patio.

"That was utter humiliation." Tori spoke in a ragged whisper.

Nicholas shrugged, as they strolled past a bubbling fountain.

"I should think you would care a bit more about your reputation than that."

"People will talk, Victoria, and say what they will." He stopped and cupped her face to place a kiss on her forehead. "There's nothing to be humiliated about unless there's something you're guilty of."

"Guilty or not, appearances can hang a person. Don't you care what people think about you? How could you not?"

"What do you think of me, princess?" His dark eyes searched hers as if trying to read her answer before she responded.

"I –"

A disturbance erupted from inside, and Tori to peered

around his shoulder. A loud scream rent the air. Tori startled, clinging to his arm. Uneasiness gripped her when she lifted her head and saw his worried expression.

"Come on." Nicholas grabbed her hand. Tori was forced to run just to keep up with his long strides back toward the ballroom.

"Lady Victoria." A gray headed man met them half-way. "You'd best come inside."

Now Tori truly was frightened. Something dreadful had happened, and she somehow knew it had to do with her father. Reentering the building, Tori immediately searched for his beloved face, but he was nowhere to be found. Turning, she implored the man to explain, tightly clasping Nicholas's hand.

"It's the earl," the older gentleman began. "I'm afraid there's no easy way to say this." He looked to Nicholas briefly before going on. "His Lordship has been abducted."

"Tori's blood ran cold as fear seized her. Faint weeping could be heard behind her. She could not summon her voice to work.

"What happened, Hamilton?" Nicholas drew her close to his side.

"The servants say the earl stepped out front to see someone who had come asking for him. He was attacked by two men and thrown into a rented hack. It sped off before anyone could stop them." The man called Hamilton gave Tori a sympathetic glance before returning his attention to Nicholas. "The authorities have been notified. I suggest you see the lady home. There's nothing you can do here. And Saberton ..." He took the younger man by the arm. "Take care."

Aurora pulled her cousin into a tearful embrace. The ground felt unsteady beneath Tori's feet. She should be crying, too. But for the moment, she felt nothing but a debilitating numbness that threatened to swallow her whole.

The easiest person to deceive is one's own self.
~ Edward Bulwar Lytton

Twelve

"Zach, have Jonas bring the carriage around." Nicholas settled his cape around Tori's shoulders before leading the two women past the nervous whispers and curious stares of Hamilton's guests.

It had begun to drizzle, and he could feel Tori trembling. Yet she stared straight ahead. Her face was as pale as an icy moon. He needed to get her seated for fear she would crumple beneath the shock. Barely waiting for the carriage to roll to a stop, Nicholas called for Jonas to throw open the door.

"No!" As if coming to herself, she pulled away from Nicholas and pushed against Zach when he stepped in to block her from returning to the grand foyer. "I'm not leaving here. My father is somewhere on this island and I'll not leave until he is found."

"Victoria." Nicholas regretted his patronizing tone

when he saw it only intensified her resolve.

"Go if you must. But I will not leave."

Though she was the subject of indelicate whispering all around them, for once it didn't dictate her behavior. Unfortunately, for all of her newfound bravery, Nicholas wasn't about to let her stay on Argyle Island as long as danger had already targeted one Haverwood tonight.

"Get in the carriage, princess. We'll discuss it on our way back to the city."

"Lady Victoria, I must agree with Nicholas. You might not be safe here." Hamilton and six other men came to form a half circle around them. "You'd do best to return to Mrs. Charlotte's and let the authorities take care of the particulars."

Tori turned an imploring face toward Nicholas. "I cannot just leave him here."

"We have no way of knowing if the earl is even on the island at this point." Hamilton stood back and lifted his arms. "Attention, please. Since this gathering has taken an unfortunate turn, I suggest all our guests make their way to the ferry for safe passage home. We will shut down the ferry with the last conveyance. Good evening and thank you for your gracious understanding."

Before Tori could argue, Nicholas scooped her into his arms and headed for the carriage with Zach and Aurora close on his heels.

"Put me down! This instant!" When Nicholas failed to comply, he got a bony little elbow jabbed into his side.

"To the Haverwood's, Jonah." Nicholas called up as

he stepped into the carriage. "Zach, get the door."

Zach lifted Aurora inside and swung the door shut behind him. Jonas set the carriage in motion.

Nicholas settled her onto the seat and she scooted over to hug the far corner when he slipped in beside her. Thunder rolled in the distance. Nicholas expected her mood to match it but was surprised when she looked out the small window and said nothing.

He knew she was furious, but his first priority was to make sure she was safe.

The sound of rain pattering on top of the rig filled the space of the carriage, along with an occasional sob from Aurora as she wept softly against Zach's shoulder.

All the while, Tori remained quiet.

Nicholas rested his arm along the back of Tori's seat, watching the lights play over her delicate profile. The carriage jostled across the planks of the ferry that took them from Argyle Island to the mainland.

As badly as he wanted to question her to try and make sense of the earl's odd disappearance, he knew this wasn't the time.

Nicholas searched his mind for anything the earl may have said regarding the danger he supposed was following them, trying to piece together some clue as to who might have taken such a risk on a plantation full of witnesses.

On more than one occasion the earl had mentioned that Nicholas must see to Victoria's safety, never emphasizing his own well-being. After the attack on the ship, Nicholas conceded someone indeed wanted her injured—

or worse. But he could have sworn they'd managed to elude that threat and left whatever peril that followed them at Wrenbrooke Harbor.

Passing under a lamplight glowing in a haze of rain, Nicholas caught sight of unshed tears shimmering in Tori's eyes. Still, she was silent.

Mulling over the facts, Nicholas had yet to make sense of the earl's disappearance. If robbery had been the motive, the assailants wouldn't have risked such a public spectacle. They would have hijacked his carriage or seized him on a deserted street in the city after dark.

If Haverwood was kidnapped, they'd done a clumsy job of it. At least a dozen eyewitnesses could describe the two that had come asking for him, not to mention the rented hack could be easily traced.

The only thing for sure was that Victoria needed to be kept safe until the earl was found and the culprits caught.

He heard her sniff but still she gazed out the side window.

"Victoria, I need you to listen to me." He softened his voice and place a hand on the both of hers clasped in her lap. "I know you're upset with me, but removing you from Argyle was for your own good. We will find your father."

He knew she heard him when she blinked back tears, but she refused to answer.

"Have you any idea who might have done this?"

"I know of no one who would wish my father harm." Finally she spoke, but her answer was quiet.

Careful not to upset her more, he nodded and let the matter drop as they pulled onto Habershire Street leading to the Haverwood house. Once stopped in front of the large steps, Zach helped Aurora down and into the house.

When Tori didn't move, Nicholas sat with an arm resting on the back of the seat as he watched her. He knew she needed a moment before going inside to face an hysterical Mrs. Charlotte. Once he was certain she was safe, he'd go in search of the earl himself.

Several minutes passed until he broke the silence between them. "I think we'd better get you inside before you catch your death of cold." Again, he noticed her shivering. "I'll see that Gabe has the house secured before I leave."

She followed him out of the carriage and up to the door, where she turned on him like a lioness. "How dare you?"

Nicholas was taken aback.

Fury blazed from her blue eyes as she suddenly advanced on him. "Because of you, I am miles from where my father was last seen. I needed to be there in case he is found." She became teary again and could barely speak, fighting for composure. "I should have been with him in the first place, not out cavorting in the gardens."

She looked away and bit her lip for a mere second.

"Now if you'll excuse me, Captain Saberton, I intend to go find my father. Which will be infinitely harder now that you've half-dragged me so far from the scene."

With that, she lost her restraint completely and spun

around to rush inside the house. Her tears, and biting words, left Nicholas completely stunned.

Flicking up his collar, he turned and disappeared down the lane, instructing Jonah to wait for Zach.

The temple of our purest thoughts is silence.
~ Sarah Josepha Hale

Thirteen

"Tori?"

Slowly, Tori lifted her eyes from a dazed stare. Someone was speaking to her, but she didn't fully comprehend until they began to jostle her shoulder.

"Please, Tori. You're beginning to scare me." Aurora stood over her chewing on her thumbnail. "Mama says you need to come downstairs. The constable is here, and he wants to talk to you."

Tori threw off the tear-stained cape that was still alive with Nicholas's spicy scent. "Has there been some news? Aurora, have they found Father?"

Aurora shook her head. "No, but he's come to help."

Driven by desperation, Tori made a brisk flight down the staircase. Anxiety hastened her steps, though she refused to let herself contemplate the worst. There was always hope her father would be returned safe and sound.

Unless he had been found ...

"Victoria, honey. For goodness sake, slow down. You're white as a sheet, child." Aunt Charlotte stood in the doorway of the dining area and took her niece by the arm to seat her at the end of the table.

Zach sat at one side of her and another man, busily eating a piece of Sally Lunn cake, sat on the other.

"This is Constable G.W. McAllister, dear. He's come over to ask you a few questions." Aunt Charlotte took a seat next to Zach. "I don't understand how this could happen. This sort of thing never, ever goes on in Savannah. I can't remember the last time." As usual, her dear aunt prattled on, not caring if anyone listened or not.

The constable slurped noisily from his coffee cup and it proved to be all Tori's shattered nerves could take. "Sir, is there some information as to my father's whereabouts?"

The rude man ignored her and took another heaping bite.

Tori took a ragged breath and glanced over at Zach.

"G.W. didn't get a chance to have dinner," Zach tried to explain. It sounded ridiculous the minute he said it.

Tori flashed the boorish man an impatient glare.

"Settle down there, missy." The constable pointed his fork at her, his mouth disgustingly full.

With a quick hand, Tori grabbed the offending utensil that he was waving in her face and set it loudly upon the table. The man's generous jowls flapped in indignation.

"I would appreciate it, sir, if you would explain what

steps have been taken to locate my father."

G.W. McAllister sucked his teeth and lifted something from between them with a thumbnail, then, took one more sip of coffee before finally looking back at Tori. "I'm going to ignore your sass, being that you aren't from around here. I imagine it's mighty scary for a little lady left all alone. But, there's no reason to panic. Everything's under control. Don't you worry your pretty little head. The old earl will turn up eventually."

"More coffee, G.W.?" Aunt Charlotte sniffed and brought the silver coffeepot over to his side of the table.

"I believe I will, Mrs. Charlotte, thank you."

What was the matter with these people?

Determined to get a decent explanation from this man, Tori was prepared to take him up by the lapels and shake the living daylights out of him. There was no time for his disregard and time was their worst enemy. She stood abruptly, stark fear spurring her on. "I'm sure you are aware, Constable, my father is an influential man. I suggest you take his abduction a bit more seriously."

The constable looked from Tori to Zach as if she had threatened his very person.

Zach sat forward and nodded. "I have to agree, G.W.. There's no time to waste."

"All right." Constable McAllister leaned back in his seat and yanked the napkin from around his neck. "First of all, I don't have to be out searching this city. I've got men to do that for me." He spoke condescendingly, much the way he would to a simpleminded child. "Secondly, who's to say the old earl didn't just decide to spend the night elsewhere." He gave Zach a suggestive wink. "He'll probably come strolling in here 'round about sunup and everyone will see there was no need for all the alarm."

Tori was mortified, unable to believe what she was hearing. "I assure you, sir. My father would never behave in the way you are suggesting. He was seen being tossed into a strange hansom. Are you suggesting he was merely topping off the evening out on the town? That is absurd!"

"Were you there when it happened?' The constable narrowed his droopy eyes. "How do you know those two fellows weren't just helping him into the carriage?" The constable shook his head at Tori's frown. "Now, there's no use getting yourself all upset. Go on up and lie down a while. We'll come across him." He stood and finished the contents of his cup. "I thank you, Charlotte. The cake was delicious as usual."

"Miss Victoria." He donned his hat and tipped it at Tori.

"Lady Victoria." Zach corrected.

A feeling of complete helplessness tightened in her chest, making it hard to draw a breath.

"Certainly, G.W. You'll be informing us now, if you hear something, won't you? If say a R-A-N-S-O-M demand comes in?" Aunt Charlotte followed him as he ambled out the door.

Blinking back tears, panic began to overtake her. It was apparent that Savannah's law enforcement had no intentions of helping. Her father was in desperate danger somewhere, and there wasn't a thing she could do to help him.

"He's right, Tori. You'll make yourself sick worrying about it. We need to pray for Uncle Edward if we want to get him back home." Aurora, seated next to Zach, looked up with red eyes that belied her brave front.

Reentering the dining room, Aunt Charlotte's shoulders slumped a bit more than usual. "I know G.W. comes across as unsympathetic, darlin'. But he's doin' his best to keep us all calm." Charlotte said between sniffles. "He's a good man, I'm sure he'll find Edward very soon and we can all get back to normal."

A tear escaped and slipped down Tori's cheek.

Aunt Charlotte patted her with a pudgy hand. "Oh dear, we mustn't cry." With that she held her hankie to her mouth and boo-hooed.

"Ladies, please. What we need is something to take our minds off this. Worrying won't bring Lord Haverwood home any sooner." Like most men, Zach would do anything to divert an emotional outburst. "Mama always used to play games with us when she wanted to keep our minds occupied. How about a round of charades? Or hearts?"

"Dottie always knows the right thing to do." Aunt Charlotte dabbed her eyes.

"Hearts sounds like a wonderful game, Zach. How do we play?" Aurora perked up.

"It's simple enough to learn. Have you a deck of gaming cards, Mrs. Charlotte?" Zach cleared the plates to one side as the housekeeper set them on a tray to take to the kitchen.

"Gaming cards! Why, if I did, I'd never admit to it."

"There's some in your thread box, Mama. I'll get them," Aurora offered.

"Dear heavens, I'll be ruined." Charlotte took up her fan. "Why, if this ever gets out, Zachery Saberton, I'll have to relinquish my position on the hospitality committee. They may boot me out of the church all together."

"I promise not to tell a soul, Mrs. Charlotte." Zach laughed.

"Tori, you're so quiet. Can I get you something, honey?" Charlotte laid the fan aside.

"I'd like to go up to father's room for a while." Tori gave her aunt a weak smile in trying to ease the concern shining in the older lady's eyes. "Please don't worry about me."

By the time she reached the door of her father's room, her frantic thoughts turned to prayer. "H-help... please." A sob caught in her throat. "Please, Lord."

Grief tore at her heart as she lit the table lamp and looked around. His belongings were all there, but she longed to see him there instead. What on earth would she do without him? How could she possibly survive?

Inside the wardrobe, his fine suits hung neatly in order. Ten white shirts, all exactly alike, were folded in a drawer. Dozens of ascots and kerchiefs, all embroidered with the family crest, were arranged in another. His jeweled comb and mirror decorated the dressing table, alongside his silver shaving mug and razor.

Everything in its place. Exactly as he'd left it.

Gazing into the cold fireplace, Tori listened to the rain patter against the window. She sank wearily into a tall leather chair. Oh, how she ached to see her father's bushy gray mustache give a twitch of reprimand at seeing her slouching so unladylike in his seat.

With eyes closed, she was overcome by loneliness that settled around her like a heavy cloak. Her father was the single, most constant, thing in her life. He was no less than invincible in her eyes. Because of his distinguished name and powerful influence, she had never lacked for anything. He saw to her every need.

"Dear Lord," Tori whispered in utter desperation. "Be with him and bring him home safely to me." Wracked with a sob, she folded her hands and brought them to her forehead. "Please, please, Lord, see that he is taken care of. I simply can't bear the thought of him suffering." Hot tears streamed down her face. "He's all I have in this world."

She sank to her knees beside her father's chair and continued pouring out her heart.

Thou shalt cry, and He shall say, "Here I am."

The scripture verse from Isaiah came to her mind over and over until there was no room for doubt. Speaking it aloud, the warmth of this promise took hold in her heart and washed over her tattered nerves. Before long, her fears began to quiet and peace calmed her soul.

Lightning flickered through the window. Tori to shut

her eyes against the blinding light. Upon reopening them, her attention was drawn to the leather-bound book on a small table next to her father's chair. She recognized it at once. *Lady of the Lake* by Sir Walter Scott, inscribed in gold lettering across the brown leather cover. It had always been his favorite.

In spite of her tears, Tori smiled when she reached for her father's cherished possession and held it to her chest. Somehow it made her feel closer to him, knowing he had held these same pages in his own hands so many times in the past.

Running her hand over the cool, smooth cover, she opened the book carefully and read the familiar inscription. "To my dearest, Edward. Forget-me-not." The signature was hidden beneath an old ink blot that made it illegible, yet Tori knew it was her mother's name scripted underneath."

Returning to his chair, she sat and read from the romantic passages as time seemed insignificant. Sir Walter's lush description of the beautiful Scottish countryside made Tori homesick for Wrenbrooke and the times spent there with her father.

Just as her eyes were beginning to grow heavy, a piece of paper fell from the pages of the book. Sleepily, she unfolded the yellowed document and glanced at the contents.

With a sudden jolt, Tori sat up. Blinking, she stared down in disbelief, the words jumped out at her. Surely there was a mistake.

The document in her hand was a marriage certificate joining her father and an unknown woman—a Lucinda Martin. Taking a second, closer, look, she confirmed the name was most definitely not that of her own dear mother, Rachelle Beauchet.

The year recorded was eighteen hundred and thirty-six. Four years before her parents had married, and five years before Tori was born. Stranger still was the location of this supposed marriage—Augusta, in the American state of Georgia.

Could this have something to do with her father's disappearance? The marriage was an obvious farce. It couldn't possibly be legal. But what if this Lucinda Martin had revenge in mind? What if she had decided to retaliate against the earl for pretending to marry her all those years ago?

With determination, Tori sprang from the chair. This was the first real clue she had and was determined to pursue it. If they located the Martin woman, it could lead to her father.

Just short of the door, Tori stopped in her tracks. She had nowhere to go for help.

Back in England, she had access to any number of advisors. But here in the Americas, she was at a loss.

Aunt Charlotte had nearly lost the family business due to lack of sound guidance. So she wouldn't do. And that inept constable was out of the question. He wasn't interested in the leads he already had.

Purposefully, she avoided the most logical choice,

hoping to come up with—anyone—else to assist her.

Driven by distress, she had been terrified for her father—and still was. Every moment he was missing meant he might be suffering unimaginable torment. His health could not possibly hold up to the strain.

The document in her hand was the only piece of evidence she had to go on. Otherwise, he was lost to her with no hope of finding him in a city full of strangers.

Thanks to her impetuous temper, going to Nicholas for help now was next to impossible. Squeezing her eyes shut, she willed herself to stay calm.

Lord, forgive me, and lead me to the help I need.

There is a wisdom of the head
and a wisdom of the heart.
~ Charles Dickens

Fourteen

Retracing her footsteps, Tori found Zach still sitting with the women in the dining area. Trays of cheese and sweets were scattered on the table around them. All three looked surprised when Tori dashed into the room.

Aunt Charlotte brought her hand to her chest. "Mercy sakes, child. Did you have a nightmare?"

Tori rushed to her aunt's side and handed her the certificate before turning to Zach. "Zach, please, I need to speak to your mother as soon as possible. Will you take me out to Brechenridge?"

Zach had risen when Tori entered the room.

"Tori, honey, where did you get this? And for pity's sake, what does it mean?" Aunt Charlotte looked puzzled as she glanced from the paper to her niece and back again.

"Let me see, Mama." Aurora reached for the yellowed document dangling from her mother's hand. "Who is Lucinda Martin?"

"A shabby girl that used to come around sellin' garden vegetables from a little farm south of here. She took a fancy to Edward the summer he came out for our wedding. But he certainly never married her. I can assure you of that." Aunt Charlotte laid the worn paper on the table. "Why, it's nothing to worry over. Obviously a forgery."

"Please, Zach. Can we leave tonight?" Tori was impatient to be on their way. The earl's life could very well depend on Zach's answer.

"Well, I suppose we could. But it won't do you any good. Mama's in Philadelphia meeting with a prospective buyer." His voice softened with consideration.

"Tonight?" Aunt Charlotte shook her head so adamantly, two long ringlets escaped the purple cap on her head and bounced down across one eye. "Goodness, no. You can't go anywhere tonight. It's rainin' out there. Besides, they're liable to bring Edward home any minute, now."

"Can I go?" Excitement lit Aurora's face.

Tori lifted her hand to still the confusion and collect her thoughts. "Please, listen, all of you. I don't know exactly what it is that I've found. But you have to admit it's something to look into. If my suspicion is correct, it may very well have something to do with father's abduction. It was in one of his books. Zach, I was hoping your mother could help me find this woman or at least refer me to someone who can. Before it's too late. Can you tell me when she is due to return?"

"Not until a week from next Monday," Zach answered.

Tori's shoulders went slack. Nearly two weeks. She couldn't wait that long. She needed answers now.

After looking over the document, Zach tapped it on the table. "You know, Tori, Nicholas has access to any counsel mother has. And then some. Why don't you go to him?"

Aurora nodded, as did Aunt Charlotte.

"Oh dear." Tori rubbed her temples. Her head was pounding. "I'm afraid I've ruined any chance of your brother ever doing anything for me. I was quite mean to him earlier."

"Nicholas isn't one to hold a grudge." Zach took his seat again. "He's too sensible for all that. How about if I take you to him first thing in the morning?"

"No. I shouldn't wait that long." Having lost the battle with her pride, Tori was prepared to relinquish it completely if Nicholas would help find her father. "Do you know where we could find him tonight? Now?"

Aunt Charlotte gasped. "Victoria! Surely you can't be thinking of seeking a man out in the middle of the night. Why, the scandal such a thing would cause."

"Please, Zach." Tori's eyes were heavy with unshed tears as she laid her hand on his arm. "This woman could be desperate. Desperate enough to …"

Finally, with a nod he was unable to refuse her.

"Mercy sakes, we'll be ruined. Never in my life have I heard of such goings-on. The world has gone mad right under my nose." For lack of anything better, Aunt Charlotte took up a napkin and fanned herself.

"Tori, can I go with you?" Aurora was on the edge of her seat.

"No." Aunt Charlotte lifted a finger to wag at her daughter and Aurora's enthusiasm wilted.

"It's settled then." Refolding the certificate, Tori pushed away from the table. "I'll go get my wrap."

Hurrying up the stairs to her room, she grabbed up the first thing she could lay her hands on. Nicholas's cape. Without a second thought, she threw it around her shoulders and headed back down to join Zach.

If he and Aurora were surprised at seeing the overly long cloak, they didn't show it. Opening the door, Zach gave Aurora an affectionate kiss on the cheek and followed Tori out to the waiting carriage. A sleepy-eyed Jonas climbed up onto the driver's seat.

As the horses trotted off, they left a deliriously happy Aurora standing in the doorway with a hand to the side of her face.

The rain had stopped but the thick night air was still heavy with moisture, amplifying the clopping of the horses' hooves along the empty streets. Tori avoided conversation by staring out the small carriage window. Their first stop was the offices of Haverwood Shipping and Trade. Tori watched from inside of the carriage as Zach tried the doors and found them locked. The high windows were darkened, and it was obvious Nicholas was not there.

Zach paused, glancing at Tori, before giving Jonas the instructions to the next destination. Climbing back inside the conveyance, Zach explained that they would see if his brother was at home. "It's half past two in the morning, Tori. Even Nicholas can't get you an answer tonight. Let me take you back to Mrs. Charlotte's. I promise to pick you up at daylight."

"What if he refuses to help me? I must find someone else and we will have wasted precious time. Please, take me to him, Zach. Surely he will be agreeable to at least giving me a simple yes or no."

With a defeated sigh, Zach tapped on the roof of the carriage to instruct Jonas that they were ready to leave. She could see that her decision agitated him but he was too honorable to question her.

So unlike his brother.

Expensive coaches lined St. James Square as they rounded a corner and came to a stop in front of Nicholas's stylish West Broad Street home.

Tori refastened a small comb in an attempt to tame her disheveled tresses. Her rumpled ball gown was hidden for the most part under Nicholas's evening cape. Still she looked a frightful mess.

No time to worry about that now.

Tori emerged from the carriage, lifting the hem of her skirts to ascend the circular stairs leading up to the darkened doorway. Rather than wake the staff, Zach used his key to let them in.

Once inside the dimly lit hallway, Zach lifted a finger to his lips, motioning for her to wait where she was. He then took the marbled staircase two stairs at a time.

Her normal curiosity to look around was overruled by the urgency of her mission.

Lord, please move on Nicholas's heart to help.

He had every reason to toss her out on her pantalets for the thoughtless way she had spoken to him. All she could do now was ask his forgiveness and pray for compassion.

Voices at the top of the stairs brought her attention to Nicholas coming toward her in a gray robe. Tori tried to read his expression but was unable to sense his mood.

"What's this about?" His question was low and direct. "Has there been news?"

"She needs your help." Zach stepped around him, obviously ready to take up her cause. "I tried to convince her to wait 'til morning but she has something she needs investigated."

Nicholas pinned her with an unwavering gaze. And though it was unnerving to the point that breathing became a challenge, she refused to look away.

"Is this true?" His voice softened.

"Yes."

"Thanks, Zach. You can go on up to bed. I'll see Miss Haverwood home." Though he spoke to his brother, Nicholas's eyes never left hers. He continued to study her face as Zach disappeared back up the stairs. A chill in the air overcame her.

"I see you've forgotten your shawl again," Nicholas drew his cape tighter around her shoulders and secured the ties at her neck.

"So I have."

Nicholas pulled open the double doors that led to a sparsely furnished parlor and motioned for her to go in before him. For an instant, being here alone with him in his bedclothes made Tori question the wisdom of seeking him out after all. Admittedly, it had been a desperate move.

He led her to a small table flanked by two leather chairs. A game of chess was set in the middle. Nibbling her lip, Tori took a chair across from him, sitting on the edge with her hands folded primly in her lap.

Nicholas sat back and rested his elbows on the arms of his chair, apparently waiting for an explanation as he brought his hands in front of him, steepling his fingers. "Start from the beginning and tell me what this is about."

Tori decided to begin with a confession. "I overreacted earlier and spoke harshly. My behavior was unacceptable. I am truly sorry."

"So you ventured all the way over here, braved the storm at two in the morning to make your apologies. Is that what you expect me to believe?"

Tori could only manage a nod in answer.

"What is this really about, Victoria?"

At this point she had nothing else to lose so she chose to get straight to the point. "I need your assistance."

"Now, that I believe."

Tori shifted uncomfortably. "You're the only person I know to ask. I really have nowhere else to turn." Tori watched him cautiously then presented the paper she had found. "Here, read this."

He took the parchment and quickly skimmed over it. He raised a brow and handed it back. "So the earl has more of an interest in Georgia than he let on."

"I need you to help me find this woman. For obvious reasons, I believe she may lead us to my father." Despite her best efforts, her hands held a slight tremble, so she clasped them in her lap.

Lightening lit the room from the corner windows.

"But I can't do it alone, Nicholas. I need your help." When he didn't immediately respond, she reached across the small table and placed her hand on his. "Please."

Thunder cracked outside and Tori flinched.

He rose and pulled her up into the warmth of his arms He held her so tight she didn't dare move. The same spiced wood scent that had lingered on his cape filled her senses and she closed her eyes to breathe deeply. Nicholas embodied the strength she needed. And in that moment, she allowed herself to be immersed in the stability of his embrace.

The tenderness he showed her, after she had all but scorned him, touched something deep inside her heart.

"All you had to do was say please, princess."

Turning her face, she looked up at him. A half-grin played at the corner of his mouth.

She tried to smile back, but it wasn't in her tonight. "Please tell me you believe this could have something to do with Father's disappearance."

Moonlight broke through the clouds for a fleeting second to shine down upon them through the high windows. "I do believe it's a place to start." Nicholas straightened the cape around her shoulders. "For now, I'll take you back to your aunt's. We can talk about our options first thing in the morning."

Tori nodded, relieved he had taken her notion seriously. For the first time since finding the marriage certificate, she felt a glimmer of hope that they might be on the right track to recovering the earl.

Exhaustion finally flooded over her. "Thank you." Her voice came in a broken whisper.

Nicholas pulled her to himself and kissed her forehead.

There is no instinct like that of the heart.
~ Lord Byron

Fifteen

The moon peered from behind the clouds and illuminated the brilliant blue of her eyes. Along the way to the Haverwood house, Nicholas watched Tori scan the empty streets and he knew she was hoping for any sign of her father. As if she expected the earl to appear out of thin air if she willed it hard enough.

Once stopped, she gave a tired smile as he helped her disembark and make their way to the high doorstep. Before she reached for the door, Tori paused.

Her eyes lifted to meet his. Nicholas didn't like what he read in their depths. Her desperation was almost tangible.

"Come on," Nicholas smoothed a curl, still slightly damp, that clung to her face. "Let's get you inside."

"You've been so kind. I don't know what to say." He pushed the door open, but she still didn't move. "Thank you, Nicholas."

"Princess, we'll find your father."

"I realize it isn't much to go on." She placed her hand inside his arm and allowed him to lead her inside. "But I feel better knowing you will be looking into it for me."

"I'll contact my attorney first thing in the morning and have him track down the woman in the document. Sound fair?"

The foyer was still lit, and before the door was closed the Haverwood ladies filed out, both talking at once.

"Oh, praise be!" Mrs. Charlotte exclaimed.

"Tori, we were scared to death. We thought something had happened to you, too." Aurora gave her a hug, then looked to the doorway. "Where's Zach?"

"Where on earth have you two been?" Mrs. Charlotte was clearly annoyed at them both.

"Victoria was with me." Nicholas passed her a look that brooked no argument. "We needed to examine a document she found with her father's things. She's convinced it is somehow connected with his disappearance. She felt she needed to act quickly, so she sought me out. Perfectly acceptable under the circumstances."

"Well, I hope none of your neighbors saw her coming to call in the middle of the night. It wouldn't matter if your father was President Abraham Lincoln himself, Tori, you'd never live it down." Mrs. Charlotte motioned for everyone to filter into the parlor, but Nicholas remained at the door.

"I'm not staying. I just wanted to see Victoria home."

"In that case, go on up, girls. I'll see Nicholas out." Turning back to Nicholas she lowered her voice, pulled him by the sleeve until he bent down to her level. "Nicholas Saberton, you better have acted in a manner befittin' a gentleman or between your mama and me, we'll take it out of your hide."

"Mrs. Charlotte." Nicholas patted her round cheek. "You know me better than that. I assure you, my neighbors saw nothing."

Charlotte Haverwood released a grateful sigh.

"I kissed her well out of their view."

By eight o'clock the next morning, Nicholas was back in his office on Bull Street. He'd sent a message to Abner Westphall requesting a meeting at his earliest convenience. Considering it was Saturday, he didn't expect to hear back from the lawyer until Monday morning, but he'd given Victoria his promise to make the contact.

Sorting through invoices, Nicholas was surprised when the front door swung open at quarter after nine and Mr. Abner Westphall came into the room clasping the lapel of his overcoat. A prominent attorney in Savannah, he'd made his mark, and was proud of the fact. He'd handled the Saberton's affairs for forty years and had known Samuel and Dottie before any of their boys were born. He and Nicholas's father had been the closest of friends.

"Good morning, Nicholas." Westphall offered his

hand and Nicholas left his desk to accept the greeting. "I got your note and came as soon as I could."

Nicholas led him to chair with a pat to the man's back. "Thank you for coming, Abner. I assume you've heard about Haverwood's abduction?"

"It's all over the newspaper this morning."

Nicholas hadn't taken time to read his copy, choosing instead to visit the constable hoping for new information. Unfortunately, G.W. McAllister posed no help at all. According to his wife, he was sound asleep after a late night and his second man in charge indicated they had nothing new in the case.

"How well did you know the earl?" Westphall asked, taking a notepad from his leather briefcase. "The word around town has it he was well liked by most, if not revered."

"I was contacted by him in March. Before that we'd never met." Nicholas leaned back against the front of his desk, arms crossed at his chest as he relayed the connection. "He's the older brother of my late business partner, Percy Haverwood. From what I understand, Mother met him briefly years ago, but I'd never personally made his acquaintance."

"I didn't handle Percy Haverwood's holdings. I'll find out who did and see if I can schedule a meeting." Nudging his spectacles with a thumb, the lawyer flipped to a fresh page in his notebook. "Now, I assume the earl had a reason for contacting you?"

"He said it was imperative that I leave immediately for

England, to see him and his daughter safely out of the country as soon as possible."

This gave Westphall pause. His hand stilled as he looked up at Nicholas over his glasses. "Didn't you find that a bit odd?"

"I did. But out of respect for Percy I decided to make the trip."

Westphall nodded and made the notation. "Did the earl ever explain his reasoning?'

"No." In hindsight, Nicholas was agitated at himself for not pressing the issue. "When asked, he evaded the question."

"Did he ever say anything or do anything else peculiar?"

"You've obviously never met the man." Nicholas couldn't help but smile. "Lord Haverwood is a dignitary of the first order. He's used to having his way and always has an agenda." Standing, Nicholas moved to the window, looking down on the square which was just beginning to come alive with Saturday activities. "The earl may come off as quirky or gruff, but he always knows what he's doing. He has a brilliant business mind and will stop at nothing to see to his interests."

"I take it his interests included you marrying his daughter?" Nicholas could see Westphall watching for an answer in the reflection of the glass.

On a heavy sigh, Nicholas turned. "Zach's the only person besides Victoria who knew about that."

Abner nodded. "I stopped by your home thinking you

would be there. Zach told me where to find you—among other things."

Returning to take a seat at his desk, Nicholas filled the lawyer in on the unusual conversation he'd had with the earl when he'd first arrived at Wrenbrooke.

"I dismissed it, of course. I figured the earl was just trying to increase his influence by having his daughter become a duchess."

"Mmm hmm." Abner had taken a page full of notes. "Are you certain he understood you were not interested in marrying Lady Victoria and reclaiming the family inheritance?"

"I don't know how I could have made it any more clear." A jab of conscience caused Nicholas to frown. He wasn't the least bit interested in going back to England to reclaim Brechenridge. But he couldn't honestly say he hadn't developed a rare fascination for the earl's daughter.

"Your message said you needed me to look over a document."

Taking the folded parchment from a pocket in his vest, Nicholas handed it across the desk. "Victoria found this among her father's belongings."

Nicholas watched the lawyer scan the paper both through his spectacles and over the top of them before finally returning his attention to Nicholas. "I take it no one knew about this."

"Victoria didn't. Neither did Charlotte Haverwood." Nicholas replaced his pen into the inkwell. "Do you think it's legitimate?"

"Quite." Westphall was quick to answer. "This is the hand and seal of Judge H.M. Lamb from Richmond County. In the year eighteen and thirty-six. Have you any idea where this woman is now?"

"None." Sitting back in his chair, Nicholas brought his elbows to rest on the leather padded arms "I was hoping you might be able to help track her down. Victoria is certain she has something to do with the earl's apparent kidnapping."

"Possibly." Abner lifted the parchment. "Mind if I keep this for the time being?"

"Please do." Weighing his next question before posing it, Nicholas narrowed an eye. "What would the woman have to gain by abducting the earl?"

"Ransom. Revenge. Possible inheritance. A number of scenarios come to mind. Since he had remarried, it's quite possible the woman is dead." Abner tucked the document into a pocket of his leather case. "And if she's not, that makes for a fairly convincing motive for murder. At least, my wife would think so."

Nicholas gave a half grin.

"Yet, since the earl felt it was his daughter who was in the greatest danger, there are evidently more pieces to this puzzle that must be uncovered. Her welfare is at stake. I suggest you hire an investigator to dig a bit deeper into the earl's disappearance. In the meantime, I'll travel to Augusta to have a look at the court records."

"Thank you, Abner." Nicholas stood. The very real

thought that Victoria could possibly be targeted next caused cold dread to grip his chest. Keeping her safe was suddenly raised to a whole new level. This had gone from an amusing diversion to a matter of life and death. "I'll see that Victoria is taken care of."

"If you don't mind my asking, Nicholas, how do you plan to see that happen?" Westphall stood as well.

"I'll move her where I can keep a closer eye on her. At my home. In my care ..."

The emphatic shaking of Westphall's head was more than annoying, especially since hearing his plan out loud sounded ridiculous.

"You have no legal right to keep her there. She isn't your legal ward, nor is she your wife. Therefore, I'm afraid you'd be asking for tongues to wag." Abner removed his spectacles and waited for Nicholas stop studying the ceiling. "You and I both know the ladies of Savannah would have a hen-fest with that."

"I can hire guards and keep her from leaving the Haverwoods until this is resolved."

Still, Abner shook his head. "Again, you have no right. Besides, I don't know anyone that appreciates being held a prisoner."

Frustration built until Nicholas swiped at a pile of invoices stacked on the corner of his desk to send them fluttering to the floor. "I won't stand by and do nothing. As long as there's a threat, she's my responsibility."

"I have no doubt you'll do the right thing." Abner nodded kindly, before seeing himself to the door. "I will send word when I return from Augusta. Good day, Nicholas."

With that he left Nicholas alone with his troubled thoughts.

Returning to the window, he leaned against the jamb, looking out over the bustle of Forsythe Square. A muscle worked in his jaw. Up until a few days ago, he would have shrugged this off as just another wild scheme the earl was becoming famous for.

It wasn't that he hadn't believed there was a threat. No, he'd seen it aboard *The Tempest*. But he had believed they'd left it behind, convinced whoever wanted to harm Victoria was an ocean away. Or so he'd thought.

Part of him wanted to toss decorum to the wind and insist she move to his home for her own safety. What other people chose to believe about him didn't concern him at all. They would always find something to gossip about, even if they had to make something up. It was the kind of thing this town thrived on, had an insatiable appetite for as a matter of fact.

But, this was different. This time it would mean hurting someone who didn't deserve it.

I know you'll do the right thing. He couldn't get away from Abner's words.

Mulling over every option, he was left with only one that made sense. Nicholas listened to the stately chime of the tower clock as it struck one from the church across the square.

By the stroke of two, Nicholas forged down the steps

of the editorial offices of *The Georgian*. Passing a couple of Savannah's matrons with barely a greeting.

Walking the few blocks to his home, he entered the foyer with a slam of the heavy wooden door and shouted for Jonas on the way to his library. "I need you to deliver a note to Zach. You'll no doubt find him at the Haverwoods."

"Yes, Sir. Mr. Ian arrived home from seminary. He's in the library."

"Good. When Zach gets here have him join us there."

Nicholas wanted his brothers to be the first to congratulate him on his forthcoming marriage.

*Perhaps it is our imperfections that make us
perfect for one another.*
~ Jane Austen

Sixteen

 $\mathcal{L}$ ady Victoria Haverwood lowered the newspaper,
staring straight ahead in absolute horror. Surely there
was a mistake. A misprint, at the very least.

Either way, Nicholas Saberton had some fast explaining to do.

"More tea?" Aunt Charlotte eyed Tori closely and
nearly scalded herself with the gold-rimmed teapot.
"Good gracious. Victoria, say something for pity's sake."

The Sunday newspaper had come earlier, followed by
a note from Zach promising to explain everything as soon
as he could. Tori's first thought was that someone might
have spotted her father. Yesterday's copy of *The Georgian* had been filled with talk of his disappearance, and
she'd hoped for more news today.

Having skimmed the first couple of pages, she was

beginning to lose hope of reading anything of interest until she turned to page three where Nicholas's public intentions were center page in bold print.

"Now, honey." Aunt Charlotte wrung her linen napkin. "I know it looks bad, but Zachery will be over later. He'll set this whole thing straight. You'll see. Why, it's not what it seems, that's all. Nicholas isn't one to do anything foolish."

Tori lifted a brow at her aunt, who rolled her eyes heavenward.

"Lord forgive me." With a grimace, Aunt Charlotte clarified. "All right, he is occasionally. But he's not a complete buffoon. I'm certain there's a perfectly good explanation for this."

The main door came open with a thud, straining noisily on its hinges. Aurora, rushed past the sitting room, calling out to her mother.

"In here, darlin'." Charlotte motioned for Flossie to set out another plate.

"Mama, have you seen this morning's—" Aurora froze when she came into the room and her gaze fell to the newspaper in Tori's hand. "*Georgian?*"

Tori gathered as much composure as she possibly could. "Yes, Aurora, we have. We were just discussing it." Laying the paper aside on the table, she rose. "I've decided not to wait for Zachery, Aunt Charlotte. Nicholas owes me an explanation face to face."

"Of course, sweet." Aunt Charlotte also stood and followed her niece to the stairway. "A marvelous idea, actually. We all need to get out for a while. No sense in sitting here waiting for news."

"I shan't be long." Tori turned from the bottom step. "However, Aunt Charlotte, I'm afraid you are mistaken on one account. If Nicholas Saberton thinks that I am going to marry him, he most certainly is a buffoon."

With that Tori lifted her skirts and ascended the stairs.

Once inside the solitude of her room, she collapsed onto the window seat, leaning her head back against the cool wall next to the open pane. The absurdity of such an announcement was almost laughable.

A special license had been procured from a Judge Henderson. It had gone on to claim that because of the Earl of Wrenbrooke's abduction and given the understandable distress of the intended bride, all concerned had decided to forego the usual betrothal period in favor of a quiet private ceremony tomorrow.

Tomorrow!

Why was Nicholas doing this? He wasn't interested in her father's estate. He certainly wasn't in need of money. She held no claim to any part of Haverwood shipping. Honestly, becoming Nicholas's wife wasn't altogether distasteful. If only he had asked.

Something stirred in the bushes directly under the window where Tori sat. Aurora's tabby cat in pursuit of another hapless mouse, no doubt.

Every girl, at one time or another, has thought about marriage. Tori certainly had. But she'd hoped her suitor would declare his undying devotion first. Then on bended knee, he would ask that she make his happiness complete by agreeing to become his beloved bride. Like a tender scene from a fairy tale.

Unfortunately, her life since coming to America had been anything but a fairy tale.

Moving from her seat, she smoothed the purple satin covering on the bed. Oh, how she wished for news of father. Every moment that passed felt like he was slipping further and further away.

Something dark in the mirror caught her eye. Spinning around, she searched the open window for a source of the odd reflection.

Nothing.

She shook her head. The pressure of the past two days was taking a toll. Now she was imagining things that were not there.

A loud knock reverberated through the room, causing Tori to startle.

"Tori, are you all right?" Aurora came into her cousin's room. "We've been waiting for you downstairs, but we can go later if you'd like."

"Oh, Aurora." Tori put a hand to her throat and felt her pulse race beneath her fingers. "Come in. I've not changed, but it won't take long."

"That's all right. I'm sure you must be completely worn out with all you've been through these last few days. I'd be in absolute ruin by now. I'll go back downstairs to wait for you."

"No, please stay. Really. I'll only be a moment." Tori

didn't want to be left alone with her wild thoughts.

Aurora dropped into a chair next to the hearth. "Please don't be too angry at Nicholas. I'm sure he has his reasons for all this. Goodness knows, plenty of women would love to be in your shoes right now. He's always one to go against the tide, and he'll push every limit to take care of you. I'll bet he gets away with it, too. Oh, it's all so romantic."

Behind the privacy screen, Tori stepped into a blue and white striped day dress while her cousin continued to make excuses for Nicholas's impossible behavior. Coming around the partition, she motioned for Aurora to help fasten the buttons in back.

Picking up her brush, she ran it lightly over her hair, before taming it into a neat chignon at her nape. "Aurora, you are such an innocent. There is nothing romantic about any of this."

All the while, Aurora rattled on about love, and—

Once more, something in the mirror caught Tori's eye and she whirled around to get a better look.

Most likely just a shadow, but Tori could have sworn she'd seen something—or someone—move. The curtains billowed a tad more than the breeze warranted but otherwise, nothing was out of place.

Rubbing away goose flesh trickling over her arm, Tori cautioned herself to stay calm. Her imagination was getting the best of her.

"Did you say something, Tori?"

"We'd best hurry before Aunt Charlotte begins to

worry. If you'll hand me my drawstring bag there on the table next to you, we can be off." Tori ushered her cousin into the hallway.

Making one last sweeping glance about the room, she closed the door behind them.

What loneliness is more lonely than distrust.
~ George Eliot

Seventeen

*A*long the way, Aunt Charlotte and Aurora chattered about a luncheon they were to attend the next day.

Thunder rumbled overhead, yet the brimming clouds still held possessively to their burden. The thick heavy air was much too warm for comfort. Everything around seemed to cry out to the sky for relief.

Tori adjusted her white scoop bonnet, tying the ribbons under her chin with a determined set to her jaw. She was still plenty perturbed that Nicholas hadn't even the decency to ask her in person but had posted a public notice *informing* her she was to be married.

She'd tolerated her father's narrow-minded disregard of her for years, but by George, Nicholas would hear exactly what she thought of his actions today.

People stopped on the street to stare as the Haverwood carriage passed. A few people waved briefly, with open curiosity on their faces. If Tori had worried Aunt Charlotte would find this dreadful situation an embarrassment, one look at her beaming face as she waved back dispelled that notion.

Aurora was equally excited as she continued her recitation on the virtues of love and marriage as she saw them through hopelessly romantic eyes.

Tori hated to disappoint them, but this farce was about to end. She had only one objective and that was to find her father. Anything else, including marriage, was out of the question.

Upon their arrival, Jonas greeted them at the door with a smile wide as the Savannah River. After showing them into the parlor, he hurried off to inform Zach they had guests.

Tori looked around the room as she removed her bonnet. She had only seen Nicholas's house briefly the fateful night of the ball and then only in dim light. Reluctantly, she admitted that he had superb taste. The Duncan Phyfe sofa was lovely with its matching chairs, all facing a fireplace made of blue marble. Dark mahogany trimmed the mantle, the moldings around the windows were hand-carved, and the wonderfully high ceilings made the space feel expansive. A beautifully stenciled long table along the side of the room held a silver coffee set.

The bayed alcove extended from the front of the room overlooking the street. It was windowed on all three sides, with a grand piano tucked neatly inside.

"Good morning, ladies." Zach appeared in the doorway, clearing his throat.

Aurora greeted him from the sofa with a radiant smile. "Hi, Zach. Isn't this a lovely morning?" Her enthusiasm made them all grin, considering the gray skies looming just outside the windows.

"I'd planned on coming over to see you just as soon as I heard back from Nicholas." He approached Tori and offered his hand. "Shall I be the first to congratulate you?"

Tori's pursed her lips at the awkward gesture. "Congratulations are hardly in order, Zachery. Where is your brother?"

Zach gave a quick glance over his shoulder to the darkened hallway. "He's, uh, he's gone riding. He should be back any time."

"Well, then, we can wait for him." Aunt Charlotte seated herself next to her daughter. "How long ago did he leave, Zach?"

"Yesterday evening." Zach smiled weakly at the incredulous looks he got all around. "He enjoys long rides. It sort of clears his head. He promised to be back by ten."

It was half past eleven.

"Well, isn't this a fine kettle of fish?" Tori crossed her arms in a huff.

Aurora snickered until the others frowned her into silence.

"We can leave him a note and go have a little somethin' to eat over at Ruthanne's while we wait." Aunt Charlotte snapped her fan and wiggled to get up from the overstuffed sofa. "That little tea room down on Broughton Street, you know the one. Jonas can have Nicholas join us there when he comes in."

The last thing Tori wanted was to be subjected to any more curious stares from the townspeople. She had no answers to their inevitable questions, except that this was the most bizarre predicament she'd ever been in.

Overtaken with a sense of despair, Tori turned from the others and closed her eyes.

Lord, please help.

Hugging her arms, she continued to pray silently. There was nothing stable left in her world, everything was completely upside-down. She couldn't lay all of the blame on Nicholas. She couldn't place all the blame anywhere.

"Princess?" Nicholas's low voice spoke quietly behind her like balm to her tattered nerves.

Turning, she lifted her eyes and was immediately taken aback. "Good heavens. You look ghastly."

At least a day's worth of stubble shaded his jaw, his hair windblown, and his clothes were hopelessly wrinkled.

"And you smell of lathered horse." She covered her nose to make the point.

Nicholas's deep chuckle filled the room as he moved to the door to call for Jonas to prepare a bath.

"Oh, no, you don't. We are going to have a talk." Tori was primed to have this out once and for all. "And you shall stay where you are and hear me out."

As Nicholas and Tori continued to stare at one anoth

er, tension filled the room.

"You know, now that you mention it, Mrs. Charlotte, lunch sounds like just the thing." Zack took Aurora's arm and helped her to her feet.

Aunt Charlotte waved him off. "Not now, Zachery. I want to hear this."

"Please don't let us keep you, Aunt Charlotte." Tori turned from Nicholas's silent challenge and forced a smile. "I know you all must be famished. I promise Nicholas and I shall have a long talk and get this entire misunderstanding worked out before you return. I'll tell you all about it then."

Charlotte allowed herself to be led to the door, addressing Nicholas along the way. "Don't you go disappearing again."

Tori waited until she heard the front door close, then reeled about, placing her hands on her hips. "It may be acceptable here in Georgia to up and announce one's intent to marry a person without even consulting them first, but I am not a Georgian, nor am I available to marry one." She paused only long enough to take a breath. "So you can just go right back over to that newspaper and make a retraction, because until my father is found, I'm not marrying you or anyone else. The whole idea is utterly preposterous."

Nicholas calmly walked to the side table and poured himself some coffee as if she wasn't even speaking. He ignored her, swirling a splash of cream around in the cup with a spoon, until Tori was on the verge of hysterics.

"Do my feelings mean anything to you? My father is missing, Nicholas. How can I possibly consider marriage?" Frustrated tears filled her eyes and she fully expected him to loathe her for it.

Instead, Nicholas barely smiled and set his cup aside. Coming to stand in front of her, he caressed her cheek. "Feel better?"

No. Actually she wanted to scream.

"I take it you have some reservations about marrying me?" He held a hand out toward the sofa. "Sit."

She stood.

"Suit yourself. I've been sitting too long, anyway. I believe I'd rather stand."

She sat.

Nicholas leaned against the mantle with fresh amusement shining in his eyes.

Tori knew she was being disagreeable, and what's more she didn't care. She needed to know why he had done such a callous thing.

"I gave your father my word." As usual, Nicholas seemed to read her thoughts.

"Your word to marry me?" Her tone implied he was lying through his teeth.

"My word to keep you safe, Victoria. To see you're taken care of, no matter what. And that's what I intend to do."

Tori laughed with an unladylike sputter. It was preferable to crying. Nicholas had offered to marry her out of some stupid sense of obligation? She almost wished it had been a prank. She could take a joke, but she couldn't bear the humiliation of his pity.

"Well, Nicholas, thank you just the same. But, in case you haven't noticed, I am a grown woman and quite capable of taking care of myself."

"I've noticed. Grown up quite nicely by the way." He smiled when she rolled her eyes at him. "But, as to your ability to take care of yourself—well, that's debatable. This way, you won't need to. I'll do it. As of tomorrow, you'll be my wife." He took the seat next to her. "Princess, listen to me. Your father was convinced you were in some kind of danger."

Tori shook her head. "He never mentioned anything of the sort."

"I'll admit, I had my doubts at first, but after the attempt on the ship, and now the earl's gone missing, I'm more inclined to agree with him."

"Then hire an armed guard. But you certainly don't have to marry me." Her pride stung as he laid out his motive for their sudden betrothal.

"It's the only way I can offer you absolute protection. Unless you'd consider moving in here as my legal ward without the benefit of marriage?"

Tori lifted a brow in answer.

"I didn't think so." Dark smudges under his eyes told her he hadn't had much sleep. His expression became serious as he ran a hand down the stubble on his cheek. "You know, your father did ask me to marry you once. Remember?"

"Only because he thought you would become a duke, making it a prosperous match. I think he came to realize after a while, however, you simply aren't cut out for aristocracy. I believe he gave up on that idea."

Nicholas took her hand. "Is the thought of becoming my wife so repulsive?"

Before she could answer, a fleeting image came back to haunt her. The movement she had seen in the mirror as she pinned her hair this morning still filled her with unease.

"Victoria? What is it?"

"Nothing." She frowned, still trying to fit the pieces together in her mind.

"If you're worried about losing your English title, forget it. You won't need one here. You'll find that being Mrs. Nicholas Saberton has all the benefits you'll need."

Tori's frown deepened. She hadn't really thought about that until now. "I suppose that would take some getting used to."

"Well, get used to this." He released her hand and loosened the stay at his collar with an abrupt flick of his wrist. "You will be my wife. And as such, you'll never want for another thing as long as I live. Is that clear? Your father asked that I take care of you, and it's become apparent you need taking care of."

"I won't." A breath caught in her throat prevented her from saying any more. It was unthinkable to marry without her father there to give her away. "I couldn't."

"I'll buy you a title and have it engraved on your forehead—in gold, if you want." He stood and went recover his coffee.

She didn't require a title to make her happy. Admitting that to herself came as a surprise, yet a tremendous relief. Her true needs were fairly basic: love, respect, a safe place to be with the people she cared for.

Why had her father asked Nicholas to watch over her? Was she truly in some sort of danger? The attack aboard ship had seriously shaken her. But now with her father's abduction, nothing felt safe anymore.

Except when she was with Nicholas.

Looking up at him, she watched as he brooded over her perceived rejection. Obviously she had insulted his pride, and to a man like Nicholas there was nothing worse. His mother had told her that his former fiancé had treated him much the same way.

Tori glanced over at his broad back. Just the sight of him, so strong and self-assured, made her believe that maybe, just maybe, he could provide the protection she needed. His connections would certainly enable her to do an extensive search for her father. That was surely more important than the silly notion of a fairy tale marriage.

"Silver." She spoke quietly, resigned to the fact that there was no other option available to her.

Nicholas turned to her, weariness evident on his face.

"I prefer my nameplate to be made of silver, if you please." She watched him through lowered lashes. "Gold is a bit much."

He set down his coffee.

"But I'll need your promise to help me. Whatever it takes to bring Father home."

Nicholas sighed heavily. "Victoria, I intend to do everything possible to find your father. My lawyer is in Augusta researching your document, and I just rode all the way to Macon and back to hire the best investigator in this entire area. He's looking into the matter as we speak."

His disclosure touched her deeply. "Well, then, if I were to allow this marriage, I suppose you really ought to call me Tori."

"Never mind that." Nicholas pulled open a drawer and removed a flat velvet box. "This belonged to my great-grandmother, the Duchess of Brechenridge. It's been in the family for years. Consider it a wedding gift."

Tori took the box from his hand and opened it carefully. She'd never set eyes on such an elegant piece. The brooch was made of one large oval sapphire surrounded by dozens of diamonds. A smaller teardrop sapphire dangled below.

Nicholas placed a hand on her shoulder. "I'd like you to wear it tomorrow."

Tori didn't know what to say. This was all happening too fast. In truth, she could marry Nicholas tomorrow and be happy for years to come, if only he'd show the tiniest bit of love for her. "Thank you. I shall cherish it."

She searched his face for what she was certain was not there.

"It's settled then. I'll clean up, and Jonas will bring

you to meet the others." Nicholas took her hand and placed a kiss on top of her head. "But first, I want to know what had you so worried a moment ago."

She had to think about what he was referring to. The image in the mirror came back to her mind.

"Well, I ... this morning, that is ... I saw something odd in my room, that's all."

His eyes darkened, and he continued to watch her with that unwavering stare that never failed to quicken her pulse.

"I'm sure it was nothing." Tori stood and retrieved her shawl and bonnet from the parlor chair.

"What exactly did you see?" He walked over and took the bonnet from her hand and set it upon her head, tying the ribbon himself.

"I'm not exactly certain. I thought there was a movement behind me, I saw it in the mirror. Twice. But when I turned nothing was there. With all that has happened, it could have easily been my imagination."

"Jonas!" There was a restless edge in his voice as he ran a hand through his hair.

Jonas came in from behind her. "Yes, sir?"

"I want Miss Haverwood's things brought over today."

Tori gasped. "Now, just a minute, Nicholas. I've barely agreed to this marriage in the first place. Tomorrow is quite soon enough. I couldn't possibly be ready by today."

The most important day of her life, and he was acting

as if they were planning a picnic in the park.

"Settle down, Victoria. The ceremony is still set for tomorrow afternoon. But I want you here where I can keep an eye on you tonight."

"I won't do it!" Tori snapped, then caught herself. She mustn't lose her temper. She had to make him see reason. "Please, that doesn't give me nearly enough time to get my things together. Besides, Aunt Charlotte would never allow it."

"Unimportant." Nicholas stepped around her. "I'm not leaving you unprotected."

Tori moved quickly to stand in front of him again. "Please, Nicholas, don't do this. Don't ruin what little reputation I have left."

His hand reached down and smoothed her hair. "No need to worry about your precious reputation, princess. It's been taken care of."

"You can send a guard home with me to Aunt Charlotte's. I promise to be on my best behavior."

He refrained from pulling her close, but kept both hands on her arms. Finally he gave her that barely perceptible smile of his and she knew she had his consent.

Barely lifting her lips, she thanked him with a kiss.

Just then, the front door pushed open and Nicholas relinquished his hold.

Zach and Aurora entered while Aunt Charlotte flounced up the winding steps that led to the entry, waving her fan furiously. The colorful hat atop her fiery hair was alive with a dozen or so silk butterflies attached to tiny springs, which bobbled in every direction with each step she took.

"This bothersome heat wears me to a frazzle." When she spotted Nicholas and Tori, she picked up her pace. "Nicholas, you dear heart. Zachery explained the whole thing. Has Dottie been told?"

"I see you two are getting along a little better." Zach grinned. "So is there going to be a wedding tomorrow or not?"

All eyes fell on Tori. She nodded in answer.

Aurora squealed with delight.

Zachery shook his brother's hand and kissed Tori's cheek. "Congratulations. A most welcome addition to the family."

Aunt Charlotte perked up. "Why, that's right, Zachery. We will all be family now." She beamed at Aurora, who blushed with a giggle.

Nicholas snapped his fingers. "I almost forgot. Victoria needs to visit the dressmaker by three. I ordered her a dress yesterday, and they need her to come in for a fitting." He smiled at Tori. "I know you're disappointed but Madame Dupree was unavailable."

"I see you've thought of everything." Tori was a tad piqued at the thought that even this had been planned without her approval. "With only two day's notice, it couldn't be much more than a potato sack."

If Nicholas heard her, he disregarded her. "Mrs. Charlotte, I was thinking of hosting a dinner after the ceremony at The Pavilion House. It's the most elegant hotel in Savannah, and their food is delicious."

"No, sir." Aunt Charlotte shook her butterflies. "You won't deny me the pleasure of having your wedding reception at our very own home. I've got it all planned in my head. Nothing elaborate, mind you, but we must invite the mayor and his wife. And three or four … or five other families."

Aunt Charlotte was so excited she was nearly beside herself. "Aurora, will help me. She's a wonderful little hostess, you know. Look at the time. So much to do this afternoon. Come now, girls."

Let morning bring me word of Your unfailing love,
for I have put my trust in You.
~ Psalm 143:8

Eighteen

 ith all the preparations and purchases to be made, the afternoon passed quickly. Much to Tori's dismay, Aunt Charlotte's tiny little reception banquet was taking on a life of its own. Her aunt had promised to keep the guest list to a minimum, but Tori hated to think about what "minimum" meant to the dear lady.

After their whirlwind afternoon, Aunt Charlotte returned home in a flurry of excitement. All she said about her talk with Zach earlier was that they'd had a wonderful chat and this marriage was certainly the very best thing for all.

Tori excused herself, right after the evening meal, and went upstairs to her room. Nicholas had brought in the burly man named Amos, whom Tori remembered from their voyage, to stand over her all afternoon. He now positioned himself on the other side of her door after personally checking every nook and cranny inside her room. The hulking fellow had secured the shutters from the inside just as Nicholas had insisted.

Tonight she was bone tired after a most exhausting day. She couldn't put a finger on when she had given in, but she had gone to Nicholas with full intentions of putting a stop to this talk of marriage before it got out of hand, but came away a betrothed woman. Just like that.

Dozing, she fell into a dream she was soon struggling to escape.

Dreaming she was in a mighty whirlpool, spinning completely out of control. She swirled past her father and he held out his hand to her, but she couldn't reach him. Finally, she caught onto Nicholas. But, Miss Mair hit her fingers with a ruler and she lost her hold. She grew so weary of the struggle, but dared not give up. An inky shadow formed in the center of the rotation, spreading toward her. She couldn't get away.

"Tori, honey, wake up. You're having a nightmare, child."

Tori's eyes came open with a start.

Aunt Charlotte patted her hand to rouse her. "Mercy sakes, Flossie's marinated pork didn't set well, did it? We heard your cries all the way down the hall. That giant out there called us up to see about you."

Aurora stood on the other side of the bed, nibbling at her fingernail.

Tori pushed herself upright. The panic of the dream

still gripped her, but she couldn't bring the gist of it back to her memory. With her heart pounding in her ears, she was shaken.

"My throat is a bit dry." Her voice was groggy.

"I'll go get some chamomile tea. Mother always makes it for me when I have bad dreams." Aurora was quick to offer her help.

"Have Flossie put a tiny bit of laudanum in it, darlin'. It does wonders for helping a body relax. You'll want to be fresh and well-rested for tomorrow." Aunt Charlotte squeezed her hand.

"Thank you."

With Aurora gone to see about Tori's tea, Aunt Charlotte shut the door and came back to the bed. "Tori, honey, there's something I've been meaning to talk to you about all day. I suppose I've put it off as long as I can."

By the way her aunt was wringing her hands, whatever she had to say must not be pleasant.

"I know I'm not your mother, but ... "Aunt Charlotte began again. "Now, I don't know how much they schooled you on this particular thing, but as your only living female relative, I feel it's my duty to help you understand what to expect. After the wedding."

Was this about her little reception again? That's all she'd talked about today.

"You may put your mind at ease, Aunt Charlotte, we have that sort of thing where I come from and I've been trained thoroughly." She preened the cuff of her night-gown.

"Oh, good gracious!" Aunt Charlotte looked appalled.

"Rest assured, Miss Mair saw to it that I've had plenty of practice, too." Tori wondered at Aunt Charlotte's look of shock. "Truly. I could do it with my eyes closed and my hands tied behind my back."

She realized that her admission might sound braggadocios, but she didn't want her aunt to worry about having an inexperienced hostess on her hands. The woman was nervous enough.

"Merciful heavens!" Aunt Charlotte picked up a book on Tori's night table and flapped its cover to fan herself. "I have heard the British are meticulous, but to train young women before they've even married. Why, I never!"

Aunt Charlotte seemed in need of laudanum herself.

"I'm rather fond of it, actually. Perhaps we can compare notes sometime."

"Be thou compassionate ... "Aunt Charlotte slumped over in prayer. Such an odd little duck.

Aurora tapped on the door, and her mother called for her to come in, giving an odd sigh of relief.

"Here you are, Tori." Aurora moved in with a silver tray and set it down gently on the table next to the bed. "What have you two been talking about? Did I miss anything good?"

"No." Her mother responded with a shake of her head. "Good heavens, no. Nothing at all."

Tori took a sip of her tea. Aunt Charlotte was certainly behaving strangely this evening.

"Well?" Aurora plopped herself on the end of the bed. "What were you talking about?"

"I was just explaining—"

"Goodness me, look at the time. Come now, Aurora. Tori needs her sleep. Let's leave her be." Her aunt hurried Aurora toward the door.

Perhaps she had sounded too braggadocios. Aunt Charlotte had, after all, come in to give her some motherly advice. Maybe she felt slighted somehow. "Please wait, Aunt Charlotte. I would love the benefit of your experience. I've acquired a great many skills, but I'm still not familiar as to how it's done here in the States."

"How what's done?" Aurora leaned in eagerly.

"Entertaining—" Tori began.

"Victoria, no!" Aunt Charlotte implored at the same time.

"Aunt Charlotte was asking if I knew anything about hostessing a large gathering. For the banquet she's planned after the wedding."

"I was?"

Tori set her cup on its saucer when Aunt Charlotte sank heavily onto the bed.

"Aunt Charlotte, I believe this has all become a bit too much for you. If you'd like, we could just abandon the whole idea. I doubt I'll be in much of a mood to celebrate anyway."

"Here, Mother, drink this." Aurora poured another cup of tea.

"No, I'm fine. Really." With a nervous laugh, she mumbled something to herself. "Yes, goodness, yes. We will ... entertain just as we'd planned."

Tori lay back onto the pillows propped up against the ornate headboard and picked up her teacup once again. Yawning, the laudanum had taken effect and she suddenly felt very sleepy.

"Aurora, go on now and get some rest, darlin'. You'll want to look your best tomorrow."

Aurora didn't argue. Tori knew she did want to look her best tomorrow, for her own reasons. "Goodnight, then. Come wake me if you get up before me."

"Goodnight." Tori's eyelids were growing heavy.

Once the door was shut, Aunt Charlotte turned to her with a serious look. "I really must speak to you about a certain task you will encounter as a wife, Tori, dear. If I don't prepare you then it will come as a terrible shock, and you'll never forgive me for not warning you."

Tori nodded.

"Now, physical differences being what they are ... "Aunt Charlotte paused.

"I see." Tori's speech turned thick, and she really only wanted to close her eyes. But she knew if she did, it was likely they wouldn't reopen.

"When a man takes a wife, er ..." Aunt Charlotte was fanning herself with a book again. "You see, God created it so that .... well ... it's the only way to make an off-spring."

Offspring.

So that's what this was about. Tori shook her head a little to clear the fog threatening to take over. The girls at school had pooled their limited knowledge about these things. She felt she had a fairly good idea what was to happen once a couple becomes husband and wife.

"Thank you for telling me about this, Aunt Charlotte. Perhaps, I'll have Nicholas kiss me first. He has a wonderful way of distracting me to where I forget my own name." Tori was too sleepy to regret her next shameful confession. "I do so enjoy Nicholas's kisses."

To have and to hold; from this day forward,
'Til death us do part.
~ Traditional wedding vows, Book of
Common Prayer

Nineteen

Church bells ringing in the distance made Tori's heart skip two beats.

From the moment she'd opened her eyes this morning, her world was set in motion. Detached, she felt as if it were happening to someone else.

A copper bathtub had been dragged across the room, and before she knew it, she'd been immersed and scrubbed rosy pink all over. Her hair squeaked after being washed in French-milled lilac soap.

Aunt Charlotte had sent up three housemaids to attend to her. Over and over they'd tried to pile her sable locks atop her head. All finally agreed to simply let the unruly tresses tumble down her back, tucking only the sides up under her hat.

Not half an hour later, Tori stood on a footstool while the dressmaker and her assistants surrounded her to pin, nip and stitch. All four of them yanking and tugging until she could barely breathe.

Once finished, Tori turned from the mirror to get the final approval from her aunt.

"I declare! You're a vision. Turn around, precious and let me see the back." Aunt Charlotte lifted the short train, setting it straight.

The white satin dress was high-collared and fitted at her waist. The full, scalloped skirts swayed gracefully with each step. Pouf sleeves ended with a lace ruffle at her elbows. A small white hat came to a pearled V on her forehead, and a demure veil covered her face.

"Don't forget to pinch your cheeks and squeeze your lips shut every now and then for color."

"Aunt Charlotte, do you suppose I could forgo walking down the aisle … alone?" She took her aunt's gloved hand in her own. "I'd rather stand with the others at the altar. It won't be the same without father."

"Don't you give it another thought." Aunt Charlotte patted her niece. "Reverend Beauregard is very understanding about these things."

"Here, Tori, this just came for you. Nicholas had it sent over." Aurora handed her a small white package wrapped with a big blue bow. "What do you suppose it is?"

"I haven't the faintest idea. He's already given me a lovely piece of his grandmother's jewelry. That reminds me, please hand me that velvet box on the dressing table. I mustn't forget to put it on."

After untying the bow, Tori opened the box. The other two Haverwood women clamored to see what was inside.

A sterling silver nameplate lay in all its polished splendor upon a bed of dark blue satin. The inscription read simply: *Victoria – My princess always.*

A grin spread across her face as she lifted the shiny piece.

"How pretty." Aurora peered over her shoulder.

"Yes, but whatever is it for?" Her aunt, as usual, was baffled.

"My forehead." Tori held it up above her eyes and burst out laughing.

"You English girls have the strangest customs." With that Aunt Charlotte helped herself to another strawberry tart.

Before another hour passed, Tori was on her way to the church, seated in the Brougham alone with her anxious thoughts.

"You all right, Miss Tori?" Jonas stopped whistling long enough to look down from his driver's perch to check on her.

Her teeth caught the edge of her lip. A nod was the only answer she could manage.

Apparently, that was good enough for him and he resumed his merry tune.

Surely this was the best thing for them all. With her

father missing for three full days now, time was of the essence. Nicholas needed to be focused on the investigation rather than worrying about keeping an eye on her.

The Brougham came to a stop at the front steps of the regal, white church on the south side of the square. Tori's insides did a flip-flop.

She chided herself to remain calm. What was there to be nervous about? Just because she was stranded in a foreign land, about to pledge love and life to a husband who felt nothing but a constant need to antagonize her. Not to mention, she'd now have to tolerate spearmint in every cup of good English tea 'til kingdom come.

Waiting for Jonas to open the door, she admired the beautiful summer day. After a soaking rain the night before, the color of the trees and flowers were vivid against the cerulean sky.

Savannah's majestic First Christian Church faced Johnson Square. Four stately pillars lined the front. Even now, the carriages carrying Aunt Charlotte, Aurora, and various others pulled in behind Tori's. A ripple of excitement filled the air.

Curious onlookers gathered in the park across the street, trying to catch a glimpse of Lord Haverwood's daughter as she arrived to wed the most notorious bachelor in the county. Between her father missing and Nicholas's unconventional newspaper announcement, the city was abuzz.

Lowering the veil to cover her face, Tori took Jonas's hand as he helped her step down.

Approaching the stately double doors, she had a moment of apprehension. What if Nicholas never grew to have feelings for her beyond the need to kiss her now and again? She reminded herself that some of the suitors who'd presented themselves to her father for her hand were far less appealing. It wasn't unheard of to marry for convenience.

The doors came open and Tori's heart constricted at first sight of Nicholas standing down front with the minister. Seeing him in his formal Navy uniform, reminded her of the night of the ball. His powerful bearing spoke of the many years he'd spent as commander of his own ship.

With one step inside, she squared her shoulders and never looked back.

A man she didn't recognize stood to Nicholas's right. Same build and posture, but his hair was more the color of polished mahogany.

Zach sprang forward as soon as he noticed her. Bounding up the center aisle, he offered her a small bouquet. "My lady, you are more breathtaking than a field full of buttercups."

"Poppycock!" She gave it her best shot at being glib despite an ache wrenching her heart. "I shall be glad for the chance to keep a closer eye on you, Zachery."

"I stand forewarned." He laughed and led her to where Nicholas stood. "I think I'll enjoy having a sister. Come on. There's someone I want you to meet."

Almost head-to-head as tall as Nicholas, the other

man wasn't immediately familiar, although his lop-sided grin was classic Saberton.

"Tori, may I introduce our brother, Ian. He's the scholar of the family."

Nicholas took obvious offense at the remark, much to the delight of his youngest brother.

"Ian, this is Lady Victoria Haverwood, soon to be our sister-in-law."

Ian took Tori's hand and made an informal bow. "A pleasure to meet you, Lady Victoria." At second glance, his steady regard was very much like his brother's.

Nicholas looked down at her briefly before a woman Tori recognized as Reverend Beauregard's wife stepped up to pin a white boutonniere to his jacket.

"Our mother is in Philadelphia until next Monday. She won't be happy to have missed her eldest's wedding." Ian shot a look at his brother, then smiled down at Tori. "But, she will be delighted to finally have a daughter."

Smiling in return, she chanced another glance at her soon-to-be husband. For once, she didn't have to avoid his midnight gaze. Checking his pocket watch, Nicholas seemed anxious for the ceremony to begin.

"Although, if my brother isn't more attentive, I may decide to marry you myself."

That got Nicholas's attention and he snapped his watch shut with a look that left no doubt as to what he thought of the challenge.

Zach gave a loud chuckle.

Aunt Charlotte entered the sanctuary spouting orders

right and left. All those following her instantly picked up their pace. Four impossibly long ostrich feathers sprang from the back of her teal blue hat, sweeping everything in their path, while two porcelain lovebirds nested on the top of her head.

"Reverend, oh, Reverend. There you are." She headed down the aisle to where the minister stood near the altar. "May I have a word with you? Nicholas, you, too, dear." Tori watched as her aunt pulled the men aside and spoke with her usual animation.

The gentle pastor nodded, then ducked as she turned to speak with Nicholas, but not before a barrage of feathers assaulted his nose and he erupted into a sneezing fit.

As the grand pipe organ struck a chord, Tori's breath caught in her throat.

Everyone made their way to the front next to the communion table, resplendent with a large arrangement of summer blossoms. Only when Nicholas offered his arm did Tori remember to breathe.

"Dearly beloved, we are gathered here in the sight of God." The minister's opening words reflected the solemnness of the occasion.

Nicholas dutifully repeated his part of the vows and, with polite urgings from the minister, Tori managed to reply at the appropriate times without embarrassing herself too terribly.

A commotion erupted somewhere behind her, but Reverend Beauregard never stopped to acknowledge it, so

Tori put it out of her mind.

A promise to love, honor, and cherish sealed the covenant between them.

Forever.

The honor part was easy. Nicholas may be reckless at times, but he was truly an honorable man. The love and cherish part were yet to be seen.

Looking up at Nicholas, she realized everything she'd ever wanted was standing right next to her. A safe place to call her home and someone respectable to share it with.

When the time came to pray over the couple, they knelt with heads bowed before the minister. Nicholas gave a gentle squeeze to her hand upon the last "amen."

A chaste peck sealed their vows and it was thus that Lady Victoria Marie Haverwood became Mrs. Nicholas Saberton.

He who finds a wife finds a good thing.
~ Proverbs 18:22

Twenty

"*L*adies and Gentlemen, may I have your attention." Ian tapped lightly against a crystal goblet with a silver sugar spoon. "A toast. To my brother, my friend, who demands the best of everything and never settles for less. And to his good fortune at finding so perfect a bride, the lovely Victoria." Ian raised his glass, and the guests responded in kind.

Tori returned their smiles, and gave a gracious nod to her new brother, though a dull ache in her heart dampened the moment. Her father should be here.

"May the Lord bless their union today with lasting happiness and may they live in the abundance of His love."

"Hear, hear!"

"Cheers!"

She lifted the goblet to her lips, but barely took a sip.

Good wishes flowed as extravagantly as the peach-flavored punch. Yet, she couldn't escape the melancholy that enveloped her.

Aunt Charlotte's simple reception boasted over seventy guests and they all descended upon her the moment she walked through the doors. Nicholas accepted congratulations with his usual composure, looking her way every now and again with an unreadable expression.

Aurora was banished to a corner playing soft music on her harp for her mother's guests, looking utterly miserable. Considering the delicate music flowing from her fingertips, her pout looked out of place. Tori knew she'd much rather be celebrating with Zach.

The gentlemen congregated in large groups near the serving tables, while the ladies exchanged tidbits of gossip around the seating area.

Tori slipped unnoticed to admire a vast arrangement of white calla lilies set in front of the empty hearth. She couldn't wait to get out of the confining, ill-fit bridal gown. A distinct stick in her ribs every time she moved was evidence the seamstress had left in a pin or two.

For the second time that day, a commotion behind her caught everyone's attention. Someone was making a fuss in the hallway. Before anyone could investigate, Felicity Jenkins Duff burst into the room like a tornado, shaking off everyone in her path.

"You!" Felicity stormed in Tori's direction, but came up short when Nicholas stepped in front of her, blocking the way.

"And you, Nicholas Saberton!" Her desperate rant brought a bitter twist to her features. "You were supposed to marry me."

Ian came to his brother's side, followed closely by Zach. Every eye was on the new groom. Whispers of astonishment circulated the room as Tori, too, moved forward to stand at her husband's side.

"That was an unfortunate assumption on your part." Nicholas fought to keep his tone civil. "I never gave you any reason to believe your delusions had any substance whatsoever." As he spoke, he took one more step toward the hysterical woman and she wisely took a stumbling step backward.

With a hand upon his arm, Tori gained his attention. The furious flash in his dark eyes gentled noticeably as he looked down into her face.

No words passed between them. None were needed.

"Felicity Duff, you no-good hussy!" Charlotte Haverwood was as riled as a wet hen, waving her arms and shaking her feathered head. "How dare you barge in here, disrupting my wedding party. You leave this instant, before I have you arrested."

Felicity twisted away and backed into the wall. "Not until I've had my say."

"You have no say." Aunt Charlotte shooed her toward the door like a pesky rodent. "Now, get!"

"Why don't you ask Nicholas the real reason he married your darling niece? And while you're at it, ask the little tramp where she's been spending her nights."

Gasps echoed through the room fueling her spiteful rage. "Why was she seen on his doorstep unchaperoned at three in the morning?" Felicity's painted lips curved, watching Tori's expression freeze in horror. "She's nothin' but an English fake."

Nicholas immediately tensed.

Tori pushed aside her panic to move in front of him, steadying him where he was as she placed her hand on his chest. "Please, Nicholas. I'd like to take care of this, if you don't mind."

With resolve, she walked over to where the waspish female watched with a smirk.

"Mrs. Duff, you have insulted me and my family for the last time." Tori refused to raise her voice. "We were tolerant with your attack in the park. However, this is inexcusable—bursting in uninvited, spewing shameful lies on our wedding day." Tori clasped her hands in front of her, noting a purple hue spreading up Felicity's neck. "I believe Aunt Charlotte kindly asked you to leave. Although, I believe you owe these good people an apology before you go."

An unpleasant squawk escaped Felicity as one by one, the distinguished ladies of Savannah came to stand behind Tori, presenting a united front.

Zach appeared at Felicity's right and Ian at her left. Each took an arm to escort her to the door.

She yanked away from them. "I won't apologize for anything. You people believe what you will. You're fools, every last one of you. This is not over." With a nasty gleam in her eye, she stormed through the entrance hall. Tori could see Amos open the front door to facilitate her exit.

As soon as heavy door closed, the room came alive with twittering and fans waving everywhere. Three toasts went up to the lovely bride.

Nicholas received several heavy pats on the back from the gentlemen, young and old, but his careful attention never left Tori. She offered a feeble smile to show she was fine, but kept hold of her hands to keep them from shaking.

Aurora intercepted her thoughts. "The things that woman said! And the way Nicholas defended you." Her cousin's dreamy sigh made Tori laugh.

"Aurora!" Aunt Charlotte's shrill voice permeated their conversation from the other side of the room. "Mrs. Dalton's grandson wants to meet you, darlin'."

"Yes, run along, now, Aurora, darlin'." Tori mimicked. "Mustn't keep dear Mrs. Dalton's grandson waiting."

The younger girl giggled at Tori's imitation of a southern drawl with a decidedly British clip. "I'll be right back, Tori. Don't leave yet." Aurora went to join her mother, calling back over her shoulder, "Promise?"

"Promise what?" Nicholas handed Tori a glass of punch before reaching to touch his grandmother's brooch pinned on her dress. "You wore it."

"Yes, of course. It's lovely."

Brushing her cheek with the back of his knuckles, he

smiled. "You never cease to amaze me, princess. Here I thought I was supposed to be protecting you."

His hand was warm where it touched.

"Go upstairs now and get your things. It's time we left."

The couple drew interested stares from around the room. Low chuckles from the men, hastened Tori's retreat to the stairway. The hulking Amos followed close behind at Nicholas's nod.

On her way, Tori caught Aurora's attention and motioned for her to come along as well.

Once in the quiet of her room, she lifted the veiled hat from her head and carefully discarded the pin-laden gown. A light gray travelling dress, with black chevron trim, was laid out on the bed ready for her.

Her trunks had already been packed and transported to Nicholas's home. She'd left her father's things as they were in his room, except his Bible and a silk ascot that smelled of his shaving cologne. Those were packed neatly in Tori's valise.

"I'm going to miss you so." Aurora sniffled and Tori gave her a little hug.

"I'll just be a few blocks away. We can have tea every afternoon if you'd like."

A loud knock took them both by surprise.

"Ma'am, the Captain says it's time to get on back downstairs." Amos announced through the door.

Aurora eyed her with something akin to pity.

"Smile now, Aurora. No looking so glum." Opening

the door, she handed her bag to Amos. "This is a happy day, remember?"

The reminder was more for herself than for Aurora.

Every eye followed her as she descended the stairs. Nicholas took her hand at the bottom step and placed it on the inside of his arm.

Well-wishers surrounded them, all vying for her attention. One by one, she greeted the townspeople, thanking them for coming and sprinkling in reminders that they stay vigilant for news of her father's whereabouts. Each promised they would.

Zach and Ian each took a turn kissing the newest member of their family before Aunt Charlotte pushed them all aside, whimpering loudly into her hankie. Her ostrich feathers hit Nicholas in the chest as she hugged her niece at the front door. "Nicholas, your mama's gonna skin you alive when she finds out you've gone and gotten married without her here to see it. Goodness knows they'll hear it clear to Charleston." She motioned for him to lean down closer. "But, for once in your life, you scoundrel, you did the right thing."

Trust me not at all, or all in all.
~ Alfred, Lord Tennyson

Twenty-One

A beautiful sunset, awash with color, welcomed them into the evening as they entered the waiting carriage. Glittering lamplights paved the way to fashionable Chippewa Square.

Tori watched beautifully dressed patrons entering the Savannah Theatre on one end, while others scrambled to attend a lecture at Chatham Academy on the other side.

Set in the middle, like a magnificent jewel, was the Pavilion House Hotel, lit up from the inside by a huge chandelier hanging in the lobby. A massive round table adorned with a beautiful array of fresh flowers sat directly beneath the fixture.

While Nicholas headed to the desk to sign the register, Tori was drawn to a collection of art lining the hotel's stately brick walls. All were painted in rich, vibrant colors by an artist unknown to Tori.

"Ready?" Nicholas waited for her beside the grand spiral staircase.

Resisting a twinge of nervousness, she gave a nod and followed his lead to their suite.

Ornate double doors opened up to reveal an elegant parlor. Directly across, tall French doors led out onto a wrought iron verandah overlooking the courtyard. Faint melodies from an orchestra filtered in from the ballroom set below their rooms. On each side of the parlor were doors leading to separate private bedrooms.

Two of them.

After directing the bellman to leave Tori's bag in the ivory-colored chamber, filled with satin and lace, Nicholas then brought his own bag into the other.

Confused, Tori didn't move. She'd naturally assumed they would be sharing one room. Apparently, they wouldn't be sharing anything tonight.

"I apologize there wasn't a maid available to take care of your dress." Nicholas removed the shawl from her shoulders. "You'll have to settle for me." Hovering over her, he began to unfasten the tiny toggle on the high collar of her jacket.

Tori brushed his hands aside, slightly perturbed, though not exactly sure why.

"Be still. These things are complicated enough without you wiggling around." He frowned in concentration, lifting a brow at her exasperated sigh.

"Will you be staying, or have you other plans after I retire?" Already, she sounded like a nagging wife, even in her own ears.

Nicholas chuckled at the implication. "What kind of man would leave his bride on their wedding night?"

"The same sort of man that sends her off to sleep alone." Tori immediately felt her cheeks redden at her brazen reply.

His deep laugh caused her to brush his hand aside. "Thank you, I can manage the fastenings myself." A lump formed in her throat that she tried to swallow away. "If nothing else is required of me, I shall be in my room." The last came only as a whisper.

It was one thing to know he had yet to profess his love for her, but she'd always assumed he at least desired her.

Nicholas grasped her arms, and she crossed them over her chest to prevent him from pulling her closer. He didn't say a word until she quit studying the brass buttons on his jacket to look up into his face. A full minute passed before she did so.

"Nothing will ever be *required* of you, Victoria." His voice was low and steady. His eyes were gentle and she avoided them.

"You're perfectly welcome to share my room tonight, but the decision must be yours. There will never be anything forced between us. You come willingly or not at all."

Embarrassment held her tongue. Try as she might, Tori couldn't say the words he wanted to hear. Instead, she turned and went to her room, shutting the door behind her.

Why couldn't she admit she would rather go to his room and be done with it? Because proper ladies didn't admit that sort of thing. Miss Mair had been perfectly clear on that point. Ladies of quality never came off as too anxious where intimacies were concerned.

Then again, Miss Mair had never married and seemed to detest everything male. And most males felt the same about her.

After removing the heavy gray traveling suit and all the stays, corsets and trappings that went with it, Tori was glad for the chance to move unrestricted in just her pantalets and camisole. She went about unpacking her bag to keep her troubled mind occupied.

Placing the discarded gown on a hook in the wardrobe, she came across the most decadent garment she had ever laid eyes on.

A sleeping gown, of sorts, made of sheer white voile and flaunting the most shamefully plunging neckline Tori had ever seen. Very unlike her soft cotton night gowns with the drawstring ribbon under the chin. The outer covering held no better coverage, as it was made of the same sheer material and showed every detail of Tori's toes when she held it up to herself.

Her first thought was that someone had left it by mistake, until she noticed a delivery slip tacked onto the sleeve.

Deliver to: Mrs. Nicholas Saberton
Bridal Suite
Pavilion House Hotel

Someone had actually sent this ... thing ... to her on purpose. It must have been Aunt Charlotte. Well, her aunt's French designers had outdone themselves this time.

Tori wrinkled her nose as she laid the decadent negligee out on the bed.

Telling herself to simply ignore it, she went about arranging her various bottles of oils and perfumes. Seating herself at the dressing table, she brushed her hair until it crackled, then went about her nightly ablutions.

Casually glancing over at the wicked creation now and again, she was interested to know why, exactly, someone would even want to wear such a thing. It couldn't keep a body warm, and it didn't look to be very comfortable with all that flouncy material.

Tori's curiosity finally got the best of her. Pulling the weightless garment over her head she reveled in the soft material as it fell lightly around her feet. Spinning, this way and that, she watched the gown float gracefully about her. She'd never seen anything so provocative in her life.

Cupping her hand, she blew out the lamp and opened French doors, letting the night air cool her room. Lying back onto the tall bed, she looked out at the stars. Dozens of twinkling lights splayed across the sky, giving an illusion that someone up there was winking down at her.

Tori smiled at the fanciful thought.

Music from the stringed instruments sounded clearer with the doors open. She closed her eyes, imagining the couples below twirling in time to the music. Laughter mingled with the natural sounds of nighttime and drifted up to where she lay taking it all in.

Once again, her thoughts turned to Nicholas. The music reminded her of how they had danced the night of the ball. Sweeping across the floor, gliding ... swaying ...

Her sweet imaginings had them dancing once more. Under the stars in the garden below surrounded by fragrant flowers.

Suddenly, something wasn't right.

An odd sound out on the verandah brought Tori's eyes wide open. A rise of alarm quickened her pulse. Though she was afraid to move, she was more afraid not to.

Her room was lit just enough by pale moonlight that she could find her way to the door.

Lifting her gown, Tori ran the short distance from her room to Nicholas's and pushed open his door. Rushing over to where he sat at the secretary, Tori stopped in her tracks, suddenly remembering what she was wearing. Unfortunately, it was too late.

If he was surprised to see her, he didn't show it. With pen in hand, Nicholas leaned back in his chair, waiting for her to state her business.

The light from the candled sconce on the wall flickered and sent animated shadows on the cream-colored rug. In horror, Tori gaped down at her revealing attire. Squeezing her eyes tightly, she prayed she was still dreaming.

"I see you got my gift. It was good of you to drop by

to say thank you," he replied dryly.

This wasn't happening. But, when she dared to reopen her eyes, he was still there. And so was she, wearing nothing but a sheer nightgown.

"There was a—a noise." She was muttering but couldn't seem to form a coherent thought. "The verandah ... you see, I was ...."

Nicholas smiled outright now. "The party below is rather loud, I agree."

Before Tori could put a plan in place to remove herself from his appreciative gaze, Nicholas extinguished the light and found her in the dark.

"Why are you here, princess?" His question caught her off guard.

"I was frightened. And ... I needed to be with you." She answered him as honestly as she knew how.

Nicholas cupped her face and lowered his lips to hers. His kiss chased away all fear, and timidity for that matter.

Lifting his head, Nicholas asked, "And do you want to stay?" The tenderness shining in his eyes, barely visible in the moonlight, was her undoing.

"Yes."

God's gifts put man's best dreams to shame.
~ Elizabeth Barrett Browning

Twenty-Two

Sunlight streamed into their private haven as Nicholas leaned against the doorframe behind his wife, admiring her in the mirror.

She was a beauty.

Yesterday after their nuptials, he'd heard it said more times than he could count. Watching her now, he was fascinated by her changeable expressions, as unpredictable as the open sea. Charmed, he took in her sparkling blue eyes and that impish dimple on one side of her mouth that was as capricious as she.

"I see marriage hasn't taught you a blessed thing about common courtesy." Tori pulled her hair over one shoulder, taming the curls with her silver-backed brush. "Spying on a person is considered ill-mannered."

"Unless that person is one's wife. According to the Good Book, that makes you fair game."

Nicholas came over to nuzzle her ear.

"Hmm. Just as I thought. You neglected to read the rest of the story." She pursed her lips and gave him a side glance. "You must first love and honor your wife, sir. I'm rather certain a marriage in name only doesn't apply."

"Ah, but ours is no longer a marriage in name only. In the Biblical sense you are now unquestionably mine." He turned her vanity seat to face him. "And I do honor you, Victoria. Never doubt that. I pledged to honor and take care of you the rest of your life. I don't make that kind of vow lightly."

"So, is that all, Nicholas? Did you merely pledge to honor and care for me?" Her voice held a hint of sadness.

He knew what she was asking of him. But the way he felt about Victoria was unchartered waters and he needed some time to weigh it out in his own mind. Even before all they'd shared last night, it would be a lie to deny she'd already stolen his heart. Still his pride wouldn't let him admit it. "I personally believe all things happen for a purpose. We have a lifetime to talk about it. Let's just enjoy today."

She didn't respond, only nodded looking down at the brush in her lap. He saw his words—or lack of words— had disappointed her.

"They're sending up some breakfast. It should be here soon."

For now, he chose to change the subject. He needed time to sort through the emotions she stirred up inside him. Yesterday, he was in full control of his growing attraction to Haverwood's lovely daughter. He told himself he was acting out of a sense of duty, nothing more. It was simply the right thing to do. This morning, however, after holding her close to his heart for most of the night, listening to the even whisper of her breath, he could no longer disregard the truth. "My attorney's office is across from here on the square. I thought we might get out this afternoon and stop over to see if he's made it back from Augusta. Would you like that?"

She perked up immediately. "That would be wonderful."

"Good. I'll check on breakfast. Lock the door behind me. Don't let anyone in."

Closing the door, Tori let out a pent-up breath. Dottie Saberton's words came to her mind. *"Nicholas is a good man. He has much love to give if he would only allow the Lord to rid his heart of the bitterness that has taken root there."*

Deep in thought, she donned a velvet robe of pale green. Opening her travel case, she took up her father's Bible and hugged it to her chest, silently praying for her father and for the man she now called husband.

Drawn by the cool morning breeze, she walked out onto the verandah to sit at the white wrought iron breakfast table. Though the sun was not at its peak, the day was already proving excessively warm. Rain must have showered the courtyard overnight as the flowering bushes and clinging rose vines sparkled with fresh dew.

In truth, a cyclone could have blown through last night and she'd never have known it. Safe in the circle of Nicholas's arms, she had slept like a well-nourished baby. Oddly enough, the memory caused her no embarrassment. As Nicholas had said, she was his. And for now, that was enough.

The sound of a key turning in the door brought Tori out of her musing. She was famished. She'd barely touched her plate of finger food at Aunt Charlotte's reception, and now she wished she had.

Nicholas entered the verandah carrying a delicious-smelling tray. "A special plate of silver dollar flapjacks with boysenberry syrup made especially for the bride, compliments of Chef Roland." Setting the platter on the small table, he poured her a cup of tea. "Along with poached eggs, honey ham, and buttermilk biscuits with some kind of flavored honey." He tasted the end of his thumb. "Pear maybe?"

Before he took his seat, Tori was already cutting into the delectable fare. "When we return to your home, you must send him a note of thanks."

"Our home."

Her hand stilled as she looked over and noticed his serious expression. "Yes, Nicholas. Our home."

They ate with a concert of birds high above flittering from tree to tree. The morning was peaceful and provided a much-needed haven from the whirlwind of the past several days.

With coffee cup in hand, Nicholas rose and moved to the scrolled railing, looking out across the courtyard. Tori watched the breeze ruffle his dark hair. She felt a curious pride in knowing this man had pledged to put her above all others. Placing her napkin upon the table, she sat back in her chair.

"I can see why Felicity fought so hard to have you." She spoke up causing him to side-glance in her direction. "You're fairly tolerable when you aren't scowling so." Tori folded her arms across her chest with a grin. "However, I do believe you frightened the poor woman. It's unlikely we'll see much of her anytime soon."

"I see. So, you're not intimidated?" He straightened from the rail and held out his hand in invitation to join him. "I've been told I can be difficult."

Without hesitation, she went to him and he wrapped his big arms around her.

"Yes, you are that." Tori nodded. "But you are also very giving when you choose to be."

A long silence elapsed between them. Tori was content to stand there on the lovely verandah in her husband's arms. The tension in his embrace told her Nicholas was at war within himself. It would take a while for him to fully trust her feelings for him.

"We really should go inside. What will people think?"

"I don't know. Let's ask them." He called down to a couple of whispering hotel maids staring at them from the gardens. "My little English wife is concerned that my holding her is disturbing you ladies."

"Oh!" Tori twisted past him and scurried back into
the room. "You're incorrigible."

"If you'll hurry, we can stop by the stationer's on the
way to the Attorney's office. You can order monogrammed stationary to send the chef your own note of
thanks."

His suggestion was highly modern and it pleased her
tremendously. "I won't be but a minute."

Looking back to see if he'd heard her, she realized he
hadn't followed her inside. Instead, he remained at the
rail, apparently lost in his own thoughts.

All the world's a stage
and all the men and women merely players.
~ William Shakespeare

Twenty-Three

Three days had passed since he'd taken Victoria Haverwood as his bride. Though the turmoil surrounding their hurried marriage was anything but peaceful, Nicholas was surprisingly content.

Holding her in his arms at night, with her head tucked beneath his chin, he'd listened as she quietly put words to the utter desperation she felt at losing her father. She told of her early years, before she'd gone off to school, when the earl had been her only family. Eventually, the demands of her father's position called him away more than he was home.

The earl's private staff tended to her dress, daily routine, and were on call through the night should she ever have a nightmare. By the time she left for boarding school at seven, she was independent but had never gotten used to being alone.

It was in those quiet moments, Nicholas caught a glimpse into the soul of a lost child.

On their second day, Nicholas had taken her to visit Abner Westphall. Afterward, they'd checked in with the investigator who assured them he was pursuing every lead. Everything possible was being done to see the earl safely returned.

Victoria had his promise, and he'd meant every word.

This evening, he had plans to take her out again, hoping to keep her occupied with less time to dwell on things she had no control over.

"I have a surprise for you, princess." Nicholas took an iron rod from behind the curtains to close the tall Grecian shutters against the bright hues of sunset.

"A surprise?" She glanced up from her book, her curiosity piqued. "I do love surprises."

"You once said you have an affinity for Shakespeare." He watched as light from between the wide slats danced across her hair bringing fire to selective strands. "Especially when you're flustered."

"You have quite a memory." Tori lowered her lashes. He loved the way that dimple peered from her cheek. "I've always had a fascination for the theater, though I've never gone."

"I have two tickets for tonight's double billing at The Savannah Theater across the square." Removing the tickets from his jacket, he watched her expression turn from curiosity to joy. Just the effect he was going for. "I believe one is a Shakespeare."

"Tonight?" Tori rose to have a closer look. "Nicholas, I can't possibly attend the theater with Father still missing."

"You won't do him any good secluding yourself. He wouldn't want you sick with worry." Nicholas began to unbutton his shirt to change into his evening clothes.

"Actually, he'd be highly disappointed if I didn't worry."

"I'd prefer it if you'd come with me. I won't press you, but going alone won't be nearly as entertaining." He had no intention of going alone. Victoria couldn't do any more than she already had to see her father found. She needed a diversion to ease her troubled mind.

"You'd go without me?"

"Only if you leave me no other choice." He took a freshly starched shirt from the wardrobe and pulled it over his shoulders, enjoying the way his wife didn't bother to hide her admiration.

"I imagine that would cause quite the stir if you showed up without me." Crossing her arms, she nibbled her lip.

Nicholas reached around her to retrieve his gold cufflinks from a valet stand against the wall.

Tori intercepted to fasten them herself. "I have wanted to see a play for the longest time. Ever since I can remember, actually." She folded the cuff, and set the link in place. "We could tell the man at the desk downstairs where to find us if word should come."

"We could."

"I don't see why not. Only for one evening." Once she had both cuffs in place, she'd convinced herself to accept his offer.

Finding her reversal adorable, Nicholas took her hand and brought it to his lips. "Besides all that, this gives me a chance to show off my lovely bride." He pulled her close with his other arm around her waist.

Tori tilted her head to accept his kiss, but suddenly drew back. "I haven't anything to wear. Not suitable for the theater, anyway."

Reluctantly, he released her. "When I ordered the tickets, I sent for Jonas to bring one of your gowns over. It came earlier when you were reading out on the verandah." Nicholas brought a box in from the common area and set upon the bed.

Lifting the lid, Tori immediately recognized her favorite gown.

"I told him which one to look for. I particularly like that dress." He tied a silk cravat around his neck. "You wore it aboard *The Tempest*. The night I kissed you under the stars up on deck."

"Almost kissed me." She smoothed the sleeves. "Father had it specially made in London for my last birthday. When he saw the iris-colored silk, he'd said it was the color of Haverwood eyes and insisted the dressmaker make it into a gown for me of the very latest fashion."

"It does match your eyes. That's probably why I'm so fond of it." Nicholas came up behind her and kissed the top of her head. An overwhelming sense of affection for her gripped his heart and the words nearly slipped from his lips. Still, caution held out. "Best go get ready or we'll be late."

Tori could hardly believe she was going to the theater. To see a play by Shakespeare was a lifelong dream. Still, a twinge of guilt at enjoying an evening out without her father nipped at her conscience.

Her only solace was knowing Nicholas had done everything he'd promised to help find and bring her father home. They met with his attorney and a private investigator the first day after their wedding. Both men were immensely helpful and assured her they would have some answers as to the identity of Lucinda Martin before the week was out.

She partially pinned her hair up in back, letting loose curls fall down over her shoulders. The duchess's brooch and the drop earrings she'd worn the day of the wedding matched splendidly. Her shawl of silver lace and elbow-length gloves completed the ensemble.

Half an hour later, they stepped from the lobby of the hotel.

Tori slowed in the bustle of the square. Out of sheer instinct, she scanned every face in the plaza, hoping against hope she might spot her father in the crowd. It was absurd to consider, yet if there was even the slightest possibility, she refused to give up.

Unfortunately, no one even vaguely resembled the earl.

On a heavy breath, she looked up at Nicholas and found him watching her. Slipping her hand to rest inside his arm, she let him know she was ready to cross the road.

The square itself was like none of the others she had seen thus far. Clearly the hub of Savannah's plush night life, it was scattered with twice as many streetlamps along widened paths. Strolling couples, the men resplendent in their top hats and the ladies in their rustling crinolines, strode regally through the square in their evening attire.

All eyes seemed drawn to them as Nicholas escorted her across the park and up the steps of the theater. Her skirts swayed about her gracefully as if she walked on air.

Two elderly matrons clucked excitedly behind their fans as they passed through the entrance of the theater. One would think as observant as these people were, someone would have seen or heard news about her Father by now.

The first play, appropriately called, *The Busybody*, was a comical farce that kept Tori perched on the edge of her seat in their box in the upper right-hand corner.

The second offering was a tearful Shakespearean classic that soon had her sniffling into her lace handkerchief, completely enthralled by the actors below.

After three encores, with roses littering the stage, the house lights finally came up. Tori sat perfectly still, taking in the poignancy of the moment. Her heart was full, almost painfully so.

Double doors opened all around the auditorium as scores of people flooded out below.

Nicholas offered to help her to her feet, and she accepted gratefully. The emotion stirred by actors in a play put Tori in a reflective mood. Her feelings for Nicholas ran deeper now than ever and she was of a mind to tell him so. Whether he was ever able to admit the same, she needed him to know.

"Nicholas, wait." They were the last to leave the darkened box and she stopped him with a tug on his hand. "I have to tell you something and it can't be put off."

"What is it, princess?" His voice was deep and quiet as he smoothed her cheek with the back of his hand.

Tori encouraged herself to be out with it before she lost her nerve.

"I-I … that is …" She stilled his hand, so she could think clearly.

"I must say … What I mean is, I've quite decided to love you."

Her gaze shot up to his. That wasn't at all how she'd intended to say it.

His steady regard made her glad for the low lights.

Finally, he spoke. "Have you now?" His tone was amused but at least he didn't laugh.

"Yes, Nicholas. I'm afraid I've gone and fallen quite hopelessly in love with you."

Tilting her chin, he brought his lips to hers in answer.

Gently at first, before his kiss became more and more demanding.

Time stood still. The feel of her husband's arms around her, lost in the warmth of his affection, made her forget to breathe.

A muted cough behind them shattered the magic of the moment. "Pardon me, sir. The balcony is now closed."

Slowly Nicholas lifted his head. "We'll discuss this more later." With a last kiss to the tip of her nose, he placed her shawl on her shoulders and took her hand.

The usher drew the curtain behind them, closing off access to the upper circle.

They were the last to descend the red-carpeted staircase into the main lobby of the theater. Through tall windows set in front, Tori could see the plaza was lit up as brilliantly as if it were the height of the day. Stately carriages passed along the street with lanterns glowing brightly. She could see the hotel on the other side of the square glittering in grand opulence.

The instant they crossed the threshold they both knew something was terribly wrong.

The acrid smell of smoke assailed Tori's senses. A general disquiet rose among the townspeople quickening their pace as they began to scatter in every direction.

Tightening her hold on Nicholas's arm, she searched his face.

"Come on." Hailing a hack parked under a street-lamp, Nicholas led their way down the brick steps to the

TRUE NOBILITY

chaos of carriages trying to pass on the road.

"Mister Nicholas!" From across the square, Tori spotted Jonas waving from the drivers' seat of the Saberton coach parked in front of the hotel.

Lifting her skirt, Tori followed her husband and dodging horses, they wove their way around the panic to where Jonas worked to steady the pair of grays.

"Your warehouse—" Jonas's voice was suddenly cut off by the sound of clanging that rent the air. A ribbon of fright slipped down Tori's back. Excited shouts broke out from the street leading down to the wharf.

Moving swiftly, Nicholas put an arm around her, guiding her toward the Saberton carriage where he opened the door for Tori to climb inside.

"Cap'n! Come quick!" Four men Tori recognized as men from the ship called from the road with torches glowing in their hands.

"What's the trouble, Amos?"

The men surrounded Nicholas, talking all at once.

"The Exchange House!"

"Gone up in blazes!"

Tori followed Nicholas's narrowed gaze in the direction the men pointed. Over the housetops, bright flames could be seen licking at the darkness.

"Dear heavens." The words escaped her as she fell back onto the leather seat.

"The warehouses are full, Cap'n. If fire gets to them, you'll lose everything." The hulking guard Tori knew as Amos lowered his voice, but Tori could hear just the same. "If you was to lose all that cargo, it would take everything you own to pay back them holders for their lost crops. Everything you've worked for could be destroyed."

"I'll take Victoria home. Ian can stay with her there."

"Mister Ian done went down to the wharf. He sent me to find you and tell you he and Mister Zach are headed to the fire and will do all they can. They said you is to stay with your bride." Jonas piped in from up top.

Though she couldn't see him, Tori knew Nicholas was torn. He'd poured his life into making Haverwood Shipping and Trade what it was today, the largest importer on the Eastern seaboard. She couldn't stand by and watch him lose it all because he felt an obligation to look after her like a bothersome child.

Pushing the door open, she saw him rubbing his forehead.

"You must go." All the men looked up. "I'll be fine, Nicholas. You must go and see to your cargo."

Still he hesitated.

She decided to take matters into her own hands. There was no time to waste. "Jonas can take me home. I'll wait there to hear from you."

Finally, Nicholas began to roll up his sleeves. "Amos, you stay with Victoria. Don't let her out of your sight. Jonas, take her to the Haverwood's and stay there until you hear from me. This could be a long night."

Tori could tell Amos felt he got the short end of the bargain.

It was a sacrifice almost too harsh to ask of a sailor. If anything, Nicholas's crew fought back-to-back for one another at all costs. Asking one to stay behind with the women was a disgrace.

Nonetheless, Amos handed off his torch and sprung up into the seat across from her.

As the carriage lurched forward, Tori watched Nicholas through the small back window until she couldn't see him any more.

"God go with you, my love," she whispered.

Abide with me from morn until eve;
For without thee I cannot live.
Abide with me when night is high;
For without thee I dare not die.
~ John Keble

Twenty-Four

The reflection of firelight flickered from the shimmering Savannah River.

As Nicholas rounded the corner of Factor's Walk, he shielded his face from the oppressive heat of the raging blaze. All along the wharf, flames leapt from blown out windows of storage warehouses. The exchange building was completely engulfed and the adjoining buildings were at imminent risk.

A wide hose spanned the short distance from the river to Bay Street, where a man-powered pump spewed murky water at the ferocious blaze.

Nicholas threw off his vest and moved to the head of the line. "Keep it pumping!" His order was swallowed by the roar of the fire.

Every available man passed buckets, one after another, to douse the flames lapping at the city's main export office. Vigorously, they kept at it for what seemed like hours. If the fire reached the outer warehouses, every plantation owner, peanut farmer, textile merchant and seaman alike stood to lose thousands of dollars in the fall trade. None shouldered more of the burden than Nicholas.

"The north side! It's coming down!"

As predicted, the building crumbled. Though devastating the exchange building itself, it gave better access to battle the blaze from within, possibly sparing the warehouses to the north.

Turning their faces from the intense heat, the men waited for the initial burst of the refueled inferno to subside, before resuming their counterattack.

As time passed, the sea breeze worked to their advantage blowing in from the north, bending back the flames and keeping them from reaching the buildings in that area.

Smoke filled Nicholas's nostrils, burning clear down his throat. Nearly every man in Savannah had come down to the wharf to battle the blaze. A fire like this would prove deadly if allowed to burn farther into the city.

Glowing cinders exploded in a firestorm, sending one man screaming from the flaming building. Those close by slapped at the burning ash as it spewed down onto their clothing.

Nicholas drew in as close as the extreme heat would allow, fortitude spurring him on.

"Cap'n, lookout!"

A fiery beam crashed to the ground pinning the man who'd given the warning beneath its smoldering weight. With a howl, the man's face twisted in agony.

"Go for the doctor," Nicholas commanded in a rasp. The combination of smoke and constant shouting had taken a toll on his voice. His lungs felt close to bursting.

Gritting his teeth, he lifted the heavy beam just high enough for the others to pull the man free. Nicholas then threw the smoking rafter to one side and away from the threat of harming anyone else. He flinched at the searing pain on the inside of his forearm where a nasty burn marred his flesh.

He dropped to his knee and looked into the dazed eyes of the felled man. Beneath the soot and grime, he saw the face of a good friend. Orville Simmons, one of his crewmen who'd been with him since day one.

Simmons trembled with shock.

An onlooker stepped forward to remove his charred shirt, eager to ease the old sailor's suffering.

Nicholas stayed his hand. "Leave it. If you peel away his clothing, his skin is likely to come with it."

The pungent smell of burned flesh hung heavy in the air.

"Simmons, hang on. The doc's coming and you're going to be fine." Even as he said it, Nicholas knew the man wouldn't last until the physician arrived.

"C-cap'n? I can't see nothin'. Everything's ... goin' black." The seafarer gasped, eyes wide. "We're goin' down, Cap'n!"

The man's panic tugged at Nicholas and he was bent on easing his friend's torment. "Simmons, man the prow. It's just a squall. We'll ride it out. There's blue skies up ahead." Nicholas spoke next to the man's ear and the sailor seemed relieved his captain had things under control.

"Aye, Sir." His answer was barely audible.

Swallowing hard, Nicholas watched the old sea dog's eyes relax into an unseeing stare as death laid claim to his soul.

Nicholas was sickened by the death and destruction surrounding him. Though smoke burned his eyes, he'd never seen things as clearly as he did in that moment.

Looking at the lifeless form of his friend, the fire and all its devastation was nothing in comparison to what really mattered—finding his wife and kissing her senseless.

Business could be rebuilt, but life was fragile. Protecting Victoria must be his first and only priority. The need for answers would be sated in time, but for now he was certain of only one thing. He needed her. He needed to hold her in his arms He'd gladly give up everything he owned to see Victoria safe and sound.

"Ian!" Nicholas called to his brother who was taking long strides toward him. "You're in charge here. I'm going home to my wife."

The smile on Ian's face told him he couldn't agree more. Nicholas slapped him on the back before turning to leave.

∾

Her room was dark and quiet.

Convincing Amos to give her a minute alone to change had been an ordeal. He took Nicholas's directive seriously until Tori wanted to lock herself in her room just to keep him from staring at her. Promising not to take more than five minutes, she'd left him at the foot of the stairs to wait for her.

Tori felt her way over to a lamp next to the bed. Once lit, she lifted the soft yellow flame to chase shadows from every corner.

Opening the French windows, she heard shouting over a billowing roar in the distance. An acrid smell of smoke invaded the room and she pulled the windows together once more.

Closing her eyes, she said a prayer for Nicholas and all he stood to lose.

A black-gloved hand roughly clamped over her mouth. "One more peep, and I'll remove your stinkin' tongue. With this."

A wicked looking dagger came up into Tori's view, and the breath completely left her. Shutting her eyes, she willed herself to be brave. Panic would ultimately be to her disadvantage.

Her silent prayer turned into a plea for help, begging

for a chance to throw this wretch off guard to make an escape. Yet, looking into her distorted reflection in the gleaming blade, the prayer froze on her lips.

"I've waited a long, long time for this." The odorous thug drew out the last "long" and it sent a surge of terror through to Tori's bones.

Opening her mouth to scream for Amos, the glove once again stifled her cry. "Hush, you dang fool," came a raspy whisper. "You keep your mouth shut or I swear I'll have your captain run clear through. An' you won't be able to do nuthin' but stand and watch."

Tori yanked the dirty hand from her mouth, "No!" She scrambled out of the way, and darted for the door.

The blade whizzed past her head, to suspend quivering in the wooden frame.

Stopping short, a scream caught in her throat.

"No use tryin' to get away. I'll stick your gizzard to the wall." The assailant came from behind her to reclaim the weapon. "I always hit what I aim for. Dead on." He gave Tori's hair a painful yank in passing. "Next time it won't be the door I'm aimin' for."

"What is it you want from me? Money? I have…"

"You ain't got nuthin'." The attacker spoke in an odd whisper, this time close enough that she was able have a better look at him.

Struck by the frailty of the man, Tori looked down at the moth-eaten overcoat covering his meager frame. A thin woolen cap was pulled down over his ears and with a threadbare scarf covered half his face.

Like the thug who had attacked her aboard ship.

Surely it was money he was after. What else would cause a person to take such drastic measures?

"Who are you? What do you want from me?" Tori inched toward the door once again, but he was ahead of her this time.

"Nothin' but what's rightfully mine." He stopped her with a hard shove back.

Catching the smelly man by surprise Tori lifted her foot to sweep his feet out from under him, sending him sprawling. She made a dash for the door, determined to outwit this mad man. Instead the rug was swiftly jerked out from under her feet and she joined her assailant on the floor.

After a brief struggle, Tori snatched at the cap covering the man's head. She froze in mid-wrangle. Before the other could react to stop her, Tori pulled the scarf away as well.

Both were astonished as they stared at one another in an icy blue daze. The aggressor finally regained control and held the knife up under Tori's chin.

Blinking, Tori tried to make sense of what she'd just seen. Apparently, her ferocious attacker, bent on murdering her before the night was over, was nothing more than a female in disguise. And judging from the way she intermittently coughed now and again, she was a sickly female at that.

"What are you starin' at?"

"Who are you?" The fact that her eyes were so like

her own, hadn't escaped Tori's notice.

"Get up. That oaf is gonna be up here any minute." She stood, yanking at Tori's arm.

"I'm not going anywhere." Tori jerked her arm away.

The girl moved the tip of the knife down Tori's neck to rest against her breastbone, inches from her heart, increasing the pressure until it punctured tender skin. "I've wanted you dead for a long time. But now they say it don't matter whether you're dead or alive. So you're coming with me. I want every penny that's mine and you're gonna get it for me."

Frantic, Tori's mind raced to find a way out of this predicament. "Do you have my father?" Standing as best she could without getting herself skewered, she tried to keep the girl involved in conversation long enough to keep herself alive.

"Move." The girl pulled Tori outside the long window onto the terrace, coughing as soon as they entered the smoke-filled air. "You'll just have to see for yourself."

"Mrs. Victoria?" Amos's voice sounded from the hall. "Is you all right?"

Relief flooded her tattered nerves. Help was so near, just on the other side of the door. So close she had to bite her lip to keep from calling out. Her mind screamed to take the chance that she might get to the door before that knife found her back.

"Don't be stupid. Come now or you ain't never gonna see that papa of yours again. Your choice." The girl's cold whisper left no room for misinterpretation.

"You know where Father is?"

"You wanna see him? Shut up and come on." She jerked her head toward the open windows.

Following her made no sense. Except this person claimed to know where her father was. If Tori let her disappear, the only clue to his whereabouts would disappear as well.

"Mrs. Victoria, I'm comin' in!"

"You'd best think fast, because if that goon comes in here it'll be just in time to meet his Maker." The blade was poised and ready to be flung at the door should Amos walk in. There was no doubt in Tori's mind that this girl had every intention of murdering him should she make the wrong choice.

Tori watched the handle of her door turn.

"No, Amos, please. I'm not dressed." Tori swallowed hard to steady her voice. "No need for alarm, I just knocked over the washbasin. I'll be right down."

The silence was thick with tension as she watched the handle slowly return to its normal position. "I ain't goin' nowhere. I'm waitin' right here."

The girl motioned with the dreaded knife for Tori to hurry.

Tori's heart sank as she weighed her options. More than likely, Nicholas would think she'd left him of her own volition. To think what that might do to him shattered her into a million pieces.

Yet, if there was the slightest chance this person could take her to her father, she had to follow.

Praying she would eventually have a chance to explain, she allowed herself to be prodded down the stairs of the terrace and shoved into the night.

My sorrow; I could not awaken.
My heart to joy at the same tone;
And all I loved, I loved alone.
~Edgar Allan Poe

Twenty-Five

Savannah lay in mournful silence beneath a stubborn haze of smoke. Distorted shadows drifted across the amber-colored moon, bathing the streets in a pallid blush.

Nicholas didn't stop to freshen his filthy garments. Instead, he strode past his Broad Street residence, traveling eight more blocks to the Haverwood drive.

Though a deep fatigue had come over him after hours of fighting the indomitable blaze, he refused to rest until his wife was in his arms He wanted nothing more than to bury his face in the sweet curve of her neck and take in the intoxicating lilac scent of her hair.

He wasn't proud of the way he'd left things between them.

Victoria's innocent admission had haunted him more

times than he could count this night. She'd deserved a better response. An honest response.

Truth be told, he did love her. Loved her with every breath. As hard as he'd tried to deny it, the more it was undeniable.

Unlike Celine, Victoria was authentic. Time and again, he'd watched her attempt to do best by everyone. Whether disastrous or triumphant, her heart was always sincere. A fact that affected him without fail.

There was something truly remarkable about her. With all her imperfections, he had no choice but to admit the truth. Victoria was indeed perfect for him.

Quickening his pace, he was eager to tell her so.

Rounding the corner, it struck him as odd that the Haverwood home was completely lit. Lamps glowed from the window of every room as if they hadn't been turned down all night. Several homes along the way had shown evidence that their Savannah neighbors were also finding it hard to sleep tonight, waiting for the final outcome of what certainly would be remembered as one of the city's most devastating fires.

Approaching hoofbeats thundered behind him and Nicholas took a step back. A single horse and rider barreled past followed by his own coach careening perilously as it turned the corner of the lane.

Narrowing his eyes against the cloud of dust, he spotted Jonas pull the horses to a skidding halt in front of the Haverwood front steps. The labored pair snorted, tossing their heads against the brutal handling of their reins.

A multitude of reasons for Jonas's haste sprang to mind. None were anything Nicholas wanted to consider.

Dashing toward the entrance, he watched the single rider dismount. The front doors flew open and the portico at the top of the steps broke out in frantic melee.

Mrs. Charlotte's garbled screeching pierced the night as she grabbed the newcomer by the sleeve, fairly yanking him inside. Jonas stood back allowing Aurora a moment more to wail into her hands.

Crackling dread spurred Nicholas on. Victoria was nowhere to be seen.

Visions of her splayed at the foot of the stairs drove him to vault over the picket fence and swing up onto the side porch.

"Mister Nicholas!" Jonas called out as soon as he caught sight of his employer.

Aurora huddled under a knitted wrap. Her shoulders quaked from sobbing. "Nicholas!

Tori ..." Again, she dissolved into incoherent sobbing.

Nicholas charged into the house. Searching only for one cherished face, he bounded the stairs two at a time.

"Amos!" His voice, still raspy from the effects of the wind and smoke, was a source of vexation as he called out for his main deckhand.

"Here, Cap'n" A burly shadow crossed the threshold of Victoria's chamber, but Amos didn't come out into the hall.

"Nicholas, thank heavens you're here!" Mrs. Charlotte hollered from below. "The most frightening thing has happened. Right under our very noses. She promised to only to go up for a second. I heard her myself." Her call got progressively louder as he continued his quest without looking back. "G.W., go catch him. He's not listening to a word."

Entering the bedroom, Nicholas found Amos pacing restlessly. The night table was flipped over on its side atop the rug crumpled in a corner. The bedcovers hung precariously to one side, puddling into a heap on the floor. Gossamer curtains billowed from the windows, opening out onto the terrace.

"Where is Victoria?" His frantic question was sharp, causing Amos to leave his vigil and face his captain.

"She ain't here." The ex-bondsman was bleary-eyed from the burden that had been placed on his shoulders. "She say she was needin' to change. Not five minutes later, I heard a questionable sound and come up to see about it. I called through that door and she say she was fine. I waited right there for her to come on out, but that was the last I heard from her. When I called out again, there were no answer. I push open the door and everything's like this. An' she ain't nowhere to be seen."

"How long ago?

"Nearly two hours by now." Amos shook his head. "I sent the stable boy down to the wharf to fetch you, and Jonas went for the constable right away. Ain't made it back yet. I didn't want to leave the other women alone or I'd of gone searching for her myself."

Nicholas brushed past the big man to scour the terrace. No sign of forced entry. No footprints on the whitewashed planks. Nothing left behind on the brick steps leading down to the unspoiled garden below. Nothing but deafening silence.

Panic threatened to engulf him as he rummaged every inch the grounds, hoping for a torn piece of fabric, an earring, or a shoe left behind in haste.

Why would Victoria send Amos away? If she'd been in trouble, surely someone would have heard her scream. If she'd been hurt, the evidence would be plain enough. Instead, nothing. Vanished without a trace.

Nicholas refused to give credence to petty uncertainties nipping the back of his mind.

Focusing on one thing alone, he grit his teeth, combing his way through a line of shrubbery. Finding Victoria and bringing her home was the only thing he'd even consider at this point. There'd be plenty of time for the whys and hows later. Right now, he needed to find her and hold her close.

And make certain whoever did this never dared to come near her again.

Emerging beyond the manicured bushes, he paused, alone in a vast field of red clover skirting the Savannah River. In the meager light of predawn, he detected no movement apart from an occasional wave of the breeze as it rippled across the grassland.

To the east, the river ran north up to Augusta, easily the fastest route out of the city. To the west, the rails of Central Railroad and roads leading over to Macon and

Atlanta with nothing but farmland in between.

Retracing his steps, Nicholas formed a plan to cover a fifty-mile radius of Savannah with volunteers and hounds, spreading in every direction until no rock was left unturned.

The action worked to sooth his temper. He wasn't used to his orders going awry, especially when it involved the well-being of those close to him. Amos would have plenty to answer for, but not tonight.

As soon as he topped the steps of the terrace, his crewman met him back at the window of Victoria's room. Nicholas could see Amos was nearly beside himself with worry. For now, he needed him to keep his wits, to try and remember as much as possible.

"You said you heard a sound?" Nicholas reentered the room inspecting every wall from floor to ceiling, hoping to come across something he might have missed.

"Yessir, a thud. Like somethin' done hit the floor. Mrs. Victoria say the washbasin fell but you can see it ain't moved." The hulking man had moisture on his face. Whether from tears or sweat, Nicholas couldn't say.

Stooping down, he examined something protruding from the furrowed rug. Last evening's playbill lay tucked within its folds. Nicholas lifted the flier as an image of Victoria filled his senses. This same paper had been in her gloved hand as she'd sat still as a mouse taking in every word of the play. Her hair gleaming in the reflection of the stage lights and her keen eyes wide with wonder.

"Cap'n, I ain't seen this before."

Standing, he turned to where Amos stood by the door. "Looks like this wood had a run-in with a knife."

Quick to investigate, Nicholas ran a finger over a clean slash marring the carved casing. "Looks like the tip barely stuck. Either they were a poor aim or it was thrown from across the room."

"I remember when they tried to hurt Mrs. Victoria on the ship, Cap'n. That man had a knife, too."

His blood run cold at the thought that the same murderous villain they'd dealt with onboard somehow followed Victoria all the way to the mainland.

Voices rose from the stairs.

"G.W., how could this have happened right here in Savannah? It's so a body's not safe anywhere." Charlotte Haverwood came through the doorway in a tizzy while Constable McAllister sauntered into the room like he was attending a Sunday social.

"Oh, I wouldn't worry too much about it, Mrs. Charlotte. Savannah's just as safe as it ever was. You've got my word on that." He eyed Amos before walking over to where Nicholas stood. "Problem is those bluestockings have made it a habit of disappearing." The Constable's crude guffaw caught in his throat when Nicholas seized the neck of the man's shirt.

"My wife is missing, McAllister. I want every available man out looking for her before noon. Is that clear?" It took every ounce of effort Nicholas had not to accentuate his point with a well-placed fist. His patience had run its course.

"Now see here, Saberton. Mind how you handle the law." McAllister's beefy jowls flapped when Nicholas released him, pushing the heavy man aside.

"Nicholas, you're beside yourself." Mrs. Charlotte chided.

Further irritated that the constable continued his lack of urgency, Nicholas turned on him again. "You're wasting time, McAllister. If I have to go wake up the mayor, myself, I'll do it. One way or another there will be a search party formed and activated to bring my wife home!"

"No need to trouble the mayor, now." McAllister finally seemed to get the point as he ambled toward the door. "If she's out there, we'll come across her."

Nicholas threw a scowl at the inept officer. G.W. McAllister was nothing more than the mayor's brother-in-law who took a salary for doing as little as possible.

Charlotte Haverwood left the room as well, clucking along behind him.

"I know you's disappointed in me, Cap'n. But I swear I woulda never let her out of my sight unless she insisted on it. Even then it was only for a few minutes." Amos was back to pacing.

"Never mind who's to blame." Shards of guilt at having ever left her spurred him on. The warehouses should never come before Victoria. "Go find Zach. Have him make sure no ships have left the bay. Tell Ian to take a schooner up the river. Check with every ferry to see if anyone has seen her."

"What you gonna do, Cap'n?"

"I'm going to find my wife." A muscle worked his jaw. "If I have to tear up Georgia to do it!"

~

The first rays of dawn splayed across the grayed horizon to reveal the smoldering remains of the once-impressive Exchange House. Charred, with its walls fallen in and its roof completely missing, the remnants of the structure groaned and popped with lingering distress.

Several men stood staring at the looming sight, shaking their heads at the terrible loss. Three men had died as a result of last night's fire, but the majority of the warehouses had been spared.

A gnarled lamp post in front of the building was a ghostly reminder of the devastating heat that had radiated from Savannah's worst blaze to date.

Watching from the parked carriage, Felicity Jenkins Duff spied Zach Saberton over on the north end of the waterfront. Nicholas would surely feel the sting of this loss for a good long time. It would serve him well to learn that no one double-crossed her without paying dearly.

She sat back into her velvet seat and smiled with contentment.

For two years she'd tried to catch Nicholas Saberton's interest. Still might have if Victoria Haverwood hadn't ruined her plans.

Now she'd fixed them both. She had destroyed the only thing Nicholas ever loved in his life. His precious shipping company.

Curling her lip, she tapped at the roof of her carriage with her parasol and sat back in smug satisfaction as it lurched forward.

*Not until we are lost do we begin to
understand ourselves.
~ Henry David Thoreau*

Twenty-Six

They had trudged for what seemed like miles through high grass and thorny underbrush, stopping every so often to let the other girl catch her breath. Tori had no earthly idea where they were going, although, the nudging of the blade to her back was an ever-present reminder of the hatred fueling this escapade. The knife had ripped through the back of her gown in numerous places, and Tori felt the sting of each slash.

Finally, when they came to a clearing of sorts, Tori collapsed onto the grass holding her side. Expecting the girl to insist that she get up immediately to continue their escape, Tori instead found the girl on her hands, and knees coughing violently.

On her feet in an instant, Tori had almost decided to break free. The farther from Savannah they'd traveled, the more convinced she was that the authorities were better prepared to track down her father. She had yet to see evidence that this person had any real knowledge of his whereabouts.

Just as she lifted her skirts to run, the other girl called out to her, stopping her cold in her tracks. "Don't ya even recognize your own … flesh an' … blood." The coughing wracked the girl's thin body.

Tori wanted to flee as fast and furious as her legs could take her. But, for some reason, she needed to know what the girl had meant by that.

Tori wrestled with her conflicting emotions. She longed to be safe again, far away from this wretched creature. Yet, if there was even the slightest possibility that this girl truly did know where her father was being kept, she mustn't hesitate to go to him.

"Are you so bloomin' ignorant you can't see it?" The girl spoke again.

Cold, exhausted, and in no humor for guessing games, Tori turned on her. Straightening her back, she rested her hands at her waist. "I see nothing. You are muttering gibberish."

The girl fell back onto the grass, barely recovering from her last spell. With a shake of her head, she wiped her mouth with her coat sleeve. "You think you're so high-falutin. You ain't nothin', you hear?"

Tori shook with frustration. Taking a step closer to the girl lying on the ground, she kicked the knife well out of the other's reach. "I demand you tell me what you

know of my father." Her tone took on an almost hysterical edge.

"That he ain't just your father." The girl spat at Tori's
feet.

Absurd. Of course he was just her father. Her mother
had died before any more children could be born.

Inching closer, she blinked against the shadows on the
girl's face to search for a clue to the bizarre accusation.
Tori's eyes widened at what she saw. Returning her deep
blue gaze with burning contempt, the other girl's voice
lowered with a touch of malice. "An' you ain't the only
one with his stinkin' blue eyes neither."

Those eyes. They were ... her father's eyes. But, that
wasn't possible. She'd never seen this girl before tonight.
Yet there was something vaguely familiar about her
mangy dress, and that voice.

Tori whirled around and grabbed up the dagger, holding it with a dainty finger poised on the top of the blade
as if she were about to cut a delicate filet. "It was you!
You attacked me aboard Zachery's ship."

The girl tried to laugh but had to pause for another
round of hacking until she gagged.

Tori poked the knife in her direction every now and
again as she scoured the clearing for some sign—any
sign—of life. Was her father here? Was this girl acting
alone? For all Tori knew, a passel of thugs were lying in
wait beyond the trees.

A small trickle of blood appeared at the corner of the
girl's mouth. Tori immediately dropped the dagger as if

she had caused it. "You're ill."

"There's ... an ol' ... storehouse ..." The girl was unable to finish before she lapsed into an unnatural sleep.

Hoping to find her father at last, Tori followed the direction the girl had pointed. She walked until she saw a filthy looking building on the other side of some bushes. Surely this wasn't the place the girl had referred to. It had been condemned six years ago, according to the posting on the door, and she could only imagine the squalor inside.

Drizzle fell and thunder sounded in the distance. They didn't have long to find shelter. Like it or not, this seemed to be the only place they could stay dry while she thought about what to do next.

Returning, Tori tried to rouse the girl, but she didn't move. Taking the ruffian by the back of the collar, Tori dragged her as far as she could before stumbling over a rock. Painstakingly, she got up and continued the effort, only to once again fall victim to a gopher hole.

By the time she'd towed the girl to the edge of the meadow, her arms were numb, and her legs cried for mercy.

"How have I gotten to the place where I am now rescuing you?" Tori muttered to herself. This same moth-eaten delinquent she was hauling through the brush had tried to murder her. And on more than one occasion. If she had half a mind at all, she'd leave her there and run as far away as she could.

It was becoming apparent the girl was no longer a

serious threat and her condition seemed to be worsening by the minute. Everything in Tori cried *run*. But she'd proposed too many unanswered questions. Besides, she couldn't just leave her here to die.

"Stop." Tori commanded herself. Her imagination was getting the best of her. "No one is going to die."

Pushing against the run-down door with her foot, she jumped back when it fell completely off its rusted hinges, and crashed noisily into the crumbling warehouse. A cloud of dust flew up from under it as the sound echoed throughout the empty building.

Completely dark inside, yet Tori heard strange stirrings and rustlings, signaling they were not alone. Fast losing her resolve, she made a wide circle around the foreboding portal, only to trip over the girl she'd left lying in the pathway.

Coming to, the girl directed a crude blasphemy at Tori's infringing backside now resting on her midsection.

Tori tried to pull the girl to her feet by the shoulder of her tattered overcoat. The thin material ripped at the seam, and the girl was hurled over by the force of it, leaving her face down in the dirt.

"Oh, dear," Tori mumbled to herself, tugging at the girl's other arm. "That couldn't be at all good for your cough."

The other one pulled away from Tori's grasp as if she were lethal. "Leave me be." She followed her weak demand with a curse.

Tori crossed her arms in front of her. Given the pains

she'd taken just to get her here, she was fed up with being the target of that hateful glare. "Surely you don't suggest we stay here for the night. Perhaps we should continue on until we come across a village with an inn."

Tori winced at the young woman's odd-sounding bark of laughter, which caused another spasm of coughing. "They don't let my kind in no inn. An' who's gonna pay for it? You?"

Tori wondered at just what kind she was, until the girl shoved her forward. Tripping, she fell onto the floor of the filthy warehouse. Slow to get back up, her body felt like a mass of bruises.

The girl went over to a bale of cotton that reeked of mildew and collapsed on top. Tori stood rooted to where she was, half out of defiance, half out of sheer terror at what might spring out at her from the darkness.

Just as she determined she'd rather sleep in the grass outside and risk getting sopping wet from the coming rain, something scampered across her foot, and she dashed to the nearest crate.

Tori's heart thudded in her ears so that she could barely hear what the hateful girl was saying. She tried to answer, but she'd been so frightened nothing came out when she opened her mouth to speak. With no exception, this was the coldest, hungriest, and most afraid she had ever been in her entire life.

For the remainder of the night, Tori pressed the girl for information at every opportunity.

After constant pestering, Tori eventually learned that

the girl, and the thug who attacked her aboard *The Tempest* were indeed one in the same. The young woman revealed that after slicing into her accomplice so he wouldn't talk, she'd then stowed away in the dank bowels of the ship for the entire trip.

Tori's guess was this was how she'd become so ill.

Although the girl's motive for wanting her dead still wasn't clear. She really didn't seem to know what she wanted. Tori knew this person hated her with a vengeance, that point she'd made perfectly clear. Yet, she'd had ample opportunity to carry out her threat but still had not finalized the deed.

With the dawn came more uncertainty.

Tori sat with her knees pulled up to her chest on a bale of hay in the corner of the dilapidated warehouse. A long stick in her hand hardly provided adequate protection from the various vermin that wriggled around her.

Filthy and hungry, she cast a wary eye out of the dirt-streaked window, cracked and weather-worn from years of neglect. Water stagnated in pungent puddles along the mortared walls. The heat inside was sweltering.

They were somewhere near the river, she'd heard the steamships bellow in passing, but this strip of the waterfront had been deserted ages ago. There wasn't a soul in sight.

Tori became leery of the girl's claim to know of her father's whereabouts.

Shaking out her skirts for the hundredth time before tucking them back under her knees.

She still tried to justify her decision to go along with this bedraggled young woman.

"Take off your dress." The captor's voice was raspy from her cough.

"I beg your pardon?" Tori was sure she hadn't heard correctly.

"Take it off. Use this 'til I get back." The girl tossed the pungent old coat at Tori. "That'll keep you from followin' me. You won't chance bein' seen out in your frilly drawers."

"Wherever it is you're going, you can take me with you."

"So you can go screamin' and get me jailed?" The girl shook her head. "Not likely. Course, if you don't want to cooperate, I'll kill you now, and take the stinkin' dress. Either way, it's comin' off of ya."

"Where are you going? And why do you need to go there in my dress?"

"Like I said. They said my contract ain't no good, so I'm goin' to the bank to get my money."

"Why do you feel you must change into my gown to go?"

The girl gave her a hateful sneer. "You think they're gonna give it to me?" She shook her head with a hateful sneer. "They won't give me nothin' but grief. But if they think I'm you then all I gotta do is sign your name and take my money."

Tori nearly laughed. "You think they'll just hand it over because you're wearing my clothing?"

"You'd best hope so."

Argument was futile. Tori needed another way to get around the girl's impossible disposition. At the very least she could follow her. And once she was led to where her father was being kept, she would go for help and never look back.

Reaching for the fastenings on the back of the once iris-colored gown, Tori couldn't quite reach the top ones. "Would you mind?" She motioned to the back of the dress, and from the girl's bewildered expression, Tori gathered that she had never owned such a garment. "Just unhook the little fasteners. See? Like this." She demonstrated with one of the lower ones near her waist.

The girl fumbled against the slashes on her back, and Tori drew a sharp breath. Holding her matted hair to the side, she felt wetness from the girl's cough spray against her neck, sending revulsion down her spine. Finally the garment came free. Tori slipped it off, careful to hold it up from the ground.

"I'd appreciate it if you would steal us a chicken or something on your way back. I'm famished." It was a crude suggestion, but Tori's stomach ached beyond endurance.

Her captor sent her a scalding glare.

"I see." Tori was tired, miserable, and becoming increasingly irritable. "So murder is perfectly acceptable to you, but thievery to keep us alive is where you draw the line? Well, fine. Point me in the direction of the nearest farm, and I shall wring the fowl's neck myself."

The girl gave an ugly laugh. "You ain't never stole nothin' in your life."

"I've never been this hungry before."

Tori wasn't ashamed that she'd been well taken care of while growing up. But, these conditions were as foreign to her as night was from day. That she was willing to steal just to make her stomach stop growling, was a humbling testament of her faith. Claiming unequivocal trust in the Lord she realized, was much easier with a full belly and a warm bed.

This girl was obviously unacquainted with such comforts. Something in her cold frown also told her that she somehow held Tori responsible.

"Why do you hate me so?" She'd asked it dozens of times and didn't know why she even bothered to try again. Knowing full well she was treading on treacherous ground, she hoped to take advantage of the girl's distraction as she tried to put on the heavy gown. If she could catch her off guard, perhaps she would answer without thinking.

Ignoring her as if Tori had never even spoken, the girl continued to fumble with the closures.

Ultimately, she tired of watching the girl and put out a hand to help. "Turn around. I'll do it for you."

The other girl immediately pulled away.

Tori's nerves were raw, and her patience had run thin. "In case you haven't noticed, I am at somewhat of a disadvantage. You need my help, and since I have no place to go at the moment, you have nothing whatsoever to lose in accepting my assistance."

"Don't you ever shut up?" The girl presented her back to Tori with a cough. "Do whatever you gotta do to this thing. Just do it with your mouth shut."

Tori felt compelled to point out the obvious. "You hardly look like me. The dress hangs on you."

"That does it. Ain't no amount of money worth all this." The girl whirled around first to the right, and then to the left. Tori assumed she was looking for the knife.

Tori caught sight of the weapon and nudged it toward the bale of hay with her foot.

"All right, then. I won't say another word." Tori nibbled her lip, and tried to act unconcerned, but her hands were trembling—whether from fear or hunger, she wasn't sure. "On the condition you take me to my father as soon as you return."

"I told you I would." Again, Tori's very presence seemed to irritate her. "But if I come back and you're gone, he's dead. Got it?"

Once finished with the fastenings, Tori cast a critical eye over the loose-fitting bodice, much to the girl's displeasure. She was painfully thin. "What did you say your name was?" Oh dear. She'd forgotten she wasn't supposed to speak.

"I warned you." She came to stand face to face with Tori, though she was no longer a threat. Without that knife and in her sickly condition, she was really more pathetic than frightening.

Standing so close, Tori could see the furious gold

flecks in her eyes—just like her father's.

Something about the exchange upset the other girl as well. She backed away with a jolt that knocked her off balance, nearly toppling over a crate.

Both were stunned for a good minute. Turning, she started to leave. But before she did, she reached out and ripped the silver cross from around Tori's neck, leaving a painful streak in its place.

Caught completely off guard, Tori shrieked as the girl also tore her beloved brooch from the bodice of the gown. "No! You can't take that." She grabbed the girl by the arm. "Please, it's not worth anything—except to my family."

"We'll see about that." The girl jerked out of her grasp and continued to the door.

"I'll pay you for it myself." Tori called after her in desperation. "Please. You must give it back."

"You just remember what I said. You best be here when I get back."

"At least tell me your name."

"Josie," the girl said before she stepped out into the blinding sunlight.

"Josie," Tori whispered.

Faint memories of her grandmother Haverwood nagged at the back of her mind. The Countess Josephine.

When my heart is overwhelmed lead me to the
rock that is higher than I.
~ Psalm 61:2

Twenty-Seven

*R*iding hard in the high sun pushed both rider and horse to the point of exhaustion. Nicholas returned to the townhouse to give the young gelding a much-needed break.

Before daybreak, he'd taken the road that led up to Millen's Junction. The Central Railroad train was due to leave out at quarter to nine. By far the fastest transport out of the city, the steam engine could reach Atlanta by evening.

Once at the depot, the porter allowed Nicholas a quick search of every car before the last call for boarding. He'd taken a good look at each traveler, hoping to find one with indigo blue eyes.

The trip had produced nothing.

Nicholas left the horse in care of the stable hands before he strode back to the main house, anxious to see if any news had come from the constable or either of his brothers.

Ian stood over several maps laid out across the dining room table.

Nicholas pulled off his riding gloves and flung them onto a chair.

"You need to get that tended to." Ian nodded at the charred marks staining Nicholas's white shirt and the raw place on the inside of his arm where the material was completely burned away. The smell of smoke still clung to him.

"Plenty of time for that after we find Victoria." Nicholas stepped further inside. "I take it you had no success in talking with the ferry operators?"

"No one's seen her." Ian resumed his study. "One tried to make a small profit in exchange for information. In the end he knew nothing – and got nothing for it."

Zach came in through the swinging door leading to the kitchen, a drumstick in his hand. "You're back. Anything at Millen's Junction?"

"No." Nicholas drove his hand through his hair. "What about the port?"

"No passenger ships went out this morning. Only a couple of barges loaded with lumber and a small sailboat headed up to Charleston." Zach took a bite of his chicken and looked over Ian's shoulder. "I just got back. G.W. took ten men or so back over to Argyle Island. Seems like he's backtracking to me."

"Maybe he can trace the hack that came for the earl." Ian murmured with a thumb over his mouth, concentrating on the maps.

Nicholas stretched his shoulders, rolling his neck. "Zach, have the cook fill a canteen for me. I'm going back out to the stable. My horse should be saddled by now."

"Where are you going?" Ian's attention turned to his oldest brother.

"To search for my wife." Nicholas's impatience was evident. "You two should get back out as well."

"Where do you suppose we look?" Ian crossed his arms.

"Anywhere you haven't already been!" Nicholas frowned.

Ian returned the glare. "How long do you plan to continue this haphazard search?"

Nicholas rubbed a hand across the stubble on his jaw, summoning every ounce of self-control he could muster.

Minister or not, Ian was about to get himself taken down a peg. His insolent tongue had gotten him pounded more than once as a kid.

"Look, just tell us where you want us to go." Zach stepped in with both arms out to stave off any more argument. "We want Tori home. All of us."

"My point is, you need a plan. You can't just go kicking down doors, hoping she's behind one." Ian settled one of the maps on top of the others. "If Tori and her abductor made it this far north, it was most likely by way of the river. The *Thorne* was the only passenger packet to come upriver since she disappeared, and I spoke with the captain last night. There were no ladies aboard."

Ignoring his brother's frown, Ian continued. "I've questioned nearly every resident along the main road from here to Argyle Isle and the answer was the same. No one's seen them. Zach covered the port. You've been down every road going out of town. And McAllister is searching the isles." Ian traced every place he mentioned with a finger.

The furrow deepened in Nicholas's brow. Reluctantly, he admitted the wisdom of his brother's reasoning. "That's not much to go on. Unless she's being held somewhere in the city. We need to search the surrounding farms and plantations."

"I doubt she's still in the city. Think about it." Ian narrowed an eye. "If you didn't want her to be recognized, you'd tuck her away somewhere remote. Somewhere most people wouldn't go."

Nicholas stared down at the map. The only unpopulated areas were a couple of abandoned industrial areas on the canals west of the river, an old cotton mill up near Anderson, a stretch of land going toward Montgomery, and the swamps. "Surely she wouldn't be taken to the swamplands. It's virtually impassable."

Zach pointed to a spot on the map. "Don't forget Somersville built all new quarters last year. The outbuildings are still in disrepair. No one ever goes out there any more."

"Mister Nicholas, you got company waitin' in the library." Jonas announced from the hall.

A surge of irritation pressed Nicholas as he tore his attention away from the map. "Who is it, Jonas?"

"Inspector Howard, sir."

Nicholas navigated the short hall to find the investigator already seated, facing the Chippendale desk. "Howard? Have you new information?"

If the inspector was surprised by his unkempt attire he didn't let on.

"I do indeed. "The inspector paused and Nicholas introduced him to his brothers.

"I hear your wife has been reported missing." His patronizing tone sounded more like an accusation.

Nicholas sat in a leather banker's chair on the other side of his desk. "She was taken from her aunt's home last night while I was down at the wharf fighting the blaze."

"Have you any proof she didn't leave of her own accord?"

"One of Zach's men is a witness." Ian came to sit on the edge of the desk facing the inspector, taking up the conversation.

Nicholas was of a mind to toss the detective out on his ear.

Ian frowned as the investigator handed him a detailed report from the bank clerk.

"A woman who called herself Victoria Haverwood was last seen at the bank at half past noon. She tried to withdraw money from the earl's account and also from yours, Mr. Saberton. The clerk refused her request."

Ian stood and passed the report to Nicholas.

A muscle in Nicholas's jaw worked as he read what the clerk had written. "Did anyone check the signature?" No one could mimic Victoria's flagrant V.

The inspector produced a withdrawal form signed in chicken scratch.

"This is not my wife's handwriting." Nicholas tossed the slip of paper back across the desk. A numbing tiredness threatened to overtake him.

"So it wasn't her." Ian also tossed the report onto the desk. "Nothing you've presented is solid as far as I'm concerned."

The investigator was wearing on Nicholas's nerves. It was nearly four and he was anxious to be out searching rather than listening to the man make accusations that didn't hold water.

"Ask your brother here. He saw her as well." The investigator nodded to where Zach listened quietly from the other side of the library.

Nicholas raised a questioning brow at his younger brother.

"It was from a distance. I was all the way over on Bull Street. She burst out of the bank and started to run."

"So?" Ian prodded. "Was it, Tori?"

"I don't think so." Zach shook his head. "It didn't really look like her, but she was wearing that dress she wore on the ship. The blue one."

Ian blew out a heavy breath.

Nicholas laid his head back on his chair, staring at the ceiling. That was the dress she'd worn to the theater last night.

"As you know, I met Mrs. Saberton the day you brought her to my office. I also saw the young woman at the bank up close. They were indeed one and the same."

Nicholas thought the investigator seemed a little too pleased with himself. He had nothing but his own testimony that the woman trying to withdraw money from the bank was Victoria.

The bank was used to dishonest people trying to withdraw funds that didn't belong to them. It probably happened on a weekly basis. The clerk had been trained for that sort of thing and he had flatly refused her the money. He would never have risked embarrassing her unless he had no doubts she was a fraud.

The real question was, who was she? And if she had Victoria's dress on, where was Victoria? The possibilities caused his blood to run cold.

"Well, I believe you're mistaken." Ian lifted an apple from the side table. "You'd do better to figure out who the woman really is and whether or not she has anything to do with Tori's disappearance. Then you might have a real lead."

"Did it occur to you to follow her?" Nicholas directed a pointed look at the inspector. "Whether she was my wife or someone impersonating her, she should have been captured and interrogated."

Ian took another hard bite of his apple.

Zach leapt to his feet, crossing the room to stand beside the desk. "I did follow her. I even called out to her and tried to cut her off at the corner of Broad Street. One second she was there. Then the big ice wagon passed, and she was gone. I asked around and no one had seen her."

Nicholas knew they were all bone tired and out of sorts. "We'll find her, Zach. Whoever she is. And when we do she can straighten out Mr. Howard, here, about who he saw at the bank today."

"She looked terrible, Nicholas." Zach softened his voice. "The person I saw was dirty and gaunt. Her hair was all cut off. And even though I was some distance away, she looked right past me as if she'd never seen me before. It couldn't have been Tori."

"Then how would you explain these …?" Inspector Howard asked in a smug tone.

Zach cringed as Nicholas lifted Tori's cross from the man's hand, followed by the diamond and sapphire brooch that he'd given her before their wedding.

"When I followed her into the bank, I overheard her asking the clerk if he knew anyone who might be interested in buying the pieces. I asked to see them and took them from her. She became nervous and fled the building before she could be apprehended."

Nicholas's mind raced. If he'd had an inkling of doubt before, he had none now. Victoria would never willingly part with her cross, nor his grandmother's brooch. They were her most cherished possessions.

"Tori isn't capable of all you accuse her of." Now Ian

was riled. It took plenty to get his middle brother's dander up. "Mr. Howard, for past four years I've attended the most prestigious seminary in the country. I believe I can discern good from evil."

"With all due respect, Reverend, you can't argue with the proof—"

Nicholas's fist came down on the desk causing the investigator to jump. "The only proof here is that whoever had these, has Victoria." He stood and braced his hands on the desk, leaning over the stricken investigator. "Failing to apprehend this person may have cost my wife her life. Your incompetence is inexcusable, Howard. I'd suggest you use every resource you have in your arsenal to locate that woman and get her back here before she harms one hair on my wife's head."

Nicholas stormed out of the room, more intent than ever to find Victoria and bring her home.

∼

Tori's eyes shot open.

It took a minute to realize she'd dozed off. Curls around her face were wet with perspiration in the stifling heat. When she tried to sit up, pain seared her wrists against twine wrapped tightly around them.

Still groggy, she couldn't remember being tied up. She must have slept harder than usual.

"Shoulda known better." Josie was back with her dagger in hand.

"What happened?" Tori kicked when she tried to grab

her legs. Her pantalets didn't provide much protection. "Did you see Nicholas?"

"Why would I wanna see him?" Josie tried again to catch Tori's kicking ankles but was too weak to put forth much effort.

"W-was it the money?" Tori decided, the bank must have denied access to her accounts. "I can get it. Let me go, and—"

Josie wasn't listening. Half slumped across a bale of cotton, her cheeks were red and she was coughing too hard to speak.

Ignoring the sting at her wrists, Tori pushed upright to lean on an elbow. There had been no reason to truss her up like a Christmas goose. If she'd wanted to escape she would have gone while the girl was in town. Surely Josie could see she was being as cooperative as she knew how. Unless they left now for wherever her father was being held, Tori feared Josie wouldn't make it. The excursion to the bank had taken a marked toll on her failing health.

"Josie, your cough sounds worse." Tori tried to keep the distress from her voice. "Loosen me so I can care for you."

Josie wiped her mouth with the back of her hand. Tori noticed it was shaking. "I don't need nothin' from you. Just what's owed me."

"Then I can help find whoever owes you." Her hands were losing feeling as she tried once more to free them from the course twine.

"I gave it a chance." A diabolical edge to Josie's voice

caused Tori to stay quiet.

I shoulda known you'd be just like him. Shoulda kilt you when I had a chance whether it got me my money or not."

"Take me to my father." The sun was lowering. They'd need to leave soon to avoid spending another torturous night in this hovel. "He and my husband will see you are generously rewarded for helping free him. Between the two, you'd be well taken care of."

"Ain't takin' another minute of your lying English tongue."

Opening her mouth to speak, Tori was suddenly gagged by a filthy scarf. It chafed her face as Josie tied it around the back of her head.

Josie convulsed in another round of coughing.

A sinking feeling washed over Tori as it became more and more apparent that Josie had no intention of taking her to her father. Cursing the tears that blurred her vision, she watched as her captor fell silent to the squalid floor.

O what a tangled web we weave, when first we practice to deceive.
~ Sir Walter Scott

Twenty-Eight

"Mr. Westphall's come to see you, sir." Jonas caught Nicholas as he was leaving out the back way.

Pausing under the arched breezeway, Nicholas rubbed at the pounding in his head. Another delay he couldn't afford. Unless, the lawyer had located Victoria there was nothing else he cared to discuss.

"Nicholas." Westphall nodded in greeting when Nicholas reentered the library. "I see it's been a long day, so I'll be brief."

Zach motioned for him to take a chair the investigator had just vacated.

"Got the report we've been waiting for, Nicholas. On the Haverwood document." Abner reached inside his black leather case for the papers he brought.

"Just tell me this…" Nicholas settled into his chair on the other side of the desk from the family's bespectacled attorney. "Will it lead us to Victoria? If not, it will have to wait. We're working against every second and I have no time to waste."

"Possibly. The marriage certificate your wife found proved to be quite interesting. Quite legitimate as well."

Nicholas frowned. "How's that possible?"

Ian and Zach both pulled chairs closer to the desk. Straddling the seats, they also waited for the explanation.

Zach "Go on, Abner."

"Well, now, the earl did indeed marry this Lucinda Martin at the courthouse in Augusta. The registers record the date as … "He adjusted his spectacles to read from his papers. "March the fifth, eighteen, and thirty-four."

Glancing up over the rim of his glasses, he cleared his throat before going on. "He then returned to England, and married Lady Rachelle Beauchet, your wife's mother, two years later."

Zach took on a look of confusion. "How can that be? Are you saying that Lord Haverwood was a bigamist? That he had two wives?"

The lawyer shook his head. "No. The aristocracy make an unusual provision in these rare cases, though it's really not done much in anymore."

"What kind of provision?" Nicholas was too tired for guessing games.

"The first marriage was a morganatic marriage of sorts. Meaning, a male member of a noble house could marry beneath his station provided the wife never assume his title, nor the arms or holdings that go with it. The marriage to Lucinda Martin was performed in a civil ceremony, vows made with left hands rather than right—a union the Church did not recognize as "holy matrimony." Haverwood was free then to make a more suitable—church-recognized—marriage at sometime in the future. Marriage was quite legitimate—to both ladies."

"Victoria was right." Nicholas stood and paced several times between the desk and the door. Flinging aside a tufted pillow off the sofa, he sat in its place. "I should have taken her concerns about the certificate more seriously."

"So we find this Lucinda Martin." Ian held out a hand. "I'd venture if you find her, you'll find Tori."

"From what I see, she's the only one with a motive to kidnap both the earl and Tori." Zach agreed. "An act of revenge for his leaving her. Do you think she did it, Abner?"

"Highly unlikely." The lawyer pulled another paper from his case, and skimmed over its contents. "Her death was recorded ten months ago."

The tiny spark of hope that brought Nicholas to the edge of his seat, was extinguished in an instant. Unable to sit anymore, he paced in restless circles.

"There is another interesting addendum to this case, if you'd care to hear it." The lawyer replaced the papers he had just finished with, taking out a contract for Nicholas's inspection.

Nicholas paused to look over the paper. "There was a child?"

"Children," the lawyer corrected. "Two of them. Therein lies your possible motive for kidnapping."

"I don't understand." Ian said taking the contract from Nicholas.

"That contract states that Lucinda's children, fraternal twins. One male, one female. Were excluded from their father's inherent titles, lands, etcetera, gaining only the surname of Haverwood. Anything associated with the Wrenbrooke holdings were forbidden them. He did provide a small sum of money to be held in their mother's name to see to their needs, but that would have easily run out by their fifth birthday. At which time, he'd become a father again by Lady Rachelle almost to the day, and evidently chose to ignore the very existence of the other two."

"I can see where his return to the States might not be welcome by some." Ian leaned forward to rest his arms on the back of the chair.

"Precisely." The lawyer took the contract from Ian. "And there's more."

Trepidation twisted Nicholas's stomach thinking of what Victoria might be going through at this moment.

"There's a clause to this addendum." Reading once more from the contract, Mr. Westphall lifted his head to peer through his spectacles. "If upon the twin's twenty-fifth birthday, the earl has no other living heirs—be it son, daughter, grandson or granddaughter—his bequest reverts back to the children of his first marriage." The lawyer pulled the spectacles from behind his ears and leveled his gaze at Nicholas. "That twenty-fifth birthday occurs in two months. Just days before your wife turns twenty."

Cold dread spread through Nicholas's veins. "The earl would have to be dead for there to be any inheritance."

And Victoria as well. What was left unspoken hung over the room like a dark fog.

"Let's pray that is not the case." Westphall spoke quietly.

"Thank you, Abner, for coming." Ian stood, extending his hand to the lawyer. "You've done a supreme job as usual."

Nicholas appreciated his brother's intervention. At the moment, he was too numb to think past his desperate need to find his wife.

Ian walked the attorney to the door while Nicholas and Zach remained in quiet thought. Just as he reached for the handle of the sliding door, it was flung open.

"Unhand me this instant! How dare you mollycoddle me. Where is the captain?"

Lord Edward Haverwood, himself, entered the room in a perpetual dither. "Saberton! What in the name of all that is sovereign have you done with my daughter?" He stamped his cane with every word.

Nicholas shot to his feet, as did Zach.

But before he could question the earl, Dottie Saberton stepped in behind him with a look that Nicholas recognized as trouble.

～

Evening shadows fell across the decrepit floor of the warehouse.

Tori's hands, bound at the wrists, scraped against the fetid hay as she struggled to work them free.

Josie stirred. The smile tugging at her lips did not soften the cold intensity of her eyes. "You a mite uncomfortable, my lady? Ain't that a shame? I hope you suffer good and proper. Just like ma and Jake."

Josie approached the bale Tori sat upon and gave it a push with her bare foot.

Tori closed her eyes rather than let the girl see her flinch.

"You always had anything his golden baby wanted while we scrounged for days just to find somethin' to make our innards stop growlin'." Josie came close until her jeer was directly aimed at Tori's face. "Now you get to know the feeling."

Josie turned, coughing again with her expended effort.

Tori used her heel to scoot herself back on the hay until she came up against the wall.

Josie was ranting again. But as long as she continued to talk, it bought time for Tori to free herself.

Finally able to catch her breath, Josie weakly slid down the wall to the floor, scowling at Tori in disgust. "Go ahead and stare. Before long, I ain't gonna need none of your hand-me-downs or your stinkin' permission to take my own money outta the bank. Ain't none of that makes you a lady." She sat with her dingy elbows braced on top of her knees, looking over the ruined gown she wore. "It'll all be mine, and I'll get everything back that rightfully belonged to my ma."

Tori squirmed as Josie carelessly slit the skirt with her knife. "This fancy material ain't no better than them calico skirts Ma used to wear. Cotton was a whole lot sturdier."

Tori frowned slightly, trying to work her hands free. Useless. Her fingers were numb and refused to cooperate. Taking a quick breath against the panic welling up in her chest, she used her shoulder to free the gag from her mouth.

Crying out at the failed effort, she gritted her teeth at the sound of Josie's laughter laced with hacking. "How do ya like not to be able to help yourself? Havin' to depend on someone else? Knowing help ain't never comin'?"

Josie was likely some sort of distant relation. Tori had known it the first time she'd gotten a good look into her eyes, but she was too exhausted and sore and hungry to unravel the fevered girl's ramblings.

"We come from the same loins. Or ain't you figured that out yet?" Josie swiped at her mouth before wiping her hand on Tori's gown. "Your papa left us here. We wasn't good enough to live in that big stone house of yours."

Tori stiffened. Her mind screamed that the girl's accusation was nothing but a cruel lie.

"Don't believe me?" Josie squinted against the faint

shards of light spilling through the broken windows. "It's on record."

Uneasiness set in. The more Josie muttered, the more she sounded like a madwoman.

Resuming her struggles, Tori was determined to flee this horrid place. To be rid of Josie and her demented prattle.

"Ever heard of Lucinda Martin?" Josie smirked at the shock on Tori's face. "Sure you have. I heard you talkin' about her to your captain."

Tori's heart plummeted at the mention of Nicholas.

Renewing her struggle, the foul gag finally came free of her mouth, though the ties at her hands held firm. "How dare you make crass accusations against my father?"

"Because it's true. Lucinda Haverwood was my ma, and she was married to your papa before you was ever born."

The words on the marriage certificate couldn't be denied. Still Tori refused to believe her father capable of such a contemptible deed. Marriage to two women was illegal. Perhaps this Lucinda woman had died before her father married her mother.

"Where is your mother now?" Tori wasn't certain Josie had heard her. She sat completely still with eyes narrowed.

"Dead." She finally answered in a dull voice. "Died a few months back. Jake's dead, too. Couldn't get no medicine to cure 'em." Josie hesitated for a long moment before a faraway look again took over her features.

In the dimming light, Tori could barely make out the girl's red cheeks, but it was enough to know that fever had her disoriented. Silently, she worked at the ties at her hands. "I'm sorry. I truly am. Can you tell me what happened?"

Josie's voice dropped to a near whisper. "Jake got the yella fever. Ma and me, we couldn't get no doctor to even look at him without givin' him money first. Ma sold Spanish moss to the townsfolk to stuff their mattresses, but she had to buy eggs with the money just to keep up his strength."

Shadows blanketed the warehouse and Tori could barely make out the moisture shining on the other girl's face as she leaned her head against the wall.

"Ma went to Mrs. Peddington over at the Somersville Plantation, beggin' her for help. She sent over an old medicine woman that wrapped him up in goose fat and onion mustard. Stunk to high heaven. Didn't help none. He died a couple of days later."

Both of them were silent.

An unexplainable sadness clouded over Tori for a boy she'd never even met. The things Josie described were unimaginable.

"Then Ma come down with it, too. I did everything I could to bring her around. Even slept with the overseer out at the Hamilton place. He promised to have her seen by the doctor himself. But when time come he just called the law. Accused me of trespassin'."

Josie's voice faded so that Tori had to twist closer to hear what she was saying. Her eyes shone bright with fever. It was doubtful she even remembered Tori was there.

"Mrs. Peddington let us stay in one of the deserted quarters. She sent someone out every other day, bringin' us food and fresh water. Ma read out of her Bible some, and prayed alot, but her God wasn't listenin' neither."

Tori didn't respond.

"And that's when she told me about him." Bitterness seeped back into Josie's speech, and Tori became instantly wary. "His honorable highness, the great Earl of Wrenbrooke."

Josie bent over in a mock bow, breathing with difficulty as she tried to straighten back up. "'Your papa's a good man,'" she'd say. "'He just comes from different folks than us.'" Josie shook her head as she went on. "He turned his back on my ma before we was born. Never even wanted to know us. Left us to scrape and beg, while he went back to his castle and married a woman more befittin' of him."

To even contemplate that she spoke of the same man who had single-handedly raised her made no sense at all. Tori wanted to scream that her father would never be so callous.

"We buried Ma under a cypress tree that had honeysuckle wrapped all around it. Ma loved honeysuckle. She showed us how to pinch off the bottoms and pull out the long sweet honey stick. It was the best treat we ever got when we found a honeysuckle bush. We'd sit there eatin' on them honeysuckle blossoms 'til we got sick."

Tori remembered the lavish confections that the cook had made for her almost daily as a child. Desserts had become so mundane she rarely gave them a second thought. Now, she wished she could have given just one to the two scraggly children Josie described.

Something told her that at least part of what she was hearing was the truth. "I never knew." The words stuck in her throat.

Josie grasped onto a bale of hay, swaying as she came to her feet. "It don't matter a hill of beans whether you knew it or not. I turn twenty-five in a couple of months, and the law says I get what's comin' to me. All of it." She started in the direction of Tori's voice. "The contract said its mine only if you're dead. Ma begged me not to do it. She said the court of law could work something out if I'd just wait a little while. But I ain't waitin' any longer."

Tori knew she meant every word.

For whatever reason Josie had chosen to spare her the night she'd taken her from Aunt Charlotte's home. Maybe a change of heart. Maybe in reverence to her mother.

Now, however, she was out of her head with fever. She hadn't been nearly this ill two days ago. Progressively she'd gotten worse until Tori was certain she wasn't thinking clearly. Josie had no qualms about killing her this very instant, as much for herself as in vengeance for her mother and brother.

If she was going to survive this night, Tori would have

to think of a deterrent and quickly.

"Listen to me, Josie. I can have it all turned over to you. It's a fairly simple transaction really. Now that I'm married, I have no use for Wrenbrooke or any of its income."

"We already tried it that way, now it's time to just get it over with." Feeling her way in the darkness, Josie came closer to where Tori was bound, her dagger poised for attack.

"Wait, Josie!" Tori screamed. "Surely you can't murder me, knowing I'm your own blood sister. Think of your mother. Lucinda sounds as though she was a wonderful God-fearing lady. She would be crushed—."

"Shut up. Don't you even speak my ma's name with that English tongue of yours." Josie screeched, then erupted into another violent coughing fit. Shuddering heaves of breathlessness brought the girl to her knees.

"Cut these cords. I can tend to you, Josie. Kill me later, if you must. Right now, let me help." Tori became frantic to get loose. Josie needed medical attention.

The awful hacking finally stilled, and Tori listened closely for the haunting wheeze that she had become accustomed to hearing when Josie was around. It was there, rattling in the quietness of the darkened storehouse.

Fireflies flitted near the fallen girl, and Tori could barely see Josie's outline on the mucky floor where she now lay unconscious. Stepping off her bale of hay, something scampered past her foot, causing her to shiver. Keeping her eyes peeled on the place she'd last seen the knife, she pleaded silently for the tiny bugs to shed their light just one more time.

When the flashes finally came, Tori reached for the blade with her bound hands, and tried to steady it between her knees while she sawed at the rope. It seemed an eternity passed before the twine fell free. Pain prickled through her fingers until she was quite certain they would never be the same.

Rubbing her wrists, Tori carefully stepped over to the girl to feel the heat of her forehead. Just as she suspected, Josie was burning to the touch. Turning her onto her side, she hoped to keep her from breathing the fetid dust from the floor.

Looking around, she decided that she would need a suitable place to leave Josie while she went for help. Somewhere away from this stinking squalor.

But first things first.

Taking the knife between her thumb and forefinger, Tori held it out in front of her as if it were lethal. Shuffling her feet loudly, she fervently hoped to ward off anything in her path as she made her way to the door.

Once outside, Tori took in a most welcome breath of air.

An uncontrollable urge to run rose from the depths of her. She wanted to be far away from the nightmare of this place. She wanted to forget about the troublesome girl lying in the rubble of the old building. Wanted to pretend she didn't exist.

Oh, how she missed Nicholas.

Why should she care what happened to Josie? The girl tried to kill her at every turn. Tori flung the dreadful weapon off to her side, listening to it clatter against something in the dark.

But what if the things she'd said were true? It was highly possible that Josie was her sister.

Tori shoved her hands into the pockets of the ragged coat, bringing the woolen material closer abound her. Though the night was warm, she felt a chill. Her hand wrapped around a folded paper stuffed down deep in the seams of the jacket. Even as she withdrew it, Tori knew the paper contained proof of Josie's allegations.

Moving to where the slivered moon could better provide its assistance, she read just enough of the contract to acknowledge the injustices her father had made. A sob escaped her. According to the document, by all rights Tori should never have been born.

Lucinda Martin Haverwood and her two children, Josephine and Jacob, had been the earl's legitimate relations—his firstborn children. Twins Tori had never even known existed.

She used to dream about what it would be like to have a brother or sister. Little did she know they were very real and living in America. Impoverished and rejected. Abandoned to a life of utter misery, in favor of Tori's own dear mother. Simply because she had possessed a more acceptable name?

Tori swallowed the hurt that stung her throat. "What am I to do now?" She looked up to the stars peering from behind low clouds. "You've known about this all along. And I believe You've sent us here to set things right." Tori sniffed and squeezed her eyes shut. A tear made a hot path down her bruised cheek. "Lord, please forgive him."

Tori only hoped she could find the grace to do the same herself.

Drawing a quivering breath, it occurred to her that she needed to recover the knife she'd just discarded. It would have to be disposed of. Josie must never have another opportunity to use it against her.

Sniffing again, she turned to either side. It seemed that she had heard it hit something when she had tossed it away. A rusty washtub leaning against the wall of the warehouse, appeared to be the only thing capable of making the tinny noise. In the dark, she found the knife resting next to the building where it would have been in full view by morning, a careless mistake that could have cost her life.

Listening to the frogs and various other creatures of the night, Tori used the knife to dig a shallow hole under a tree. Dropping the weapon into it, she hesitated a moment before adding the worn contract as well. Just for safe measure. After filling the hole back up, she disguised her work with brush and leaves.

Josie couldn't kill her without a weapon. She was entirely too weak. And she wouldn't dare knowing Tori was the only one that could tell her where to find her contract. A second bit of insurance.

Returning to collect Josie, Tori lifted the girl under her

thin arms and dragged her across the floor into the fresh night air. She couldn't do anything about the injustice done to Lucinda or her son, but she was determined to see everything possible done to save Josie.

Panting and taking a moment to catch her breath, Tori let Josie lie on the grassy knoll that lead down to the riverbank. "You are terribly heavy for someone who doesn't eat enough to sustain a bird."

Her own stomach grumbled in protest.

With no idea where to go next, Tori settled her hands on her hips. She obviously couldn't drag the girl all the way back to Savannah. Nor could she leave her here alone in her deteriorating condition.

A palmetto tree, down by the waterfront would have to serve the purpose. At least, it was in a sandy area, void of the monstrous crawlers from the storehouse.

Josie moaned as Tori continued to drag her down toward the tree. Once there, Tori ripped a large piece from her petticoat. Kneeling to moisten it with the cool river water, she couldn't keep from thinking about all Josie had said.

It was no secret that her father was deeply loyal to station. Endless generations before him had been as well. He was bound by honor to protect the dignity of his title.

But going so far as to leave a woman he obviously cared for a great deal in favor of keeping with convention? In effect, denying his own children?

If true, it would take a force much stronger than herself to forgive him of this pretense they'd lived all these years.

Without warning, a sharp pain in the back of Tori's head brought complete darkness swirling in around her.

Child, wait patiently when dark thy path may be,
And let thy faith lean trustingly on Him who cares
for thee.
~ Fannie Crosby

Twenty-Nine

Nicholas saw the urgency in his mother's eyes as she strode purposefully into the library. "Have you any idea what this man has done?"

Icy fingers of dread crept up Nicholas's back. "We were just listening to highpoints before you arrived."

"Why are you people just sitting here? Get up!" The earl rattled his cane against the bottom of Zach's chair until the young man sprang to his feet. "Fetch my daughter, at once!"

"Will someone please explain what's going on." Nicholas's voice grew louder with every word.

The lawyer fidgeted, replacing his papers into their case.

"Now see here, Saberton, I hold you responsible for

this. As my daughter's husband, you were required to see to her welfare."

Nicholas cast an impatient glance at the earl and his flailing cane.

"Edward, please." Dottie's eyes never left her son's. "Nicholas, there's good reason to believe that Tori's life is in jeopardy. We mustn't delay a moment longer."

"We've been searching all night." He was tired and agitated, desperate for answers. "Do you have any idea where they've taken her?"

"Dottie, good to see you." Abner discretely made his way to the door. "I'll let Nicholas fill you in on our visit."

"Thank you, Abner. Say hello to Eleanor." Dottie doors to close behind him and turned back to her son. "Edward wasn't kidnapped. I found him out at Brechenridge when I returned from Philadelphia this morning." She came to stand in front of her son. "He decided to force your hand. He knew Tori's birthday was fast approaching and felt she would be better protected under your care. As your wife. He felt you weren't inclined to marry her soon enough with him here to keep a watch on her, so he removed himself from the picture. Knowing I was out of town, he made himself at home at Brechenridge. I'm sure that dear girl worried herself sick over his disappearance."

The earl harrumphed loudly.

"She was frantic." Nicholas could barely contain his fury at so careless a move.

"When I got home, Edward was there waiting for me

and told me what he'd done. He also told me you were married while I was away." Her tight-lipped account told them all she wasn't happy about any of it. "Though I'm delighted you've decided to settle down and take a wife, I would have liked to have been there." Nicholas caught the ominous look his mother sent his way. "However, under the circumstances, I believe you did what you thought best."

The dull ache in his chest wouldn't let up. Nicholas moved around his mother to stare out the window. Victoria was out there somewhere. He wasn't about to lose her. If he had to move heaven and earth so be it.

"When Edward revealed this scheme of his, I was quite upset. I despise his method—it was deceitful, and I've told him as much. But what's done is done, and now we must do whatever we can to find Victoria. She's in terrible danger, son."

He turned from the window and lifted Tori's cross and chain from the desk. "Someone tried to hawk this at the bank today. And tried to withdraw fifty thousand from the earl's account. She also tried to peddle Grandmother's brooch to the first taker."

The earl's mustache twitched.

"Apparently this person has a resemblance to Victoria. Any ideas where I might find her?" Nicholas didn't trust himself to say any more than that to Victoria's father.

Haverwood took the cross from Nicholas's grasp. "Lucinda wrote to me and warned me the girl had found out about her possible inheritance. She advised me that

Victoria was in danger. You were supposed to see that she was kept safe." His accusation was hollow in light of his own transgressions.

Nicholas had to look away to keep from strangling the man.

"Lucinda never would have contacted me unless it was a matter of life and death. We had that agreement. I wrote to her saying Victoria and I were coming to America where we would have all this addressed in a court of law and be done with it. I would see that Lucinda's children were taken care of so that they would not feel the need to harm Victoria or myself. Unfortunately for all of us, Lucinda died before she ever received my letter."

"Do you have the address where you sent the letter, Edward?" Dottie wanted to know.

"It was in care of Somersville Plantation. She must have been employed there."

"Somersville is over near Bloomingdale. I'll go with you." Ian was up and ready.

The earl came to his feet as well. "I must warn you—the girl made one attempt on Victoria's life already. Thankfully she was away at school at the time. Because of Lucinda's letter, I was able to prevent her from murdering Victoria right in her own bed." The earl's mustache twitched as he addressed Nicholas. "Now you've gone and handed her over on a silver platter."

Haverwood could have saved his breath. Nicholas's own conscience screamed louder than anything the earl could dish out. Stark dread and anger welled up inside of him. He'd put his business ahead of Victoria's safety and now her life was at stake.

"Do you know if this girl looks anything like Tori?" Zach asked.

"I've no earthly idea. I've never seen her. But I can tell you her mother was lovely once." The earl spoke quietly.

"Sounds like the young woman I saw bounding from the bank could very well be Lucinda's daughter." Zach started for the door, but halted when his mother put her arm through his. "I need you to stay, son. Aurora may need you when we bring Edward home."

Nicholas grabbed his revolver from an engraved case on his desk and disappeared from the room.

∽

Another cool splash hit Tori full in the face and her head lobbed to one side. A searing pain vibrated behind her eyes.

The ground beneath where her pitched violently, dipping without warning. Trying to hold on, she reached out but found nothing solid to hold on to.

A moan reverberated in her ears, the voice sounded much like her own. A swaying light penetrated her consciousness even from behind closed lids.

"You rung her bell good, Billy Joe." An unknown voice spoke above her in graveled tones. Why'd you have to knock her plumb out?"

"So's she wouldn't get away." Another voice spoke

from the other side of her.

"Leave her be. I'll tend to her." Tori knew that voice. "Just you get us upriver like we agreed."

Josie! Tori attempted to open her eyes. The blinding glare of a lantern close to her face sent pins of excruciating light through her head. Her empty stomach lurched as a result. "Get the light out of her face, you nitwit, or she ain't never gonna come around."

Splashing sounds, in time with the swaying she felt beneath her, brought her to the conclusion that she was on a water craft of some sort. But, where was she going? Were they heading back to Savannah?

"Nicholas." Tori tried to speak but it came as a quiet murmur.

The graveled voice was first to respond. "What'd she say? Somethin' about a necklace?"

"Prob'ly lost it when she fell," the other man snapped. "Get to rowing!"

"Go on." Josie still stood over her. "You'll get what was promised soon enough. Let her wake up first."

Tori listened as heavy footsteps shuffled away. She made another painful attempt to open her eyes now that the light wasn't in her face. The sky was blanketed in black, completely void of stars. A faint smell of something burnt assaulted her nostrils and again her stomach lurched.

"Where are we?" She asked into the darkness.

"On the river." Josie stepped into her view, blocking the glare of the lantern.

"I gathered that much. Where on the river? Are we going back to Savannah?" She was careful not to sound too hopeful.

Josie gave an ugly laugh before convulsing with a spell of dry coughing. Her breath was labored as she wiped a smearing of blood from her lips. In the dim light Tori could see the drawn, haggard look on the other girl's face. She needed medical attention—and soon.

"We're headed in the opposite direction of Savannah, as a matter of fact." Josie managed with a smirk.

Trying to sound indifferent against a wave of panic, Tori pushed herself upright. "Have we passed the Brechenridge plantation, yet?" Her heart raced knowing Nicholas's land was somewhere along this route. "We would be safe there." The dizzying pain in her head returned and she slumped back against the wood planks.

"We're long past it." Josie spat over the side of the raft.

Whether it was the truth or a lie didn't matter. Tori needed to get off the unsteady craft or she would be sick from its constant motion. Her empty stomach couldn't take much more. "Tell them to let us off here just the same. We can find our own way. The sooner I return to my husband, the sooner you can have your money—" Her words were choked off as Josie yanked the collar of her tattered woolen jacket up at her throat.

In that brief moment, she had a liberating discovery. She no longer feared Josephine Haverwood. Knowing that Josie was her own flesh and blood, she felt an odd responsibility to see past her bullying—to try to reach a forsaken soul.

Not only that, she'd buried that dreadful knife. Josie couldn't harm a fly without it.

"You can't kill me, Josephine. I'm the only one who knows where your contract is." Tori felt the grip at her throat relax a bit, so she pressed on. "And you must learn to behave in more civil a manner if you are to be present-ed to polite society once you return to England as mistress of Wrenbrooke. For that, you need me." Her chin lifted a notch higher with an assurance she didn't feel.

"I don't need you for nothin'." Josie released her coat. "Ain't nothin' special to bein' a lady." Though her words were defiant, Tori saw a flicker of doubt cross her face before she turned away.

"Certainly there is. One infraction to the rules, no matter how minor, could result in unconditional elimina-tion from elite society as a whole."

That ought to give Josie something to think about. At least it distracted her from wanting to kill her. For the moment.

The ache in Tori's head eased enough for her to take in their meager surroundings. She was leaning against a rustic hut set in the middle of a timber raft. The two male voices she'd heard earlier were now at the end of the watery platform. She could hear their oars slapping against the choppy water.

"How did we come to be on this rickety craft, any-way?" Tori spoke in a careful undertone. Something told her the less attention she drew from the scraggily strangers, the better off she'd be. "The last I remember you had fainted from all that hideous coughing."

Laughter came from the two men huddled in private conversation. "Who are they?" Tori asked, with more than a touch of irritation. She was tired, her head hurt, she was hungry and in terrible need of a bath.

"They agreed to take us upriver to Augusta."

"Augusta? I promised to give you my inheritance. But in order to do so, you need take me back to Savannah." Tori tried to turn so that she could better see Josie's face, but a sharp pain hampered her curiosity and she rested her head back against the wooden hut.

"Look, I thought I made it clear." Josie resumed her threatening stance. "I ain't inclined to trust you or anyone like ya. Especially with that stupid stunt you pulled back there. Good thing I thought to check for my paper after I flattened ya. Unless you want to give it back, we're goin' to the records department in Augusta to get me a new one."

Tori felt the heat of Josie's glare.

"Why didn't you kill me when you had the chance?" It was a serious question. Josie had been given the perfect opportunity to kill her and had not done so. Perhaps she wasn't as depraved as she tried to pretend she was.

Josie offered no explanation. She stood and yanked Tori up by the coat sleeve, nodding her head silently at the shoreline coming closer into view.

"There's the tradin' post." The man with the gruff

voice called out. "I expect we'll be collectin' our fare now."

The men exchanged crudities that Tori couldn't hear clearly.

"What fare? I thought we didn't have any money." She whispered but Josie shushed her with wave of her hand.

"I promised 'em somethin' else."

Ignoring the girl's warning, Tori raised her voice a bit to be heard over the lapping waves. "What could we possibly possess that those two would be interested in?"

"They think we're harlots."

Tori was too stunned to respond. With a sudden jolt, the crude raft collided with a small dock. Once moored, the deck swayed precariously as each one stepped from its platform.

Tori shot Josie a scathing look.

One of the two shabby men grabbed her arm and pushed her forward. "Get along there, missy. I ain't got all night." His lewd chuckling caused Tori's skin to crawl. His breath filled the heavy night air with a sickening odor of soured wine.

"Harlots?" Tori murmured through gritted teeth as she passed Josie. "Wouldn't a simple IOU have sufficed?"

"Just go along." Josie whispered back. "We'll get rid of 'em as soon as we clear the shoreline."

Before she could react, Tori was abruptly spun around and a hideous face with rotted teeth was descending upon her. Abrasive lips scuffed across her mouth and she quickly turned her head.

"Hey, now! That one's mine. I saw her first." She was snatched back so hard her aching head snapped.

"Don't go gettin' selfish on me, Billy Joe. We can share. Two for the price of one." The one who spoke slapped her hindside with stinging assent.

Shudders of panic surged through her entire body. "Josie!" Surely this was a perfect time to make their escape.

Tori held back a cry, as her half-sister came into view. A low fog misted off of the water and the heavy moisture had Josie doubled over in uncontrollable hacking. She appeared weaker than a half-drowned kitten. Her quivering shoulders were covered in a feverish sheen.

Both men now focused their blurred attention on Tori. Tugging the shabby coat from their greedy paws, she tried to shield her exposed limbs as best as she could. This game seemed to amuse them, and it became rougher as it went on.

The sound of the threadbare material giving way rent the stillness of the night. Desperately, Tori clung to the remaining cloth, holding it across her bosom to cover her thin camisole. How could she have let Josie talk her out of her dress?

"Enough of this. Time to pay up." A menacing hand closed over her upper arm in a painful vise. Another filthy arm came around her waist, snatching her breath as it hauled her backward.

Flashing a brimming plea skyward, Tori kicked wildly,

making contact with at least one shin.

The blast of a shotgun burst upon the riverside, echoing across the water.

Tori's stifled a scream at the unexpected blast. Taking only a second to rally her senses, she caught her captors off guard, quickly twisting from their clutches.

"Get from around here." A toothless old gentleman with bristly white whiskers wearing a red nightshirt tottered down the bank from the outpost. "Go on. This ain't no place for the likes of you two."

Thank heavens.

Tori rushed to Josie's side. When they returned to Savannah, she would see that this wonderful man was rewarded for saving them from those stinking brutes.

Josie was wobbly, but conscious as Tori helped her to her feet.

"Leave 'em be, old man. We were just seein' to some business here."

"Ain't puttin up with no shenanigans on my pier. Maude and me runs a respectable outfit. Now git, you hussies!" The barrel of the gun was centered on Tori.

In utter astonishment, Tori's back went stiff. This person wasn't here to save her from these brutes at all.

He actually thought to save those drunken creatures... from *her*!

If thou shouldst never see my face again,
pray for my soul.
More things are wrought by prayer
than this world dreams of.
~ Alfred, Lord Tennyson

Thirty

" I beg your pardon?" Tori was so dumbfounded she could barely get the words out.

"Ain't gonna do you no good to beg. You cain't go traipsin' all over creation lookin' like that. We got laws you know."

"Who is it, honey?" A woman, as short as she was round, was picking up momentum as she bobbed down the grassy bank.

"Couple of floozies from town. These two fellers brung them here and I was just runnin' them off." He pointed Tori out to the woman with the end of his shotgun.

"Land sakes." She narrowed her eyelids to near slits.

The wages of sin is death and from the looks of it, that other one there's about to get her just reward."

The hair stood up at the nape of Tori's neck. These people obviously had no idea who she was.

Her gaze darted toward the woods just past the outpost. Josie was in no shape for a quick escape. She'd have to use her head to borrow some time. "You are shamefully mistaken. I'll have you know, my husband is a very influential man in Georgia."

"Hush-up, Jezebel. Take your friend there and go on back to wherever you come from. We don't need your kind 'round these parts."

Tori leaped backward as the old man spat a stream of tobacco juice at her feet.

"We'll see that they're taken care of, won't we Billy Joe?" One of the men from the raft moved toward her.

"Billy Joe Daughtery, is that you?" The woman's loud high-pitched screech brought about an ear-piercing retort from a donkey somewhere behind her. "You get yourself back home to your wife, you worthless cheat. Or I'll be tellin' her why."

The man responded with an angry slap to his leg. "Maude, you ain't nothin' but a tail-bitin' gossip."

The pudgy woman stood up straight and looked proud to hear it.

"You go on back. I'll take her with me." Again Tori was yanked back by the arm.

"Oh no, you don't. If I ain't havin' her then you ain't neither."

Ambling their way back to the wobbly raft, the two argued between themselves. Finally they gave up on collecting their fare and pushed off into the rippling current.

Tori sidestepped the spittle to come in closer to the couple, determined to make them understand her plight.

In unison, they each took a step back. "Get thee behind me, trollop." The old man lifted his gun higher to ward her off.

Josie cursed loudly. That didn't help their cause one bit.

"You really must listen. This is not at all what it seems. I've been abducted, you see. And this is ... well, this is my abductor ... my sister ... sort of. And she's taken ill. Surely you can find it in your hearts to give her a bit of nourishment."

The couple looked at each other and nodded in smug agreement. "Foreigner."

"Oooh!" Tori was completely exasperated.

The woman's beady eyes tried to get a better look at Josie. "Appears it's a mite too late for that one." The woman's jowls bounced when she swung her head. "Looks like she's got fever. Get her off our post. We don't need no fever spreading from here. They'll put us under quarantine."

"The craft we arrived on has now departed." Tori pointed out, folding her arms "Have you a horse and carriage we might borrow?"

"Horse thieves to boot." The old man waved the barrel of his shotgun.

"That's preposterous." Tori prayed for patience. "I'd purchase them outright but I seem to have misplaced my purse."

Josie snickered causing the man to point the gun in her general direction.

"Run 'em off and be quick about it. We can't have folks seeing trash like that around here. They'll sully our good name. After all, a good name is to be chosen rather than riches and gold." His wife's sing-songy ridicule sounded like a spoiled child as she lifted her dingy white robe and rambled her way back up the incline to the box-like outpost at the top of the embankment.

The man was obviously not going to budge as long as he thought her a strumpet. Hanging her head in mock shame, Tori imitated the actors she'd seen at the theater.

Sniffing back pretend tears, she sobbed theatrically into her hands. "Oh, sir. I am so ashamed." She clasped her hands together in front of her bosom. "Your truthful words have made me see the error of my ways. Won't you please take me to the local authorities? So that I may confess and pay for my misdeeds?"

Josie laughed loudly behind her, wheezing with the effort.

Once again, the shotgun rang out and Tori jumped out of her skin.

"Lyin' hussy!" The old man started after her.

Taking off in a full run, Tori grabbed Josie's arm and dodged his blundering approach. The only protection in sight was a wooded area to the right of the trading post. Half dragging her sister, Tori hid behind the base of a huge oak, praying they wouldn't be seen.

They watched as the old codger ranted, poking his gun into every bush surrounding the clearing.

More than once, she held her breath as Josie's tight coughing nearly gave them away. By the time he gave up his search and staggered back inside, Josie lay exhausted on the floor of the undergrowth.

Tori fell in beside her. Not only did her head throb from the earlier abuse, her stomach gnawed and every muscle in her body screamed for rest.

Looking up, Tori observed the long ivy that hung in graceful garlands from the tall pines that left ghostly shadows in the dark. She was suddenly overcome with an uncontrollable urge to laugh. She wanted to laugh uproariously until tears streamed down her chafed cheeks.

Then, she wanted to bawl like a newborn lamb. For herself, for Nicholas, for Josie, for her father. For hours on end.

Instead, she just lay there, stiff and for the most part beyond feeling any emotion at all.

"Do you think they was right?" Josie's voice was raspy in the dark.

"Who?"

"Them outpost folks back there. You think God cursed me from the day I was born?"

Tori rolled onto her side, looking for her sister's face in the darkness. "God doesn't curse you, Josie. He loves you. You can't gauge His love by indifference shown by your earthly father."

Nor from overindulgence of the same.

They both lay silent for a long while. Tori wasn't certain if Josie was deep in thought or if she had lapsed into unconsciousness again.

Listening for her labored breath, Tori knew she must lend all of her strength to seeing them both through this alive. Despite her exhaustion, an unchecked tear trickled slowly down the bridge of her nose.

Please help Nicholas find us ... and help Josie make it until he does.

"Love give me back my heart again."
~ *George Granville, Baron Lansdowne*

By the time they'd made Somersville, lamps had been lit inside the main house. Nicholas let Ian do the formalities of explaining their visit while he turned his horse toward the old field quarters.

Dark and dank, he'd gone room by room, lifting a torch to illuminate every corner. Each shotgun shack stood empty. Deserted with no trace of recent intruders.

Mrs. Peddington remembered Lucinda Martin. Said she was a kindly woman and was sad she couldn't have been more help to her. She also remembered Lucinda's girl. Wild little thing. Hadn't seen her since Lucinda passed.

Just before midnight, they'd made a sweeping search of Somersville land with the help of the owner's three sons and ten field hands. On Nicholas's order, no rock was left unturned. If Victoria had been anywhere near the

Somersville place, he was bound and determined to find her.

Nicholas booted the crude gate of the last deserted shack beyond the northernmost rows of bedded cotton, sending it crashing in on a rotted fencepost. Thick cobwebs covered the entrance from years of emptiness and neglect. Angry frustration fueled each step as it became apparent this too would end with no answers.

Gathering his horse's reins, Nicholas left alone, walking back down the desolate road in silence.

The torment of knowing his wife was in jeopardy but beyond his reach exasperated him beyond anything he'd ever endured. Even in the throes of a raging hurricane, he'd managed to bring his ship safely into harbor.

Ian had returned to Savannah, intent on coming up with another fine plan.

Nicholas's plan was to continue south to the deserted rice fields deep in the swamp. However, he'd have to wait for sunup to avoid stepping over a slumbering reptile.

As unlikely as it was that he'd find Victoria hidden in the marshlands, he refused to give in to his own weakness. Exhaustion wracked his body, but he'd be hanged before he'd stop searching every length of Georgia's crimson soil to bring Victoria home.

Sitting in his saddle on a high bluff overlooking the Savannah River, Nicholas could detect no visible signs of life apart from the slow current below. Soon, the first rays of sunlight would beam across the eastern horizon. With it fishing boats and steamers hauling cotton to market would fill the waterway as the sleepy, fog-draped river was put to work once more.

Tired and heart-weary, Nicholas slid to the ground, leading his horse to the water's edge. Kneeling on one knee, he cupped a drink for himself before letting it splash over the top of his head, dripping down into his burning eyes.

The frenzy of the past twelve hours since leaving Savannah now simmered to a gnawing agitation that ate at his core. Victoria was close, living and breathing. He sensed it with everything in him.

With maddening force, Nicholas hurled a rock across the expanse of the water. If he thought she'd hear him, he'd shout her name until he had no voice. So close, yet elusively out of reach.

Alone with his tortured thoughts, his heartbeat magnified in his own ears. Passages from the Bible played over in his mind—scriptures he'd learned in childhood. Until he had no choice but admit he was powerless to save her on his own.

Sinking onto the sandy loam, Nicholas sat with legs bent and forearms resting on his knees. In alternate prayer and reflection, he watched the oppressive darkness give way to an azure glow of dawn. With the dawn, came peace. As if a heavy burden lifted, he knew he no longer fought this battle alone.

At morning's first light, he heard the approach of hooves thundering on the river road just downstream. Coming to his feet, Nicholas squinted to see a horse and rider looming his way. Swinging into his saddle, he led his mount up the bank to the where the road took a sharp curve.

"Nicholas!"

He recognized Ian's voice before he could fully see his face.

"What have you heard?" Nicholas calmed his horse as Ian's came to a skidding halt.

"Tori may have been seen last night at Crested Bluff Trading Post."

Nicholas's pulse surged as he looked across the river to the wooded area on the other side. Crested Bluff was almost due east on the middle tributary.

"The nearest crossing is Johnson's ferry. Let's go." Urging his horse forward, the animal took off in a gallop, with Ian's close behind.

They rode for less than an hour before taking the turnoff that led down to the dock.

"Who saw her?" Nicholas wanted to know as soon as he dismounted to lead his horse onto the weathered planks of the ferry.

"Big Amos." Ian gave two coins to one of the cable operators. "His cousin is up at Poplar Grove, over at Judge Hale's place. The judge asked for permission to borrow Amos's services last night to help man a political party he was hosting. His foreman came in at about three this morning and said he'd heard a ruckus down by the Crested Bluff Trading Post. Shotguns and raised voices."

"Amos went down to investigate? Nicholas pulled his

horse to the rail and wrapped the reins. Ducking under the animal's head, he met Ian between the heaving steeds.

"He did, but he never saw her himself. By the time he got over there, everything had gone quiet and there was no trace of her."

Nicholas threw him an annoyed look.

"The foreman, however, described what he'd seen. The postmaster and his wife, two other men, and two bedraggled young women who fit Tori's description."

Surveying the piney woods as the east bank grew closer, Nicholas couldn't contain a twinge of anticipation that quickened in his chest. "They couldn't have gotten far."

Pushing away from the rail, he led his horse to edge of the platform, ready to disembark the moment it touched the bank.

The best protection any woman
can have is courage.
~ Elizabeth Cady Stanton

Thirty-Two

The strange noise sounded again.

Barely awake, Tori's eyes grew wide when met with a rattlesnake coiled inches from her face. She watched lying, perfectly still, afraid to even breathe. The flat head rose slowly from its scaled body, vicious yellow slits taking in her every move. The serpent's forked tongue slithered from a mouth that seemed to smile in conquest.

Without warning, Josie gave a brash cough behind her, and Tori squeezed her eyes shut waiting for the inevitable strike.

Instead she heard a twang. And a thump.

Cautiously, she opened her eyes one at a time to the sight of the snake lying slack and unmoving a few yards from where she'd last seen it. By all appearances, it was dead.

Tori pushed up to rest on an elbow, searching for an explanation for her astonishing good fortune. Her answer popped out from the bushes in the form of a young boy of perhaps seven years of age.

Excitedly, he ran over and grabbed up the lank snake by the head and shook it to make the rattle clatter. He wore no shirt beneath his overalls, and his hair was uneven and scraggly. Bronzed skin gave evidence that he'd spent plenty of time in the sunshine. His lack of shoes hadn't hampered his agility one bit. With a snaggle-toothed smile, he lifted the wretched creature over his head. His round, almost cherubic, face beamed.

When she finally caught his attention, she greeted him. "Hello, there."

He smiled, but just until he caught himself. The sling-shot tucked inside the back pocket of his britches spoke well of his sharpshooting abilities.

"I suppose I have you to thank for saving me from that ghastly beast."

Carefully, Tori rose to her feet, still rather shaky. Dusting loose leaves from the worn coat, she clutched the front lapels together.

"It's not a beast. It's a snake." He lisped through missing teeth while blatantly rolling his eyes.

Tori wondered why a little boy would be foraging through the thicket instead of attending school.

"You speak very well. You must make high marks in your lessons."

He picked up a stick and threw it toward a tree, but ignored her assumption.

"Hmm, I see. And is that where you are supposed to be right now?"

The child still didn't answer, but the way he screwed his lips over to one side told her volumes.

She waited while he looked over a few rocks, slipping ones that pleased him into his pocket. Finally, he lifted his tentative gaze to her.

Tori tried running fingers through her tangled hair but winced when she came across an immovable knot.

"Mama weaves hers." He still kept his distance. "And winds it up at the sides."

"That sounds like a very clever thing to do. I wish I had thought of it earlier." Tori picked handfuls of leaves and straw from the tangled mass. "I'm afraid it's rather hopeless now."

Josie shivered with a sharp wheeze. Tori immediately went to her side, smoothing the remnants of her prized gown over Josie's bare legs.

"What's a matter with her?" The boy used another stick to point.

Her condition had worsened overnight. Without water the fever would eventually consume her.

Deciding it was best not to alarm the boy, she kept her voice light. "She's a bit under the weather today."

His look of misgiving told her he knew better.

"The truth is I'm afraid she's terribly sick. I really must find her some water."

His face brightened and forgetting himself, he approached her. "I know where some is. You want me to go get it for you?"

The prospect of drinking something other than the muddy river water was more than she could hope for. "You know where there is fresh water?"

He bolted off like lightning, racing nimbly through the brush as fast as his feet could carry him. Tori stood with a hand held to her brow, shielding the sun from her eyes. She wished he'd let her go with him, curious as to where the source of this water was.

All of a sudden, as if a veil of despair lifted from her eyes, his casual statement came back in a rush. His mother. That dear, precious, magnificent child could quite possibly hold the key to her freedom. Instantly, Tori felt lighter.

"Lady!" The little boy came running back through the brush with an earthen container rocking in his pudgy hands. "It's cold. I got it from the well."

Taking the jug, she looked down at the sparkling clear water. Tori was never so glad to see anything in her life and she couldn't resist another minute. Lifting it to her parched lips, she indulged in the pure wetness of it as it soothed her burning throat.

"Oh!" She finally took a breath. "I could kiss you."

His eyes grew wide as he backed up. A look of repugnance tightened his little face.

"Or ..." Tori laughed, offering a hand instead. "Perhaps we'll just shake hands." He watched her carefully before quickly leaning out to accept her thanks and get it over with.

"You haven't told me your name." Again, she smiled at his heightened color. "How shall I know what to call you?"

He hesitated, obviously not sure he wanted her to call him at all.

"If you don't tell me, I shall just have to make one up for you." Tori tapped a finger against her chin. "Now let's see. I believe you look like a Horatio."

He shook his head.

"Egbert?"

He shook it again, smiling this time.

"I've got it. I shall call you Barnaby S. Binglehopper."

He fell into a fit of giggles as he continued shaking his little head.

Tori went over to Josie and knelt by her side. Lifting her, she gently slipped an arm around her shoulders. "Here, Josie. Drink."

Josie's eyes barely opened as Tori raised the earthen vessel to her mouth. She drank deeply. Tori was cautious about letting her have too much, too soon. Her empty stomach would likely reject it. "There now. We'll have a bit more later."

"Go away. Leave me alone." Josie turned her head and reclosed her eyes. A most welcome sign. As long as she was still able to hurl insults, she still had a fighting chance to come through this.

"Barnaby? Would you set this in the shade for me? It

should stay well out of the sun over there." She held out the water pot and pointed in the direction of a large live oak sprawling nearby.

He was still given to fits of giggling. "My name's not Barnaby."

"Oh?" Tori slowly pushed to her feet. Her body ached profusely with the abuse it had taken over the last three days, and the constant rumble in her stomach was painful.

"It's Hickory."

"That's a fine name, Hickory. You may call me Lady ... umm ... Mrs. ... Perhaps you should just call me Miss Tori for now. Do you think you can take me to meet your mother?"

His expression grew cautious.

"You see, Hickory, we've gotten ourselves lost." Tori tried to ease his apprehension. "I thought perhaps she could help us get back to Savannah."

"She's not in Savannah."

Tori could tell immediately that he was avoiding the truth, but she was too weary to figure why. "No matter where she is just now. Could you please take me to her?"

He was shaking his head, even before she'd finished what she was saying.

Sitting down on an old tree stump, Tori patted a place next to her. "Hickory, come here." He kept his eyes from her as he fidgeted with a stick, drawing designs in the dirt. "I promise you'll not be in trouble. I want to thank her for raising such a wonderful, helpful boy."

A flock of seagulls cried in the distance. He took a moment to weigh her words for the truth. Finally, his eyes lifted and met hers. Tori was amazed at the uneasiness that she saw shining in their depths. She patted the stump again. Hickory dropped the stick and this time he did come over to sit next to her.

"Does your mama know where you are?" Her soft question caused him to shake his head so slightly, Tori almost missed it.

Something incredibly delicious assaulted her nostrils, and Tori lifted her head higher to take it in. Her mouth watered and her stomach lurched.

Tori lifted his chin with her fingers. "It's awfully important that I get home, Hickory. You see I—we … "She nodded toward Josie. "We're lost."

He looked into each of Tori's eyes in turn. "I'll take you home."

Tori wrapped an arm around him, until he finally relaxed against her.

"Won't you take me to you mother, Hickory? Please." Her voice remained tender. "I promise to do what I can to make sure she understands what a brave defender you are to have saved me from that horrid snake."

"Really?" He perked up. "You think I'm brave as David? I bet I could slay a bear."

"Most definitely!"

Hickory jumped to his feet and lifted his head. "Smell that?"

Did she ever. Her hand went to her middle as it rumbled loudly in answer. A luscious aroma filled the air.

Hickory grabbed her other hand and pulled her along toward the bushes he had disappeared into earlier to get the water. Once there, he pulled her down onto her knees. "Look."

Tori parted the brush and spotted the outpost from the previous evening, set upon the bluff. A well was off to one side and around back there was a chicken house with several pigs fenced in a yard surrounding it.

From where they were crouched, Tori spotted a half-open window and three steaming pies sitting on the sill to cool. She nibbled her lip, almost able to taste them.

Hickory tapped her arm and nodded toward the tempting sight. "I'll go get us one."

Just as Tori was about to launch into a lesson on the evils of stealing, the woman who had been so exceptionally rude the night before set out another freshly baked pie and again the smell of it mercilessly attacked her senses.

"Do you think you can shoot this?" Hickory held out his slingshot in one hand and some round pebbles in the other.

"Certainly." After all, how hard could it be?

"Good, 'cause I can run faster than you."

Tori slanted a glance his way.

"I'll go unlatch the gate, then all you gotta do is shoot this and hit one of those pigs. It'll squeal so loud, all the others will stampede the gate trying to get out," he explained in loud whispers.

Tori looked from one hand to the other. Rock, slingshot, pig. Seemed simple enough.

"Then," Hickory continued, "when the big lady comes out to see about the ruckus, she'll see all her pigs running loose. That'll keep her busy while I run around there and snatch us a pie."

Lord help her, Tori didn't think twice before agreeing. She was too hungry to argue.

"Ready?" Hickory waited for her approval.

She lifted the slingshot to peer at it through one eye, gathering her aim.

"You gotta put a rock in it." He gave her an annoyed look. "And pull it back like this. Now, remember to wait 'til I open the gate." Hickory leapt over the shrubbery.

Quiet as a mouse, he bowed low, deftly making his way over to the fence and unwound the wire from a peg holding the gate shut. He waved Tori on as soon as it was open.

As instructed, Tori came through the brush and took aim at the largest hog in the yard. With a dainty pinkie finger lifted, Tori pulled back and let the pebble fly.

It completely missed the intended hog, bouncing off of one wall and then one more, to hit another unsuspecting pig square on its head. The ensuing squeal could be heard for miles. Just as Hickory had said they would, the other pigs joined the protest and stormed the gate.

"Pa!" A yell came from inside the dwelling. "Those blasted pigs are loose again."

Tori held her breath, looking around for the white-whiskered old man to appear with his shotgun. He never did.

Instead, it was the woman who eventually came waddling down the steps to investigate, wiping her hands on her apron. "Do I have to do everything around here? Just once I'd like to see ..." Her complaint faded as she moved farther away to corral the wayward pigs.

Hickory was around the side in an instant, lifting a delicious-smelling pie from the windowsill. He slipped back, undetected, to where Tori stood waiting.

Just as they were turning to leave with their prize in hand, the woman's shrill voice could be heard once more. "Pa! Where in tarnation are you?"

Without thinking, Tori raised the slingshot once more. The woman, bent over trying to restrain a stubborn piglet, was sent squealing across the yard.

Tori immediately felt contrite as she met Hickory's wide-eyed gaze. Lifting one shoulder higher than the other, she whispered, "Oops."

*The pain of parting is nothing
to the joy of meeting again.
~ Charles Dickens*

Thirty-Three

They rode fast and hard to make Crested Bluff in an hour's time. Nicholas was fierce with intent. Turning off the main road that led down to the trading post and pier, he immediately became alarmed by a commotion coming from below.

Nicholas leapt from his horse and made his way through the thick greenery, careful to keep the element of surprise in his favor. He pushed back a heavy vine to find a woman chasing pigs around the yard. Not the view he'd hoped.

Dropping the vine, he resumed his search. But then something else caught his eye. A movement up near the window. Taking his captain's spy glass from his pocket, he decided it was worth a closer look.

Nicholas smiled as he spotted a small boy, helping

himself to a pie. Grinning from ear to ear, the kid turned and waved to the bushes on the other side.

Scanning the scope to where the boy was waving, Nicholas froze as he came upon a half-dressed woman that looked suspiciously like—

Victoria!

Beckoning the boy with both hands to hurry him along, she kept one eye on the dumbfounded woman. Hair in wild disarray, she hugged the child as he made it safely back over to where she stood.

Nicholas slowly lowered the scope. He had a hard time believing his eyes and had to resist the urge to rub them. Lifting the scope again, he watched her disappear into the woods with the boy.

Nicholas was quick to move, until it occurred to him that the hoyden he'd just seen may be the other girl, the product of the earl's first marriage.

He refocused the glass just as she lifted her weapon. Nicholas's heart stopped in his chest. In her brief moment of concentration, there, just to the side of her pursed lips, the quick flash of an exuberant little dimple confirmed her identity. It was Victoria. There was no denying it. And his prim, oh-so-proper wife had just waylaid the postmaster's wife with a slingshot in her underclothes, no less.

Ian, beside him with his own scope raised, had apparently seen everything. And much to Nicholas's aggravation, he was making no effort at all to contain his amusement.

Nicholas dropped the vine and made his way back through the brush, anxious to find Victoria and see the whole ordeal resolved.

"Who should we rescue first, big brother? Your wife or the postmaster's wife?" Ian laughed as they made their way to the thickly wooded ridge.

"I'm not positive it was my wife. It could easily be the other female." Nicholas took unwavering steps.

"Well, now. If it is, I surely want to meet her." Ian smiled, not at all affected by his brother's scowl.

Tori and Hickory sat upon the stump devouring their blackberry pie with the same gusto they would a four-course meal. It tasted divine.

Without the benefit of utensils, they used their fingers, so that by the time they were close to the bottom of the plate they were completely covered in the rich juice and laughing at one another.

Josie glowered at them from her pallet, nibbling her own small piece of the bounty. Though drained of strength, she still refused Tori's help in sitting up.

All at once, the bushes rustled behind them.

Tori dropped her pie and went to Josie's side, whispering for Hickory to make ready to run if need be. If the merchant's wife had come seeking vengeance, she would not allow her to take it out on the child, nor on one too ill to defend herself.

Fully prepared for battle, Tori shielded her charges

like a mother hen.

Her breath escaped her in a rush as the thick under-brush parted and Nicholas burst through into the clearing.

She was transfixed, half-afraid to believe her eyes, yet unable to look away.

His glossy black hair ruffled in the breeze as he strode in her direction. Even as her heart soared, her mind screamed caution. This must be an illusion. Nicholas, her Nicholas, could not possibly be less than six feet away.

Nearing, Nicholas smiled and held out a hand to her. "Pardon me, ma'am. I was looking for my wife. Have you seen her by chance?"

The sound of his voice sent shivers down her spine, and his smile nearly brought her to her knees. She was in his arms in an instant, covering his face with blue-tinted kisses. Joy bubbled in her laugh and as a cry of relief broke through her lips. He had come for her. By some merciful act of heaven he had actually come for her.

Nicholas lifted her feet off of the ground as he caught her up and spun her around, burying his face in the thick tangle of her hair. "I'll never let you out of my sight again." His breath teased against her ear.

Jubilant tears filled her eyes as Tori shook her head in absolute agreement. The sound of his deep voice flowed over her like a soothing balm.

"Nicholas, I believe you're being called out." A smile played about Ian's lips as he came to his brother's side. "Shall I stand as your second?"

Tori followed his gaze and had to cover her smile. Hickory stood with his slingshot poised, ready to defend her from the stranger. "Hickory, this is the man I was telling you about. This is my husband, Captain Saberton."

Even as she said it, she searched Nicholas's beloved face, but he was focused on the boy.

Hickory wavered briefly, before he finally lowered his arm. In a flash the child took off in a full run, darting into a copse of trees before Tori could stop him.

"Hickory! Come back." Tori called after him to no avail. "I promised to have a talk with your mother."

He left as fast as he'd appeared. Her little angel in overalls was gone without a trace.

"Hello again, sister." Ian greeted Tori with a kiss to her cheek.

"Hello, Ian." Tori crossed her arms at her middle, pulling the slight coat closer around her. "I shall thank you to turn your head."

"Yes, ma'am." Ian obediently turned around, looking suspiciously like he wanted to laugh.

Nicholas held her out by the shoulders to look her over. "Are you all right?" Then, he eyed Josie where she coughed on the ground. "I suppose she's the one responsible for all of this?"

Tori knew she'd better start explaining before he followed through with the threat in his eyes. "Yes, but you mustn't upset her, Nicholas."

Nicholas looked at her as if she'd just grown another

head.

"Please. She's very ill. She's become much too weak to take care of herself."

"Let me guess. She needs you." Nicholas shook his head when Tori slowly nodded in answer.

Weak or not, Josie spat an impertinent curse at him.

"You really shouldn't make her expend her strength like that, Nicholas." Tori admonished quietly.

Ian laughed at the impervious look on Nicholas's face.

Tori rushed forward to rest her hand on his arm. "She'll need it for the trip back home. You see, she'll be staying with us awhile."

"Now, just a minute."

He needn't have bothered, Tori's jaw jutted a notch higher. "Just until she's well enough to travel. To reclaim her rightful place at Wrenbrooke."

"I'm taking you home." Nicholas's patience had obviously worn thin.

"She didn't mean to do me any harm." Tori's voice rose as she struggled to make her point amidst the overwhelming evidence to the contrary.

"Yes, I did." Josie replied in a weak tone. Thankfully she lapsed into a coughing spell before she could completely destroy Tori's argument.

Glancing up at Nicholas, Tori gave a sheepish shrug. "She doesn't mean it. It's the fever." Quickly, Tori turned from his doubtful scowl. "Besides," she rushed on, "she's the only one who can lead us to my father."

Nicholas relaxed his stance.

Tori saw what looked like pity cloud his features. Finally, he held out an arm, enfolding her once again as she moved into his reach. "Has something terrible happened to Father?"

"Princess, there's something you should know." His voice grew quiet and Tori was instantly apprehensive. "Your father is home. He's in Savannah safe and sound. He was never abducted."

She pulled back to study his face, trying to understand what he was saying. "He concocted this kidnapping scheme to force us to marry. Unfortunately, he didn't consider the repercussions and heartache you might suffer at such a foolhardy move."

"No. Why?" Pain gripped her heart and she was unable to say any more.

Her father's questionable motives had once again wreaked havoc on the lives of those who loved him. Nonetheless, relief washed over her just hearing he was safe.

There would be plenty of time to confront her father later.

Right now, the sheer euphoria she felt in her husband's arms, knowing he'd searched high and low to find her, gave new meaning to the word contentment. Here, next to his heart, she'd finally found a place she truly belonged.

"The budding rose becomes the rose full bloom."
~ William Wordsworth

Thirty-Four

*N*icholas settled back into his favorite leather chair, relaxing in his master's chamber, taking in his wife's beauty from across the room. She sat at a dressing table with her back to him where she was determined to master the art of braiding.

Holding the heavy rope of hair out to one side, she plaited and unraveled several times until she finally reached the end of the braid. A smile of satisfaction played about her lips as she wound it into a roll on the back of her head and set it with pearl studded pins.

Victoria was an enchanting woman. And she'd never looked lovelier than when he' had pushed aside the vines and found her covered from head to foot in blackberries. Relieved beyond words, there wasn't anything he would have denied her at that moment.

Once again, he noticed the angry bruise just above her

eye. Upon closer inspection, he noticed numerous cuts and scratches crisscrossing her delicate skin, and his heart ached at the puffy red slashes marring her back. He could only imagine the suffering she had endured in the past week.

Since their return to Savannah, she'd said little about the experience. She was much more concerned with caring for the female reprobate she'd taken under her wing.

Having come so close to losing her, Nicholas was determined that she would never be put in harm's way again. And if that meant bringing harm home with them in order to keep a better eye on it … well, so be it.

From first glance, it was plain to see Hickory was completely enamored with Victoria. The boy obviously had good taste. Though her concern for him was admirable, he, like so many others along the river roads, had been raised to live off the fertile land. They were heartier than most and had no problem taking care of themselves.

For the ride home, Nicholas had paid the postmaster an overly generous sum for a mangy buckboard while Victoria had seen to it that Josie rested in the back.

Each time the conversation turned toward the events of the past few days, Victoria had been quick to direct his attention to something else. He still had no idea how she'd come to be in the state she was in. One day she would talk about it, but he decided not to press her until she was ready.

A newfound maturity had carried her through all this. Her resolve to see her feral half-sister taken care of was done with no thought to social implications. From what he could tell, her decision had been solely for the good of the one involved, with not a single thought given to appearances.

Quite a change, indeed.

Nicholas smiled at the memory of her dirty little chin set at such an angle as not to accept any argument. She'd sat ramrod straight, perched next to him on the buckboard, face smudged, hair full of grass and twigs, and covered only by a borrowed coat. Even so, she was a perfect example of ladylike elegance down to her frilly drawers.

Watching her now, Nicholas was nearly overcome by his feelings for the beautiful lady in the mirror.

The doctor had been called immediately upon their return and Victoria had not left the ailing woman's side. The physician eventually emerged from the room with a grim diagnosis, Josie Haverwood had the consumption. The infection had advanced, and her inflamed lungs were more than half full of fluid.

In hushed tones, they'd been informed she needed rest. A sedative had been administered to help her sleep and now it was just a matter of time.

In the wake of the fire, when he'd originally found Victoria missing, he'd ridden hard through the night, terrified she might be lost to him forever. Eventually he'd made a promise, to himself and to her Maker. If she was returned to him, he would hold her above all else in his heart and always make certain she knew it.

Drawn to where she sat, he came from behind to help her place a jeweled comb atop her carefully wound braid.

"Thank you." Tori turned her head to the side to look over the new style. "I was beginning to think my only recourse would be taking a good pair of shears to it."

Nicholas lifted a disapproving brow at that remark, taking her hand and raising her to her feet. She melted into his embrace. "Nothing could take away from your loveliness, princess."

"Nicholas?" Her voice became quiet as she snuggled into his arms "I've quite decided to keep you."

Nicholas let his fingers slide over her arm gently, a smile on his lips. She smiled back when he caught her watching him in the mirror. "I'm afraid you're stuck with me for a long, long time."

"I look forward to it." He placed a kiss on the top of her head.

"I do love you so." She spoke softly.

"And I love you, princess."

Blessed are the merciful,
for they shall receive mercy.
~ Matthew 5:7

Thirty-Five

Rolling up the familiar drive to the Haverwood house, heavily lined in azalea bushes blooming in vivid pink, made Tori's homecoming complete. Oh how she'd missed Aurora and Aunt Charlotte.

And especially her father.

Even Aunt Charlotte's garish green couch would be a most welcome sight.

Gabe appeared in the doorway. "Mrs. Charlotte, ma'am, you have guests. Shall I show 'em in?"

"Tori!" Aurora bounded from the parlor. Her squeal resounded throughout the marbled vestibule.

Meeting Aurora's animated embrace with equal enthusiasm, Tori was nearly swept off her feet when Aunt Charlotte joined the exuberant hug. "Oh, my poor, sweet darlin'."

It didn't escape Tori's notice that her father chose to watch from the parlor doorway rather than greet her himself.

After releasing her niece, Aunt Charlotte homed in on Nicholas. "And you. Zach was just telling us about how you came about finding our precious Tori. Lord have mercy!"

"When we discovered you were gone ...." Aurora spoke through barely controlled sobs. "We thought you were lost forever."

"I'm fine now, Aurora. Really." Tori cupped her cousin's sweet face in her gloved hands and smiled into her brimming eyes. "I'm home now. No need for tears."

She waited for Aurora's nod of agreement.

"Good. Now, I want to hear all of the latest news. Start from the beginning and tell me everything that has happened while I was away."

Nicholas helped her off with her satin shawl. The duchess's brooch lay amidst the creamy froth of lace at her throat.

"My, oh my. I can see you haven't been using your parasol. You look like a little gingerbread man with rosy cheeks." Aunt Charlotte led them back into the parlor, chattering all the way. "Considering the hideous ordeal you've been through, I'm just happy you're home where you belong."

Accepting Zach's kiss to her cheek, Tori smiled up at him, patting his arm. Eventually, looked back at her father who still had not moved from his watch in the doorway.

Without a word, he turned back into the parlor.

She knew it was his way of expressing his displeasure at having been put off from seeing her for nearly a day and a half. After Josie had been put in the care of a nurse, Tori had practically fallen into Nicholas's oversized bed and slept for twelve hours straight.

Once awake, she'd needed time to think—and pray—about what she would say to her father. So much had changed. So many lives hurt. She wouldn't make things worse by casting careless accusations without at least hearing him out.

Except now she was beginning to wonder if he intended to speak to her at all.

Tori would have smiled at his familiar petulance if she'd been able. She was thrilled to see him here and alive. But his haughty air only caused her immense sadness.

"Come along you two. Have a seat. You must conserve your strength." Aunt Charlotte met Tori at the parlor door and took her by the arm. "Move aside, Zachery. Give them some room."

Zach cleared his throat at being caught off guard as Aurora beckoned him to sit beside her. Nicholas gave his wife a lop-sided grin that went straight to her heart.

Aunt Charlotte's outlandish pumpkin-colored room was awash in afternoon sunlight. Tori watched each one glance over at the earl who silently gazed out of a long window, leaning heavily on his cane.

Tori knew she should, but she couldn't make herself

go to him just yet. Part of her wanted to pretend the awful things she'd learned had never happened. Yet, another part of her wanted to demand the truth.

It had taken her most of the morning to convince herself to see him at all. And were it not for Josie lying so gravely ill, Tori wasn't certain she would be here now. With all the wrongs done to Lucinda and her twins, she was determined to make him acknowledge Josie as his own flesh and blood.

All in good time.

The instant she'd seen Aurora with her pale blond ringlets and Aunt Charlotte in her frightful green dress, she'd realized how terribly important the two had become in her life.

At school, the other girls came and went with each passing year. Tori had learned early on not to get overly attached to anyone in particular.

The highlight of each term was her visits to Wrenbrooke, where the servants politely did their part in making her holiday comfortable. Yet something was always missing.

Looking about at the smiling faces of her newly acquired family, Tori knew that each one, in their own individual way, truly cared for her.

That was the difference.

Her eyes were drawn to Nicholas as he studied her from across the room. A familiar delight gripped her heart. Tori had felt a change in him. He'd admitted his love for her. A casual mention to him, but one that meant the world to her. The mere thought of it settled about her like a warm cloak on a frosty winter's day.

"Oh, Tori! What a commotion you missed over at Widow Harrington's garden luncheon on Tuesday." Aurora sat on the edge of her seat, between Ian and Zach. "You'll never guess who had the nerve to show up."

"Felicity Jenkins Duff!" Aunt Charlotte provided, with a pert nod of her head. "*Un*invited I might add."

"No sooner had she arrived when Constable McAllister and four of his men barged right there into the Widow's courtyard and arrested her!" Aurora quickly rushed on, before her mother had a chance to take over her story.

Tori's eyes widened.

Both Haverwood ladies began talking at once. Tori looked from one to the other, trying to piece together the fractured story as best she could.

From what she gathered, Felicity's driver had attended a card game where he proceeded to drink a bit too much. By the wee morning hours, he was bragging about his part in setting the entire riverfront ablaze. With a little encouragement and a few more drinks, he implicated Felicity as the main instigator, citing her plan to get even with Nicholas as the motive. Unfortunately for the both of them, not only was Constable McAllister's driver in attendance, but the mayor's stable keep and Judge Hale's foreman.

Tori's gaze flew to where her husband stood near the mantle. Nicholas could have been killed.

When she'd mentioned the burns on his arms earlier, he had downplayed the fire and its damage. She'd been so happy to be home, that it hadn't occurred to her to question him further. The magnitude of Felicity's need for revenge hit Tori full force, and she rose to stand by his side.

Nicholas gave her a characteristic shrug and slipped an arm around her shoulder, pulling her close and placing a kiss of reassurance to the top of her head. The steady sound of his heart beat satisfied her that he was alive and well, and that neither Felicity, nor anyone else, could ever take him from her.

Momentarily overwhelmed by her feelings, she felt as if she would burst if she didn't say what was in her heart. She lifted her head to look into his warm gaze. "I love you." Her voice was raw with emotion.

"It's a good thing," came the confident answer from lopsided lips. "Because I've decided to keep you."

Smiling, she rested her head against his chest until she caught a glimpse of her father still standing at the window. Slowly, she raised her head. She glanced up at Nicholas for support, and he nodded, releasing her. Tori wasn't sure she wanted him to.

Gathering her courage, she slowly made her way over to him. "Father?" Her tone was intentionally void of emotion.

He didn't bother to turn.

"You can't ignore me forever. We both know it's best to say what needs to be said and have it done with.

Though, I prefer that we speak privately."

He turned abruptly, stamping his cane in the process, startling them all.

"Dare you come here and presume to reprimand me in front of these good people?" He assumed his most daunting parliamentarian tone. "Have you forgotten your place?" His r's dramatically rolled off his tongue.

Tori's eyes filled with tears, but her gaze did not waver. She knew he was trying to intimidate her into submission, thus escaping her inevitable questions—a tactic he'd used well over the years.

This time, however, she would not allow him to push her aside so easily. He must learn he couldn't treat people with the cold indifference that had already ruined so many lives.

Conversation around the room quieted as the others stopped to witness the earl and Tori's unpleasant reunion. Nicholas's eyes narrowed.

This was an important stand she was taking, one that went against every well-bred fiber of her being. Yet, her determination to right the situation far outweighed the consequences of his anger.

"I'll see you in the study, Father." She calmly caught up her skirt and walked from the room.

She heard the earl clop noisily behind her as she headed down the hall to the study. Her father remained a half pace behind her, and Tori nibbled her lip for just a moment before entering into what had once been her uncle's study. Waiting for her father to pass, she pulled the heavy door closed.

Bleak from lack of use, the richly paneled room was dark except for a narrow ribbon of early afternoon sunshine that splayed across the burgundy carpet through a split in the gold velvet draperies.

Tori opened the curtains and tied them back on either side. The full view of the gardens was beautiful. Her mind returned to the perfectly manicured gardens at Wrenbrooke, teeming with magnificent hues of every color. Her memory settled on the small white cross and headstone set just above the rose garden, protected there by a large marble angel.

"Rachelle Marie Haverwood." She repeated the name that was engraved in stone there. She had studied that angel so often as a child.

"Blast and confound it, Victoria!"

Tori was startled out of her reverie.

"At least have the decency to speak to me directly. Don't stand there muttering out the window." With an exaggerated twitch of his mustache, the earl chose his brother's large leather chair facing an empty hearth. "Now explain yourself. At once." He didn't look at her as drummed his fingers on the hilt of his cane.

A sadness she hadn't expected tightened her throat when she began to speak. The leather creaked as Lord Haverwood shifted. Still he remained aloof while she fought to collect herself.

"Why?" Tori asked in as reasonable a voice as she could manage.

This gained his attention. He cast a wary eye at her but did not speak.

Clearing her throat, Tori closed her eyes to begin again. After all she had been through, she refused to shy away from his disapproval. She needed some very direct answers, even if it meant asking some very direct questions.

"Why was I never told about Lucinda Martin?" She took a shuddering breath, at the deep unfamiliar pain in her breast. "Nor of her two children?"

The earl irritably waved off her question. "'Tis irrelevant."

"They were not irrelevant." She snapped before she was able to catch herself. Her voice was so tense it sounded strange in her own ears. "And you owe me an explanation at the very least."

Coming to unsteady feet, her father glared at her with a look full of reproach. "He has done this to you! That libertine you married." He came toward her, whipping his cane with each step, obviously forgetting that it was he who had practically forced the marriage in the first place. "I shall not stand for this, Victoria. We shall start with divorce proceedings at first light tomorrow morning. We shall send for your things this very afternoon."

Typical avoidance, but Tori was having none of it. "My marriage to Nicholas is not up for debate. And neither of us is leaving this room until you've answered my question." She folded her arms in front of her and lifted her chin, meeting his incensed gaze without flinching. The mention of her husband had fueled her courage.

"The devil you say?" He waited, challenging her to make good on her threat.

"Were you in love with her?" Arms still crossed, Tori moved toward him in an unhurried pace, coming to rest on the arm of a side chair set directly in front of where he stood.

He sputtered as she neared.

"I found your copy of *Lady of The Lake* while you were supposedly kidnapped." Tori met his eyes with calm resolve. "The marriage certificate was tucked inside."

Tori watched as the earl began to resemble a cornered fox. While it was his nature to put up a fight, he was clever enough to know when to make an escape.

"Yes, well, the others will be wondering what has become of us, my dear. So, let's you be a good girl now, and come along." He started to turn, but Tori reached out and grasped his hand.

"Did my mother know about them?" Her voice softened.

"Good heavens, no." It was the first genuine answer she had gotten from him.

Encouraged, she gently pulled him down into the seat across from her, keeping his hand in hers. "Please." She appealed to his father's heart.

Before he knew it, he spelled out all the sordid details that her endless questions brought about, in their entirety.

"Yes, I loved Lucinda very much. Your grandfather threatened to cut me off completely if I didn't end the dalliance with a colonial girl posthaste. It seems that news of it had reached the House of Lords and we'd become a laughingstock of sorts. A recognized smirch on one's good name would never survive the rigid hierarchy of the *ton*." His fingers caressed hers, though she was certain he wasn't even aware of his actions.

"It had since become apparent that Lucinda was with child. I'd felt an obligation to see her taken care of, and so we married. She'd known going in that it would be in name only and that neither she, nor the child, would inherit a ha'penny."

He sighed heavily.

"A suitable marriage was hastily arranged between Lady Rachelle Beauchet and myself, and I was ordered to return to England at once—never to look back. Though I was nearly forty-three at the time, I knew better than to risk my standing in Parliament. It simply wasn't done."

At Tori's obvious distress, he added, "In spite of my father's dictate, I did provide for Lucinda and the child. Set it up with a solicitor, since deceased. But once I'd returned to England, I vowed to put the past behind me. I simply had no way of knowing the solicitor had forged an addendum on his own, cutting off their funds upon the children's second birthday. Though the funds were transferred in good faith from my bank in England once a year, they never got past the solicitor's own pocket."

Tori sat silent throughout her father's explanation, pained by the regret she sensed in his voice. Finally, she had to clear her throat in order to speak. There was something she needed to know. "Did you ever love my mother?"

Tori watched his face cloud over with emotion and just as quickly, he regained a tight hold on feelings long repressed. "She was young but a beautiful girl. You have her smile."

"But did you love her?"

"Love matches were not the thing, Victoria." The earl looked away from the tears shining in his daughter's eyes. "We hardly had time enough to know one another. If we'd had longer... who knows? After Rachelle's untimely death, I doted shamelessly over you trying to make up for the various voids I suppose, until several dowager matrons descended upon me insisting that I send you to a finishing school where you could be properly trained."

Tori realized how painful it was for him to relive those years and was grateful he was finally being honest with her. She felt utterly sickened at how so many had been hurt in all of this. All in the name of nobility.

"So there you have it, my dear." The earl was back to himself and standing in front of her.

"Thank you, Father. I know this wasn't easy."

"Rubbish. No point in going on about it. It is ancient hist'ry as far as I am concerned, so we will speak of it no more." This time he made for the door in earnest.

"I agree, and we shan't. Just as soon as you come to visit Josie and acknowledge her as your legitimate daughter."

Tori rushed to his side when he stumbled over his cane.

The music in my heart I bore,
Long after it was heard no more.
~ William Wordsworth

Thirty-Six

"P-preposterous!" the earl stuttered with an undignified squawk.

Tori lifted her skirt to make her way back down the corridor. Before this evening's end, her father would come face to face with Lucinda's daughter.

"Victoria! Here, now, this is far from settled." Lord Haverwood made a terrible racket as he swatted everything within reach with his trusty cane. "Come back here, I say!"

"I wish you no disrespect, Father, but the matter is settled as far as I'm concerned." Though her voice was raised a bit to offset his clamor, Tori remained remarkably calm as she summoned Gabe to bring her cloak. "Dinner will be served at eight. I'll be expecting you by seven." She accepted her wrap without even glancing back at her sputtering father.

After a short pause, she heard him start noisily up the stairs. It was by no means gracious, but Tori found his surrender encouraging nonetheless.

Knowing from where her help had come, Tori lifted her gaze to the high ceiling and whispered her thanks. She found the others having tea in the parlor. Immediately, she spotted Nicholas and presented him with a most triumphant smile.

"Aunt Charlotte, I'm afraid we're not prepared to stay." She knew her aunt was bound to be disappointed. "I know it's rather short notice, but we would be honored if you and Aurora would join us for dinner this evening."

"Oh, my, yes." Aunt Charlotte was quick to accept. "We'd be delighted. Will Edward be coming?"

"Mother," Aurora half whispered before curiosity got the best of her. "Is he, Tori?"

"Certainly, father will be there." Tori knew her next revelation would keep them twittering until dinnertime. "He has another daughter there to attend to, you see."

"Lord have mercy, child! You don't mean to tell me you've brought that heathen girl into your home." At Tori's nod, Aunt Charlotte dropped her painted fan and closed her eyes, reaching for her throat. "We'll all be killed."

"She has taken ill. But I expect it won't be long before she makes a full recovery." Tori fastened the toggle of her cloak, ignoring her aunt's dramatics.

"Yes, darlin', but, I've heard she's ferocious. Why, she

could sneak in to murder you in your sleep and you'd never even know it." Aunt Charlotte was clearly aghast. Turning to Nicholas, she tried to reason with him. "Nicholas do something, it is your home."

Nicholas shrugged.

"She's hardly as ferocious as all that, Aunt Charlotte," Tori met her husband's grin with one of her own. "She's fairly tame without her knife."

Charlotte Haverwood gulped.

"And once she is well, we can go to work on her social skills. You can help with that. She intends to take over the household at Wrenbrooke, you see. I'm afraid she has yet to learn that strangling the help is not an acceptable way to gain their cooperation."

By all appearances, Aunt Charlotte fainted dead away in her seat.

Zach was on his feet in an instant, calling for smelling salts, while Aurora sat with her mouth gaping.

Amusement danced in Nicholas's eyes.

Tori moistened her lips to cover a smile. She had thought it only fair to prepare them, after all. Once Josie was up and around, this little spectacle would seem mild in comparison to the commotion she'd likely cause.

"I believe your aunt has fainted, princess." Seeking his wife's side, Nicholas plucked a white carnation from a floral arrangement on a marble pedestal. Lifting it to his nose, he came up behind her and presented it to her around her shoulder. "Surely you haven't intentionally mortified the dear woman?" He spoke softly next to her ear. "Not Lady Victoria Goodness and Virtue—Miss Sarah Hale's most loyal student."

Zach attempted to follow the moaning lady's nose with a silver vial of smelling salts as she rolled her head back and forth.

"Certainly not," Tori replied in a hushed tone. "Besides, she's not really suffering an attack of the vapors. Her eyelids are wiggling."

Nicholas's brow rose.

Tori dipped her head in the direction of the ailing lady. Indeed, Aunt Charlotte struggled against the foul odor, even pushing at Zach's arm.

"Ah, I see." Nicholas straightened to his full height and clasped his hands behind his back. "Take heart, love, not all are as talented as you in covering their fluster. Maybe later you could give her a few lessons."

His teasing was rewarded with a small elbow to his ribs.

"I really don't see why all the fuss. It's hardly a secret." Tori twirled her carnation between two fingers and Nicholas watched with a grin. "And here I've not even told them about my adventure with Hickory yet."

Lord Haverwood arrived on the Saberton doorstep at exactly two minutes to eight.

Tori met her guests at the door and watched as her exasperated aunt was left to see herself down from the carriage.

A virtual fruit basket was knocked askew from the top of her aunt's head as she descended from the conveyance into the evening drizzle. The headdress hung precariously over one eye with a hapless banana dangling from the side of her head.

Thankfully, Aurora helped assuage her mother's ruffled dander. Righting the unfortunate hat, she managed to convince Aunt Charlotte all was well. That is, until Aurora tripped on her mother's billowing green skirt and the basket took a tumble once again.

At Tori's prompting, Jonas trotted down the steps to offer his assistance.

"I don't know what Edward's in such an all-fired hurry about." Charlotte allowed the footman to take her arm and gingerly help her up the spiral brick steps leading to the double front doors. "Mmm. Something smells divine. I do hope Tori has borrowed a cook from Dottie's place. They always serve the most delectable dishes. Jonas, have them set out extra butter."

"Yes, ma'am." Jonas nodded, then shook his head as he followed the ladies inside and closed the door behind them.

Tori greeted her with a quick hug, never letting her father leave her sight. "I've given instructions to go ahead with dinner, Aunt Charlotte. Father and I will join you shortly." She hoped her aunt wouldn't take offense, but there was something far more important to be done at the moment.

To her relief, Nicholas and Zach stepped forward and

each gallantly offered an arm which the Haverwood
ladies accepted with enthusiasm.

Tori found her father just inside the drawing room
and slipped her arm through his. "Thank you for coming."

He answered with a snort.

"I must warn you, Father, Josie's not well." Tori
walked him to the stairway and caught up her lavender
skirt before continuing their unhurried pace. She'd worn
his favorite gown as a show of appreciation for his
coming, knowing he'd more readily receive a silent
gesture than an awkward display of affection. "I hope
when you see her, it will explain my urgency in insisting
that you come at once."

He was awfully quiet as his feet shuffled upon the
dense emerald carpet running up the center of the
polished wooden steps. Painful memories he'd thought
never to rehash awaited him on the upper landing. Tori
felt for him. The stairway must seem a mile long.

They followed the narrow path of carpet down the
hallway to the last room on the left. Without delay, Tori
pushed open the carved door before her father could
reconsider.

The air inside the darkened room was moist and thick.
An iron kettle filled with mint and herbs was set to boil
continuously over the grate in the fireplace. The added
humidity eased Josie's breathing somewhat yet felt heavy
to Tori's healthy lungs.

A trickle of summer rain pattered against two windows hung with diamond-patterned lace. A canopy of matching lace covered the tester bed at the other end.

The nurse that Nicholas had hired to look after Josie stood up upon their entry, taking her leave so that they could visit alone.

The earl remained rooted to a spot just inside the door.

Tori went around to the opposite side of the bed and adjusted the floral quilt around Josie's shoulders. She knew better than to rush him. In truth, she was thankful he had come this far.

Josie made a choking sound and Tori raised her pillow to allow her to gather in enough air to cough. The lamp on the night stand flickered casting a distorted shadow of the earl onto the far wall.

Opening her eyes, Josie saw Tori and scowled. Appearing even more gaunt than usual, her blue eyes looked enormous against her thin, pale face.

The earl took a hesitant step forward then stopped.

"I've brought someone to see you, Josephine." Tori glanced the earl's way to see if he'd caught the use of her full name.

Following his cane, he took another step in the direction of the bed.

Josie, whether completely disinterested or simply too weak to care, turned her head away from Tori and reclosed her eyes. "Leave me be."

Tori lit a beeswax candle and cupped her hand around it as she moved to light two of the four etched glass lamps hanging on each wall. The room progressively took on a rich amber glow, bathing the bed in soft light.

Standing back, Tori blew at the flame in her hand and watched her father take the three remaining steps to the platform at the foot of the bed placing him at eye-level with the girl wheezing upon the pillows.

His shoulders seemed to sag beneath the weight of his past as he stared at this daughter of Lucinda's, this child he'd disregarded all these years. He watched with sad eyes as she struggled with each breath.

Reaching for the footboard, he quickly pulled his hand back as Josie's eyes fluttered open at the movement. It was obvious she was making a great effort to focus on the stranger at her feet. "Who?" Her voice was raspy and after several attempts to clear it, she gave a choked cough and laid back, giving up the effort.

Tori rested her hand on Josie's shoulder. "Father has come to visit." The girl tensed under her hand. "You mustn't try to talk. He's just come to be properly introduced. It's necessary, after all, if the two of you are to live together at Wrenbrooke."

The earl's gaze flew to that of his youngest daughter. "This is news to me."

Tori brought her finger to her lips to hush him, before rushing on. Stubborn determination to see the thing through spurred her on. "And just as soon as you're up and around again, Father will take you down to Bond Street in London to see you fitted with some—"

"Get... out!" The order was weak, but the sneer on

Josie's face left no doubt as to her meaning.

Biting back a feeling of despair that threatened to crush her hopes for reconciliation, Tori stood ready to intervene on her father's behalf.

Lord Haverwood, however, needed no such help as he straightened his shoulders and addressed the young woman frowning at him. "Your mother would not approve, my dear."

Instead of backing away from her heated gaze, Tori watched as he took a step around the side of the bed to come closer. "Lucinda deplored rudeness. Never hesitated to remind me of it."

Josie opened her mouth to speak, but a rattling cough consumed her.

The earl looked on as Tori dipped a cloth into the wash basin and bathed the girl's face in cool water. Josie was too frail to put up a struggle.

"I shan't pretend I never knew of your existence." He ignored her glare. "Lucinda was heavy with you the last time I saw her."

Tori saw a look of remorse cross his face, but only for an instant.

"She was a rare and engaging woman, had a unique ability to see only good in people. Idealistic to a fault." His gruff voice softened as if he'd called up an image of her face in his memory. "I scarcely understand it, even to this day, but somehow she fancied herself in love with me. I did my best to discourage such a foolish notion, for it simply had no place in my life at the time. It was my impression that love was for ignorant buffoons with no immunity toward a cleverly hitched skirt. I rather prided myself as being something of an unlovable sort, actually."

Josie closed her eyes to his words, though the rapid rise and fall of her chest told them she wasn't sleeping. Tori saw regret cross her father's face and she swallowed hard against the sorrow she felt for him. He needed to say these things as much, if not more, than Josie needed to hear them.

"I had a devil of a time convincing Lucinda of it, however. Meek as she was, she was terribly insistent. She used to say, 'Edward, if you'd just show folks the sweet, caring man you are underneath, they'd elect you King of England for the sheer pleasure of being at your service.'"

The earl came out of his musing when he caught Tori's understanding nod. Clearing his throat, he waved a hand to dissuade her from commenting. "Yes well, that's neither here nor there. The point is, eventually I succumbed to her obvious charms and found I'd come to care for her deeply."

Josie opened her eyes to that, glaring her mistrust.

"'Tis true, but there wasn't a blessed thing I could do about it." The earl stepped closer. "She wasn't of any particular lineage, American or otherwise. My peers, you see, simply wouldn't stand for it. I married her, to give you the Haverwood name, but it didn't mean a thing. She wasn't welcome where I came from and I chose not to put her through public humiliation. It was best she go on without me. Lucinda agreed."

A tear fell down the side of Josie's face when she closed her eyes once more. Tori reached to wipe it away, but the other girl flinched as if her touch was unbearable.

"I made provisions for the three of you. I would not have had it otherwise. Unfortunately, I had no means of knowing that my wishes were not being carried out, nor that the funds set aside for your welfare were being pilfered by an unscrupulous solicitor." A hint of despair rose in his voice. "If only your mother had written me."

Shifting the cane to his other hand, the earl spoke again as if to himself. "But she wouldn't, of course. She'd given her word." He cast a weary eye at the frail form of his older child and shook his head regretfully. "For that, my dear, I most humbly apologize."

Josie remained quiet with her eyes closed.

Her father nodded and turned on his cane, indicating that he'd finished what he'd set out to do.

Tori blinked rapidly to clear the tears that clouded her vision. When she looked down at Josie, she realized the girl was trying to speak. Lifting the pillow, she cradled her head to make it easier for her.

"Father, please wait. I think there's something Josie wants to say to you." Tori called out, suddenly over-whelmed by the possibility that the breach between these two could be spanned in a matter of moments. One word of forgiveness from Josie was all it would take.

The earl inched closer, looking from one to the other in anticipation.

"Rot... in...." Josie managed to spit out, before another attack of hacking seized her. Her meaning was plain enough.

Tori was stunned. She quickly looked up to see deep lines of pain settle on her father's face, then disappear beneath a carefully controlled expression. He turned once again and moved out the door.

Glancing down in disbelief at the choking girl, Tori was cast aside when the nurse came in to take over her care. Her mind raced as she was promptly ushered from the room.

This was not at all what she had expected. Nicholas was right, she should leave things alone that were none of her concern. But she'd been so sure she would be able to bring the two together, so sure that giving Josie the things she'd felt cheated of all her life would bring them all closer in the end.

Instead, it had only deepened the chasm of Josie's bitterness and brought misery to her father.

Standing alone in the hallway, reverberating with the sound of Josie's desperate gasps for breath, Tori held her arms and trembled uncontrollably. The sound of Nicholas's voice calling her name brought her brimming gaze to the top of the stairs where he appeared. She wanted to run to him, to be completely engulfed by him, but she couldn't get her legs to move.

With long determined strides, Nicholas was at her side in an instant. He pulled her into his arms without a word. She was shaking all over so he held her closer.

Smoothing her hair, he spoke in soothing tones.

"Shhh."

She tried to speak, but a whimper of desperation was all that escaped her lips.

"Madam."

Tori froze. Recognizing the voice of the nurse, she peered over Nicholas's arm and realized the corridor had gone completely still. No more coughing. In fact, no sound at all came from the sick room.

"No." Her mouth formed the word without sound.

"Madam, I'm terribly sorry. The young lady has expired. Shall I send for the undertaker?"

He is happiest, be he king or peasant,
who finds peace in his own home.
~ Johann Wolfgang von Goethe

Thirty-Seven

"Thank you. We'll see to it," Nicholas answered. "You can go now. I'll see that there is extra compensation sent over with your pay."

Thanking him, she headed off down the hall.

Nicholas glanced down at his wife. She held fistfuls of his shirt in each hand and her face was buried in his chest. Slowly, in waves, grief washed over her until violent sobs gripped her. She mourned, not just for the sister, but for her brother and their mother as well. And for a past that could have been.

Nicholas buried his hand in her thick curls to cup her head against him, allowing her all the time she needed to grieve. He understood the pain in her tears and talons of protective anger tore through him. He would not let her shoulder the blame of this girl's death.

363

Misplaced guilt could cause him to lose her forever to the kind of cold isolation he'd seen rip others apart. He wouldn't let it happen to Victoria. She was the least responsible for this tragedy.

"Oh, Nicholas." Her breath caught and hot tears streamed down her cheeks. She lifted her head to search his face. "What have I done? Josie died hating us. I'm afraid bringing her here has hurt father more than he can bear. He'll have to live with knowing Josie wouldn't forgive him and she all but cursed him before she died. His health can't take it." With that, she dissolved into another rush of tears.

If he was going to get through to her, he'd have to see that she calmed down first. Slipping his arm around her shoulder, he led her back down the hall.

"If anything happens to him, Nicholas, as a result of my insisting ... no, I practically demanded he come."

He handed her a handkerchief to dry her tears.

"What you've done is completely inexcusable." Nicholas crossed his arms and stood back from her.

"And I ... what?" Her mouth gaped for a second, before she looked up at him.

"Really, Victoria. Bringing the girl here to receive proper medical care, surrounding her with clean sheets, a warm blanket and a pillow for her head." He clicked his tongue and shook his head. "What were you thinking?"

She didn't respond, making a study of twisting the handkerchief in her hand.

"Offering her a chance at a privileged life after all her

years of poverty. Providing her the love of a father, repentant and willing to try to make up for his absence in her life."

"Yes, but—"

"But nothing." Nicholas was having none of her arguments. "You did what you thought was best—more than most would do. It was her choice to throw it all away. Her choice to embrace hate over the love you freely offered."

Tears shimmered fresh in her eyes. "But I've hurt Father deeply."

Nicholas placed his hands on her arms, forcing her to meet his gaze. "Your father has done this to himself, Victoria. No one knows that better than he does. He knows you, and he knows your love for him. And he depends on that love too much to jeopardize it. Unfortunately, his deeds have yielded consequences he must live with. Only God can give him the peace and forgiveness he needs."

Tori sniffed into the cloth, and Nicholas placed a kiss on her forehead to soften his words. "You must be strong now, princess. Show your father he was right in coming, and that his effort to right the past would have pleased Lucinda very much."

Tori spoke quietly. "And me, too."

"Don't you think you should tell him that?" Nicholas straightened.

Tori hesitated for just a moment before she nodded.

"You'd best be quick about it. He was calling for his

cape when I passed him in the hall."

"Oh, no." Tori lifted her skirts with both hands and ran for the stairway. "Father! Please Jonas, don't let him leave."

Jonas nodded at her frantic call and rushed out to the street where the earl was just climbing into the carriage at the bottom step.

⁓

Tori paused before starting down the stairs and turned back to Nicholas who took her by the hand. "Come on, I'll walk you down." The strength in his hand gave her confidence to face her father.

Music from the grand piano drifted up the stairs. Despite her grief, Tori was at ease. Her life, with all the special people in it, had become as full and vibrant as the melody filling the house.

Heaven had blessed her, and she was content knowing that whatever the future held, a force bigger than them all guided her path. Before joining their family, Tori gave her husband her most charming smile and he returned it with a squeeze to her hand.

Zach stood at Aurora's side, watching every move her fingers made across the ivory keyboard.

Aunt Charlotte, having sufficiently satisfied her hunger with Tori's menu of lobster salad and melon balls, now pointed out various degrees of difficulty in Aurora's performance.

Zach, though nodding respectfully, centered his attention on Aurora's face, looking suspiciously smitten. A wave of excitement hit Tori at the prospect.

Ian sat near the hearth, absorbed in yet another book. Something needed to be done about finding him some female companionship.

Finally, she spotted her father seated next to the door in the entry hall. His hat and cape still in place. He rested his gloved hands atop his cane, obviously anxious to be on his way.

Nicholas released her and went into the drawing room to join the others.

Slowly, Tori walked to where her father avoided her gaze, trying to sum up his mood. "Thank you for waiting. I needed to speak with you."

He didn't respond.

Tori knelt in front of him and laid her hands on top of his. She leaned in close so that he could hear her over the music. "I don't quite know how to begin."

He certainly wasn't going to make this any easier for her.

Rubbing his hand, she said what was in her heart. "Growing up, you were by far the most important person in my life. I lived for the times we spent together."

He blinked. It was the only sign that he had heard her at all.

"Josie hasn't changed that."

His mustache twitched. It was a wonderful sight to Tori and she took reassurance from it. "My heart breaks that she was so eaten with bitterness. She missed out on knowing a wonderful, caring father."

His tired eyes fell to his daughter showing the pain he carried.

"I also need to tell you how very proud I am of you for coming here to make peace with her. It was an honorable gesture."

He harrumphed, and Tori grinned.

"I know you did it mainly out of love for me—and Lucinda—and I appreciate it."

The earl nodded and averted his eyes once more. Tori knew it was to hide the moisture in them.

"I pray you seek forgiveness from the only One who really matters, whether Josie forgave you or not. God will. And He can put the past behind us and give us a blessed hope for the future. If you'll only ask."

At first she thought he was going to ignore her again, but then he nodded.

She put her arms around his neck and placed a kiss on his wrinkled cheek.

To her utter astonishment, she felt a hasty peck against her own cheek and he patted her arm. Holding back her tears, she laid her head against his shoulder.

"Here, now. No use in getting my good cape thoroughly soggy. For goodness sake, Victoria, remember yourself." He cracked a brief smile at the sound of her giggle.

"Father, do say you'll stay with us for a while. At least until your first grandchild has an opportunity to meet you." Tori smoothed his cape.

"Grandchild you say?" His eyes brightened as he brushed off her hand.

"Not right away, but eventually." She stood and waited for him to relent.

"May I take your cape, sir?" Jonas offered.

He hesitated for only a moment before loosening the strings at his neck.

"Good! I'm famished. Jonas, please have the maid prepare a plate for us. We can take it in the drawing room with the others." Slipping her arm through her father's, she walked with him to join the rest of the family.

"Do you by chance play chess?" Ian sat before a glass chess set laid out on a round table.

"I could be persuaded." Despite the twitch of his mustache, Tori knew her father wouldn't put up too much of a fuss. Chess had always been his favorite pastime.

"There you two are. Did you hear that last piece? Aurora, honey, play it again. She's not as accomplished at playing the piano as she is at playing her harp, but I believe she's doing very well. Don't you think?" Aunt Charlotte swayed with the music, waving her hankie in time. The colorful hat atop her head slipped more with every beat.

"Very well, indeed." Tori agreed noting the look Zach wore as he watched her play.

"I'm glad the instrument is getting good use." Nicholas motioned for the housekeeper to set the tray of food on a side table and instructed her to make a plate to bring over to the earl.

Tori filled a plate for herself. With all that had passed, she finally had peace.

Though death had taken Josie before she'd had much of a chance to know her, she refused to burden the others just now with the unavoidable news of her passing.

She would mourn, as would they, but for this short, perfect moment of time, Tori simply wanted to watch the smiles of those she loved and listen to them mingle.

"By Jove, I do believe that's a checkmate." The earl was actually smiling.

"Good game, sir. I hope you'll give me the chance to win back my watch in the near future." Ian winked at Tori.

Charlotte Haverwood nearly choked on her cider. "Gambling? In this house? Right here under our very noses? Edward you should be ashamed. And you, too, *Reverend* Saberton. Why I never..."

"That reminds me, Mrs. Charlotte. Might you like to play a round of hearts?" Zach casually opened a drawer on the side table and produced a deck of playing cards.

"What's this?" The earl cocked a brow.

Aurora snickered, and Aunt Charlotte adamantly shook her head, flinging the banana across the room. "Zachery, you scoundrel. You're actin' more like your brothers every day."

"They are teasing you, Aunt Charlotte." Tori went to her aunt's side amid the deep laughter coming from the brothers. "And they wouldn't bother if they didn't love you dearly. Can I get you more tea?"

"Why, thank you, darlin'. And maybe just a nibble of that sweet bread from dinner. Your cook is excellent, Nicholas. Did I tell you the new chef over at the Pavilion House Hotel once trained in Richmond under a man all the way from Europe whose name I cannot even pronounce?"

Tori glanced around, and contentment filled her heart as she watched each smiling face. At last, she'd found what she never knew she was missing. A place to call home.

Catching the warm gaze of her husband, she was immediately drawn to the welcoming fire in his dark eyes. As always he made her pulse quicken with just a look.

Ian casually thumbed through a leather-bound book he found in the cabinet d'affaires.

Zach and Aurora had eyes only for each other and Tori tried very hard not to take credit for that. She had promised, after all, to make him take notice of her little cousin. Of course, Aurora had taken it from there and charmed him all on her own.

Her father and Aunt Charlotte sat next to one another, bickering as usual. But, since there were plenty of other seats they could have taken, Tori was convinced they actually enjoyed each other's company. Some just had an odd way of showing it.

Home. Her home.

"Mrs. Tori." She turned as Jonas came to her side. "Mr. Nicholas needs to see you in the next room, ma'am."

Leaving the cozy gathering, Tori stepped out into the hallway and was immediately surprised by a huge arm that reached out and swung her into the library.

Stifling her scream with his hand, Nicholas replaced it with his lips after she had a chance to comprehend that it was her husband that held her.

"Nicholas!" Her breath had caught in her throat. "Must you always surprise me?"

"I hope to." He pulled the pocket doors together.

She could barely make out the lazy grin on his lips in the faint light streaming in from the lattice inset on the door.

His features grew serious as he smoothed down her curls. "They came for Josie while you spoke with your father. She'll be taken care of."

"Thank you."

"I see it went well with the earl." He played with a stray curl at the nape of her neck and smiled at the resulting shiver.

Tori nodded. "Yes, quite well."

"Good." He placed a kiss upon her cheek.

"We have guests." She reminded him with feeble resistance.

"Mmm hmm." His lips nuzzled her ear.

"You are shameless, Captain Saberton."

His deep rumble of laughter filled the small space between them. Taking her hand, he raised it to his lips. "I love you, princess."

"It's a good thing."

"Because you plan to keep me?"

"Indeed. For a very, very long time." Tori smiled sweetly and pulled his mouth down to her own.

Epilogue

Savannah, Georgia, 20 December, 1860

"...And may they find lasting contentment in the betrothal they've entered into today."

"Here, here."

Tori lifted her glass to the newly engaged couple, before sharing a private look with her husband over its brim. The cranberry punch smelled wonderful, but didn't sit well on her stomach so she quietly set it aside.

She searched the ballroom of the Pavilion House Hotel until she came upon her father, happily surrounded by his usual brood of adoring widows.

"Oh, my goodness!"

Tori turned to see her aunt chasing a man in white uniform. "You, there, this will never do. These cream-puffs are chock full of olives. I can't eat olives, they make me swell up like a blowfish."

Jean-Pierre had produced his most outlandish creation yet. In keeping with the season, Aunt Charlotte wore what suspiciously resembled a small pear tree upon her head with a small stuffed partridge perched on top.

"Hideous, isn't it?" Dottie Saberton stood just to Tori's right, sipping her punch. "The woman is as gullible as a lamb."

Tori smiled. "And every bit as lovable."

"Every bit," Dottie smiled elegantly at her daughter-in-law. Her own hat was an exquisite ice-blue pillbox from Boston. Small feathers adorned one side in snowy white. Her gown, in matching blue and white striped taffeta, was infinitely chic to Tori's trained eye. "Now let's hope Aurora doesn't share her mother's odd tastes and allow the Duprees to decorate the wedding next Spring."

Standing back to eye Tori's rich mulberry gown, Mrs. Saberton ran a white-gloved hand over the loose-fitting waistline. Her face immediately brightened. "Honey! I'm so happy!" Mrs. Saberton set her glass aside and rested her arm around Tori's shoulder. "Does Nicholas know?"

"I haven't had a chance to tell him, yet. Truthfully, I wasn't entirely certain myself, until I had the chance to visit with the doctor yesterday morning. And what with the betrothal dinner party this evening, I didn't want to take attention from Aurora and Zachery."

Dottie pressed her cheek against Tori's. "I'm over-joyed. But promise you won't wait too long. Men like to feel a part of these things."

"I promise." Tori accepted another hug before Dottie was called away to another group.

The magnificent hall was resplendent with the oversized chandelier gracing the center of the gilded ceiling. Tori noticed Aurora was over to one corner trying to gain her attention.

Going over a mental checklist of the various wedding preparations ahead of them, Tori tried to estimate which might be causing her cousin such anxiety. Aurora crossed the room and took Tori's arm to bring her in close.

"What on earth?"

"Tori, mother just said the most peculiar thing." Aurora bit her thumbnail.

Tori patiently took Aurora's hand away from her mouth. "What did she say?"

Aurora frowned in concern. "Mother says I oughtn't kiss Zach. She says I might decide I like it."

"I see." Tori smothered a grin.

"And she said no matter what I'm not to ask you for advice about kissing and such." Aurora brought her thumb back to her mouth. "But I already like it. I've loved Zach since I was twelve years old." Aurora's eyes sought out the object of their conversation. He was smiling as he talked with three other young men. When he caught her watching him, his eyes softened as he excused himself to come to her side.

"And does he love you as well?"

"Yes." Aurora answered with a whimsical note.

Tori had to wonder if she'd ever been so enchanted at the mere sight of Nicholas. "And, you say you like it when Zach kisses you?"

"Yes, very much." Aurora nodded.

"Good. Then ask him to kiss you often and trust the Lord to take care of the rest."

Thankfully, the stringed orchestra began a waltz just as Zach joined them.

Tori had completely eluded the issue, but some things were best left unanalyzed.

Nicholas came into view as she watched the engaged couple sway to the lilt of the music. In rapt in conversation with men Tori knew to be investors, he stood head and shoulders above them. He'd donned his Naval uniform for the occasion and his virile bearing affected her without fail. He flashed a smile at her before she realized she was staring.

Pulling her eyes away, she grinned at having thought Aurora silly for the very same thing. She patted the curls at her nape. With her hair piled high, pearled pins dotted throughout, her head felt a bit top-heavy.

"Pardon me, ma'am. I believe this dance is mine." Nicholas offered his hand.

"Certainly, sir. But we must be careful." Tori slipped her hand into the bend of his arm and hid her mouth with the other white-gloved hand. "My husband is very jealous, you know."

"With good reason." came the easy reply. "You are undeniably the most ravishing creature in attendance." He pulled her into his arms and swept her into a waltz, allowing other couples to follow suit.

Leaning heavily on him, Tori felt dizzy at first. The sudden motion nearly overwhelmed her.

"Are you feeling all right?"

Tori heard the worry in his voice. She supposed this was as good a time as any to break the news of their impending arrival. Nodding, she opened her mouth to do just that, when his resonant voice interrupted her.

"Good, because I have something to tell you that I think you're going to be thrilled about."

That was what she was going to say. Tori looked up at him, awaiting his explanation.

"It looks as though we will be opening an additional office in England. We've got our backers and your father generously offered to let us have a warehouse on his lands near the port. This could possibly open trade with China and then to India. Haverwood Shipping could have offices worldwide in the very near future."

Tori could feel his excitement in the exuberant way he held her. She wondered at how he would take her news, now that he had such impressive plans. Certainly, this meant he would have to be away for a time to set up this new office. She wasn't sure how he would take what she had to tell him.

"What is it, princess?"

"Will you be leaving, Nicholas? I mean to travel back to England for a time?"

"Not without you. I suspect we will make the trip between here and there often. That's why I thought you'd be pleased. You can keep your ties here as well as there."

She missed a step and gave him a faltering grin. "I'm sorry. I'm a bit preoccupied." Her eyes rose to his as she tried to gage his reaction. "It seems I have a bit of a surprise myself, Nicholas."

His brow rose.

"Although, you'll have to wait another six months before I can actually give it to you."

Nicholas stopped their dance.

Tori was caught completely off guard and had to grasp onto him for support. Glancing about at the curious stares they received in every direction, Tori tried to take his arm so that they might finish this in private. She didn't want to overshadow Aurora and Zach's betrothal announcement with her own good news.

Nicholas wasn't going to budge until she explained herself. "What sort of surprise is it that you have for me, princess?"

"A pink one." She watched hope gleam in his eye. "Or possibly a blue one."

Lifting her, Nicholas swung her around as pairs of interested dinner guests waltzed past. "I'll take one of each!"

Highly improper, but she'd come to discover the only opinion that truly mattered his. The height and depth of Nicholas's love for her would take a lifetime to fully comprehend. A lifetime to feel safe in the circle of his arms.

Her home.

A Note from the Author

From my first visit to the cobblestoned squares of Savannah, I knew I wanted to write a story set within her magnificent oaks. I visited each square and the grand houses for which this elegant city is known, many of which make an appearance in this book. Some, however, like Charlotte Haverwood's home, are a conglomeration of several. And her unique eye for decorating was a quirky figment of my imagination.

The first place I go on a research trip is to the local library. Fabulous gems can be found among diaries, family collections, historical tomes and archived county registers. I went through mounds of material at the Georgia history and genealogy room of Washington Memorial Library in Macon. The stately building itself was the home of a former mayor, and I was inspired from the moment I walked through the doors.

Savannah was indeed devastated by fire—twice. The great fire of 1796 left 229 houses destroyed including the City Exchange building and 400 citizens were left homeless.[1] Then, again in 1820 another sweeping fire took the city, every bit as crippling as the last. I couldn't help but wonder how my hero might react, knowing what ruin the city had suffered in the past as he faced another deadly blaze. The what ifs began to take shape.

I then came across an account of Prince Henry of Battenberg, a morganatic descendant of the Grand Ducal House of Hess who later became a member of the British Royal Family, through his marriage to Queen Victoria's daughter, Princess Beatrice.[2] That fueled my imagination and I began to dig deeper into the complex structure of royal protocol. At the time of the proposed marriage of Edward Haverwood and Lucinda Martin, though not unheard of, morganatic marriage was not as common in Britain as it was in Royal houses of other countries. While never formally named as such in British law, morganatic marriage did exist between people of unequal social rank, which prevented the passage of the husband's titles and privileges to the wife and any children born of the marriage.[3]

While it's not my intent that the legal content of Josie's contract be taken as absolute, or even typical, I took storytelling liberties to enhance actual addendums to benefit the story as a whole.

My imaginary people sort of took over from there. Fictional circumstances, as historically accurate as I could make them based on countless hours of research, evolved to portray a parable. Inspired by both historical accounts and fictitious events, *True Nobility* was embellished only to edify certain Biblical truths, which are unchanging and eternal.

My sincerest hope is that this book resonates with you as much as it has with me.

REFERENCES

1. William Harden, *A History of Savannah and South Georgia, Volume I*. Lewis Publishing Company, 1913.

2. *Battenberg family*. Encyclopædia Britannica, July 20, 1998.

3. www.newworldencyclopedia.org/entry/Morganatic_marriage

My Heartfelt Appreciation

It's hard to believe Victoria's story has been with me for over twenty years. The market for Christian fiction wasn't nearly as supported back then as it is today. Even so, our spirited heiress managed to capture the interest of a couple of secular publishing professionals in the late 1990s. Unfortunately, they proposed changes (remember the bodice ripper genre?) that I wasn't willing to make. So, I put my manuscript under the bed and put my lifelong dream on hold.

A dear friend, who happened to be a bestselling author at the time, was my first mentor. Full of wisdom and plenty of sass, she saw something in my writing and made me promise not to give up. Since then, she's passed on but I will tell you all about her someday—quite a testimony. I'd be remiss if I didn't thank her here. I'm asking the Lord to give her a big hug for me until we meet again.

A couple of years ago I joined American Christian Fiction Writers and attended their local chapter meeting. There I met my second cherished mentor, Lena Nelson Dooley. She invited me to be a part of her critique group where week after week, I learned the craft. Thank you, Lena, Julie, Lisa, Patty, Jackie, Betty, Sydnie, and all the rest who put a colored pen to my pages.

To my writing partners, Conni Cossette, Tammy Gray, Dana Red, and Laurie Westlake. There is no way to adequately express my gratitude for the way you challenge and inspire me to stretch beyond good enough to make my work better. Each one of you has an intuitive gift for story that never fails to amaze me. I love you dearly.

Thank you to my agent Tamela Hancock Murray for taking me on and always believing in me. You are simply the best.

My gratitude to Roseanna White of Roseanna White Designs for your stunning cover design. I'm amazed how you created so perfect a likeness from an image held only in my mind. I am blessed by your many talents.

Early readers, Carol Bates, Cindi Cannon, Erica Wright, Sheri Raymer, Roxanne Wright, Bonnie Sanchez, Tonda Hargrove, Charlotte Kretzschmar, and Betty Wimpy. Your feedback was invaluable and your excitement contagious. Thank you, sweet friends.

To my wonderful mom, dad, husband and family who put up with plenty of fast food dinners and movie nights without me. You never complain about the hours I spend immersed in my world of make believe. Instead, you've always been my greatest encouragers. I love each one of you to the moon and back.

Finally, I am forever indebted to my daughter, Ashley Espinoza, who played an important editorial role in this book. You have a knack for seeing the big picture when I get bogged down in details. Your natural skill and eagle eye for inconsistencies helped me color inside the lines. Your keen ability to understand my characters and know what motivates them added dimension. Your genuine, overwhelming love for this story helped bring it to life. I am sincerely grateful for you, Sis.

Father, to You be the all the glory. Always.